HARRY'S DREAM

Sheila. R. Kelly

In memory of my Dad, who was the inspiration for Harry.

CONTENTS

Acknowledgments I

Part One: Growing Up

1 Moving From Collyhurst 9

2 Exploring 26

3 An Invitation for Grandma 39

4 Whit Walks and a New Baby 47

5 Picnics and School 57

6 Clayton Vale 73

7 the Dog 84

8 Another Baby 97

9 Leaving School 108

Part Two: Dreams do come true

1 Bad Things Come in Threes 131

2 Changes 143

3 Training and Postings 159

4 The Dream Girl 168

5 More Changes   183

6 Overseas   204

7 Moving on to Italy   219

8 Into Austria   250

9 Home at Last   278

ACKNOWLEDGMENTS

Until the advent of the World Wide Web, I don't think I would have been able to write this novel, or, at least, it would have taken years of research.

Firstly I want to thank the members of the Facebook group "Newton Heath Remembered", who always had an answer to my questions within half an hour of my posting them, and who provided links to fascinating websites. In particular, the BBC "WW2 Peoples' War" has many personal accounts from the time.

Similarly, the members of the Skewen group, who gave me valuable information about anti aircraft sites in the area during WW2, and solved the mystery of what my father was doing there at the beginning of the war..

For personal information about growing up in Newton Heath in the 1920s and 1930s, I am indebted to my late father, my late Auntie Nora, and my Auntie Jean.

What would I have done without Wikipedia? Any information that I couldn't get elsewhere, I could get from this fantastic website, and, yes, I have sent them a donation.

I want to thank my three proofreaders; my sister, Karen and my sons, Michael and Stephen, for their encouragement and constructive criticism. I love you all.

Finally I want to thank my beloved husband, John, for supporting me, for doing most of the housework and bringing me endless cups of coffee when I am writing. It goes without saying that I love you, but there, I've said it anyway.

Part One:

Growing Up

1 MOVING FROM COLLYHURST

"You'll be living on clean teeth!" roared Grandad Roberts, glaring at his son. "Ten bob a week for a council house when you've got a perfectly good terraced for five bob. You must be barmy!"

Harry's clear, grey eyes travelled from his dad's face to Grandad's, both men glaring at each other. Then he turned to his mother, who was sitting as far back into the corner as possible, as though she was trying to become invisible. Harry would be four next week, but, even at this young age, he had an uncanny knack of knowing how his mother felt. He went over to her now and cuddled into her side. It seemed that he was giving her comfort, rather than seeking it. She hugged him gratefully. He could sense waves of anxiety easing as he hugged her.

Harry was alarmed, but not surprised, by the raised voices. His male relatives always seemed to be shouting at each other. He was puzzled though. How could you live on "clean teeth"? You lived in a house, didn't you?

He pictured a floor made up of enormous gleaming white teeth, with white tables and chairs, and a white fireplace. He turned to his mother with a questioning look, but she silenced him with a glance. He knew better than to speak.

He had felt the sting of his dad's hand on his bottom on more than one occasion, and he realised that this was not the time to ask questions.

Bill Roberts faced his father with an expression that matched the older man's.

"I don't really care what you think Dad. I am not having my family living in a slum. I want them to have a garden, and fresh air. Newton Heath is only three miles away. We'll have a new, three bedroomed house with a bathroom, and fields all round us. I've got a good job on the railway, and I don't see why we shouldn't have somewhere nice to live. We're as good as anyone else. Even Fred Kerr is putting in for one.

"Fred Kerr! He'll have got the idea from his stuck up mother. She's always had ideas above her station, she has. Bob Kerr has rued the day he married that woman. His family, and ours, have lived in these terraces since they were built for the mill workers. They've been good enough for us, and they should be good enough for you."

"Actually, Fred got the idea from me. I told him about the houses first." Bill replied. "I've been watching them being built these past few months"

Grandad looked taken aback for a second, but then turned his piercing gaze towards Alice, still cowering in the corner with her arm around Harry. "She put you up to it, didn't she? Little miss goody-goody. Collyhurst has never been good enough for you, Miss holier-than-thou, has it?"

Harry felt his mother stiffen with indignation, but she still said nothing. She rarely spoke to grandad, except to ask if he wanted a cup of tea. As usual, she allowed her husband to speak for her.

Glaring at his father, Bill said, "Alice had nothing to do with it. In fact she's been worried sick about the rent too. So you are in agreement for once. Though I don't suppose you are very happy about that, are you? That would never do, agreeing with someone else, would it?"

"Well, you cheeky young bugger! You never would have spoken to me like that before you married that stuck up madam." The accusing finger was pointing threateningly at Alice again. She shrank into the chair, squeezing Harry so tightly he could hardly breathe.

"I may not have stood up for myself when I was younger, Dad, but it's 1923. I've fought in the war to end all wars and I'm 28 years old. You can't tell me what to do any more. Come on Alice. We're going!"

Harry squeezed his mother's hand as they walked the few yards back to their own little terraced house. She looked down at him lovingly. He was so sensitive and mature for his years. He was completely different from her older son, Billy, a typical boisterous seven year old, who took after his dark haired Dad in both looks and nature. Harry knew that Alice adored her firstborn. He was born when Bill was away at war. He also knew that she loved and understood him, Harry, who had inherited her love of animals and who always seemed to know how she was feeling.

oOo

After Bill opened their front door, Harry jumped over the step into the hall to avoid standing on the gleaming white step, which his Mother had donkey-stoned earlier. This was another difference between Harry and his brother, the way he noticed things, and acted in a way that was extremely mature for such a young child. Billy would be home from school soon, and his muddy footprints would be all over the step and the hall, and he would be cheerfully apologetic when his mother reminded him to wipe his feet, but he would still forget next time.

"We are definitely going then?" ventured Alice

"Don't you start as well, Alice" Bill replied. "I'm adamant. In fact I went up to the town hall today and paid the first week's rent. We can move in next week. You'd better ask at the corner shop for empty boxes. It won't take long to pack."

"It's quite a way to walk to Newton Heath, Bill. Will you borrow the handcart from Tom?" this was the way most people moved house, but mainly they were only moving a couple of streets. Families tended to stay close together. Alice could understand her father in law being angry. He felt that Bill was abandoning the family. Harry could see, though, that his mother was pleased to be moving. He tried to imagine a house with a garden and a bathroom. It was difficult, because he had never seen one.

"No, we won't be using Tom's handcart" Bill looked proud. "My mate Fred has got a motor lorry from his uncle. He's planning to start a removal business and he said we can be his first customers. We only need to pay for the petrol and buy him a pint, as long as we recommend him to all the other people who will be moving into the new estate." Bill rubbed his hands together with satisfaction.

Alice went through to the scullery to put the kettle on the gas, and Harry, realising that Bill was in a good mood, ventured to ask a question.

"Dad, what did Grandad mean, we'll be living on clean teeth?"

Bill laughed. "It's a saying he has. It means that he thinks we won't be able to afford food, so our teeth will be clean.

"Will we be able to afford food then?"

"Of course, I've worked it all out. We'll manage easily."

"Oh, right," Harry didn't ask any more questions. He knew well that Bill got annoyed if he asked too many questions. He also knew that Billy could ask as many questions as he liked, and his Dad would delight in giving the answers. Of course, most of Billy's questions were about football or the railway. These questions were easy to answer. Harry asked questions that were surprisingly deep for a four year old. Things like, "What does god look like?" or, "Why does Grandad shout so much?" Harry's questions made his Dad uncomfortable.

They were sitting in the kitchen, drinking tea, when Billy came bouncing in. They heard the key being dragged through the letterbox on its string, the door banged against the wall and Billy was in the kitchen almost before the front door banged shut.

"Did you wipe your feet?" Alice asked.

"Oh, sorry mum, I forgot." He looked down at his boots and then gazed up at her, his bright blue eyes shining through his incredibly long lashes, giving her his smile that always melted her heart.

"Never mind love. Try to remember next time," she said.

Harry was nearly bursting with the news. "Billy, we're moving to a new house. It's got a bathroom and a garden too!" he cried. "It's a long way away, near some fields."

Billy looked at his dad. "Will I have to change schools?"

"Yes, there's a good school called Brookdale Park. You'll be going there, and Harry will start there in September."

Billy looked crestfallen. "Won't I see Joe again? He's my best friend."

"Don't you worry, son. The Kerrs are moving too. They've got a house just up the road from ours."

"Wow, that's great! When are we going?"

"Next Thursday. I've got some leave, and we are going in a motor lorry."

"Ooh, can I go in the lorry too, Dad?"

"I think there'll be enough room in the cab for you, but your mother and Harry will go on the tram."

Alice looked up quickly. "Next Thursday is the 15th of March, Harry's Birthday. I was going to make a cake. There won't be time if we're moving." Harry looked crestfallen.

"You can make a cake in your new gas stove on Friday or Saturday. Harry won't mind, will you Harry?" said Dad.

"No, it's ok Mum," said Harry, choking back the tears. Alice ruffled his soft, brown hair and gave him a hug. Billy was skipping around the room with excitement. He hadn't realised that Harry was upset. He loved his brother but he didn't always understand him.

"C'mon Harry, let's go and play football," said Billy.

"Put your coats on, "said Alice, "winter isn't over yet".

They grabbed coats, but they didn't put them on. They would be used as goalposts. There was so little traffic in their street that they could play football for hours without seeing so much as a horse and cart. Billy and Harry were soon joined by Joe Kerr and his little brother, Bobby, and several others from the houses around. Their mothers were quite glad to get them out from underfoot while they were getting tea ready.

oOo

When they were in bed later, Billy was still too excited to sleep. "What do you think our new house will be like, Harry?" he asked.

"Mum says it's got three bedrooms, a bathroom and an inside toilet. I wonder if the bathroom has got a fire, cos it's nice when we have a bath in front of the fire, isn't it? It's got a garden too, and Dad's going to plant spuds and carrots, and we might get hens too."

"Wow!" breathed Billy, trying to visualise all this while he was drifting off to sleep.

oOo

The next few days flew by in a flurry of activity. The boys were sent round to several of the nearby corner shops to beg cardboard boxes. Bill managed to get some tea chests too. On the Monday he arrived home from work carrying a great sack full of straw. "I went to see Farmer Richards, who owns the land next to the new house. He's a bit abrupt, but he did give me this straw, and he said he'll be cutting his privets in a couple of weeks and we can get some cuttings."

"That's good, I can use the straw to pack the crockery," said Alice. She was standing at the kitchen table sorting towels and bedding. "I've changed the beds today, and the March winds have been very handy. This washing is all dry. I won't iron them until we get to the new house, so they don't get creased in the packing."

"I don't know why you iron sheets anyway," said Bill, "They get creased as soon as you lie on them."

"I just like to see them smooth, and it airs them if there's any damp left on them," she replied. Like most women around there, Alice was very house proud, and she wouldn't dream of using anything that hadn't been ironed. Apart from towels though, even though some of her friends ironed these too. She thought the iron took the fluffiness out of them.

Harry listened to this conversation as he was helping Alice to fold the washing. He liked the sheets ironed too. He loved getting into a newly made bed and feeling the smoothness of the sheets. He brought a pillow case up to his face and inhaled the lovely, fresh smell. The sublime look on his face made his mother laugh. She didn't realise that he had copied the action from her. "We'll go up to see Grandma Davis tomorrow," she told Harry. He smiled. He loved to see his gentle grandma, so different from grandma Roberts, who could be a bit stern.

Alice's widowed mother lived in Cheetham Hill, in the house where Alice was born. Alice's brother, Tom, and his wife and two children lived there with her. They were always complaining that the house was too small, but they didn't seem inclined to move. Tom was a tram driver, based at Queen's road depot, just a five minute walk away, so it was handy.

oOo

Tuesday dawned dry and blustery. After Billy had left for school and the house was as neat and tidy as it could be, with boxes and packing cases everywhere, Alice and Harry set off to visit Grandma Davis. It didn't take long to walk through the streets of Collyhurst to Queen's Road. Then they just had to walk uphill for a while until they reached grandma's street. It looked very similar to the street they lived in. The terraced houses all opened directly on to the pavement and each step was either white or cream donkey-stoned. Every window had clean white net curtains. All the women around here were as house proud as Alice and her mother. It would take a very strong minded, or very lazy, woman to go against the grain.

Alice knocked at the door. "When I was living here the key was on a string like ours, but your auntie Elsie likes to see who's at the door before she lets them in. You wouldn't think that it's Grandma Davis's name on the rent book." Harry had heard her say this before, but he nodded to show Alice that he was listening.

"Oh, hello Alice," said Elsie as she stood blocking the doorway, "I thought you'd be too busy to visit us this week, what with the move and everything."

"I'm never too busy to see my mum, and you," Alice added hastily.

"Well you'd better come in then." She opened the door wider and led them through the hall to the kitchen. Grandma was sitting in her usual corner by the stove. Harry ran to give her a hug. "Hello lovey," she said. "You've got rosy cheeks is it cold out there?"

Alice answered for him, "It's fresh and windy, so it's blown the cobwebs away." Harry agreed, smiling and nodding his head. "How are you, Mum?" she looked carefully at grandma, who was looking a bit pale.

"I'm fine, and all the better for seeing you and Harry," she replied. "Shall we have a brew?" She started to rise out of her chair.

"I'll do it," said Elsie, "it's no bother." Grandma reluctantly sat down again.

"When are you moving?" asked Elsie.

"On Thursday. Bill's mate, Fred is taking all the furniture in his lorry.

"Oh, Thursday is Harry's Birthday," said Grandma. Seeing he looked upset, she quickly said, "That'll be really special, Harry. There's not many boys can say they got a new house for their birthday. You'll never forget the day you moved in." She gave him an extra cuddle as she said this, and he smiled up at her.

Alice and Harry stayed for an hour chatting to grandma, while Elsie bustled about, looking busy. Elsie looked relieved when Alice got up to go, saying, "I'll come next week, Mum, on Tuesday. I should have the new house straight by then, and maybe you'd like to come back with me to see it?"

"That'd be lovely!" she replied. "Happy Birthday for Thursday, Harry. Here you are," and she pressed a two shilling piece into his hand.

"Ooh thanks Grandma," said Harry, and gave her another cuddle.

Elsie came to the door with them. Alice took the opportunity to ask, "How is Mum. Is she getting out much?"

Elsie replied that Mum didn't need to go out much now. Elsie had taken over all the housework and shopping, leaving her with very little to do.

"It's such a shame, though," Alice replied, "My mother is turning into an old lady and she's only fifty five!"

"You ought to be glad I'm looking after her! There's not many get such care at her age."

Alice didn't argue. She just turned away. "Oh, by the way," said Elsie, "Tom's getting the rent book changed to his name." before Alice could comment she continued, "We thought it would be best, now your Mum is getting on a bit." Alice just got hold of Harry's hand and walked quickly away.

Harry could feel that his Mum was angry. He hadn't really understood the adult's conversation, but he knew that auntie Elsie had done something that his Mum didn't like, and it had something to do with his lovely grandma.

"Is Grandma getting old?" he asked.

"No, she isn't!" Alice said quite abruptly, "She would still be doing her own shopping and housework if Tom hadn't got married. Don't worry, lovey. I'm not cross with you."

Harry knew this, though he didn't know how he knew it. It just seemed that he could feel the same feelings as his mother. It was the same with Billy, to a lesser extent. Billy was always happy anyway. His Dad was harder to fathom, though he always knew when Dad was angry, even when he wasn't shouting.

Harry could feel Alice calming down as they walked home and by the time they turned into their own street she was humming a little tune. It was "All things Bright and Beautiful", his favourite hymn, so he joined in, skipping along and swinging their joined hands.

The rest of the day flew by, with Mum packing the remaining boxes and Harry helping where he could. Before they knew it Billy was home, banging the front door and shouting, "I'm starving; can I have a jam butty?" Alice laughed and Harry joined in.

oOo

Thursday came around and Fred arrived early, his lorry making a tremendous noise in the narrow street. When Alice opened the door, Harry jumped out on to the pavement. He could see that several of the neighbours had decided to donkey-stone their steps. Well, it wasn't every day that a motor lorry came down there, and it wasn't often that people moved out either. So everyone was interested.

Everything was ready. They had all been up for hours, stripping the beds and dismantling them, rolling up the front room carpet and packing the final few things into boxes. It didn't take long for Bill and Fred to put the furniture in the lorry and pack all the bags and boxes round it. Alice swept the floors and then handed the brush and shovel to Bill to put in the lorry. A very excited Billy was lifted up to sit between the two men, and Alice locked the front door. She gave the key to Grandad, who was going to pass it on to the rent man. Grandad was still looking quite stern, but he had made his peace with Bill and had promised to visit sometime. The lorry drove off amid cries of good luck from the neighbours, and Alice had a few words with each of her friends as she and Harry walked down their street for the last time.

They crossed Rochdale road and made their way through the warren of terraced streets until they reached Oldham Road. They were lucky to see that a tram was just coming. Harry was excited, as he hadn't been this way before. Alice told him that this tram went all the way to Oldham, but they would be getting off in Newton Heath, just a few stops further on. They sat on the right hand side so that they could look out for the co- operative building on the corner of Church Street. They soon saw it, and, as they got off the tram, Harry stared up at this massive red brick building with its tall tower on the corner. They walked up Church Street. There were lots of different shops on this street, and they saw that there was a canal passing under a bridge. Alice pointed out the market just up a street on the left. It wasn't open today, but she promised that they would go on Saturday. They reached a church and Alice said that it wasn't far to get to the new house. They continued along Culcheth Lane, with houses on the left, but, on the right, just after a pub, Harry could see fields. Then there were more terraced houses like the ones at home, and then they turned on to Amos Avenue. "This is our street now," said Alice. Harry looked down what seemed like a really long road. There were a few terraced houses on the right at first, and then what looked like a vast expanse of mud, with very clean, brick houses on the left, a few feet from the road, and half built houses on the right. They could see Fred's lorry parked outside their new house and they soon reached it. There was a path up to the front door, which was wide open. They could hear Billy's excited voice, sounding hollow in the near empty rooms.

Bill came to the front door. "Oh good, you're here. We're gasping for a brew. Can you get the kettle on? It's already unpacked." Alice and Harry gazed around as they passed through a small, square hall into a lovely, bright room with a large window showing another sea of mud ending in a field of wild flowers and then what looked like a steep drop into a valley. "The railway's down there but you can't see it from here," said Bill. They passed a large fitted cupboard behind the door as they turned to the right to go into the kitchen. This had a window to the front and a door at the back that led to a coal store and amazingly, an inside toilet! Next to this was the back door, which was actually on the side of the house. Harry could see that his Mum was delighted with the kitchen. As well as the back to back oven, which connected to a back boiler and the living room fire, there was a gas stove with two burners on top, a grill and an oven below. The kettle was already sitting on the stove, but not filled. Alice picked it up and went to the sink. She stood staring for a few seconds. There were two taps! Bill came in just then and grinned as he said to her, "Yes, we'll have running hot water, as soon as I've lit the fire. There might even be enough hot water for a bath tonight. The tap with "C" on the top is the cold water!" they both laughed, and Harry joined in. "And, look at this!" Bill flicked a switch on the wall and a bright light came on near the ceiling. Harry was amazed!

"Electric light!" breathed Alice, "No more lighting gas mantles or trimming wicks for oil lamps." She exchanged a grin with Bill. Harry wondered what other fantastic things they would discover in this house.

Just then Harry heard Billy shouting from upstairs. "Come up Harry!" he called, "Come and see our bedroom!" Harry ran up the stairs and saw Billy standing in one of the four doorways. They went into the room, which had a window to the back of the house. They skirted around boxes and the pieces of their bed, which hadn't been put together yet, and looked out of the window. The muddy area to the back of the houses could be clearly seen from up here, and the wild area beyond that looked very inviting to the boys. They heard the sound of a train and they could just see the top of the engine with steam billowing out of it. "Wow! I think we're going to like living here," said Harry.

They explored their parents' bedroom and the smaller room to the front, which had a tall cupboard in the corner, and then Billy said, "Wait till you see this, Harry," as he opened the bathroom door. There was an enormous white bath with feet like a big cat, and a white sink, both with two taps. "Is that a bath? It's not like our tin bath that we had at home," said Harry. He couldn't believe how big it was. "There isn't a fire though. How will we keep warm?" Bill came in at that point and told them that there would be so much hot water, they wouldn't feel the cold, and they could empty the bath just by pulling the plug out. "Anyway," he said, "get downstairs now and help your mother to put stuff away. Then me and Fred can put the beds together without you getting in the way."

They clattered down the stairs and ran into the kitchen, shouting, "Mum, Mum, we've got a massive bath upstairs!" Alice laughed and ruffled their hair. Harry could feel the happiness emanating from her.

oOo

Bill got a lovely fire going after Fred had left and it seemed very soon after this that they had hot water coming from the kitchen tap. They all had a feel of it and the boys said it was like magic. Mum left off unpacking to peel some spuds for tater ash, the boys' favourite. She got that going on the stove and then continued putting her kitchen straight. The boys had discovered the pantry in the front corner of the kitchen, under the stairs. It had a stone slab for keeping things cold and several shelves. Mum gave them the job of putting things away on the lower shelves. Their kitchen table just fitted under the window, leaving a space for the pantry door to open. They were all hungry by the time tea was ready. They sat round the table and soon devoured every morsel. Alice then reached under the table and brought out a brown paper package. "Happy Birthday Harry. You see we didn't forget, and I'll bake a cake tomorrow," she said. Harry opened the package and found a red fire engine. It was wonderful! "Thanks Mum and Dad," he said.

"And me!" said Billy, "I helped to choose it."

"Thanks Billy," said Harry.

Harry suddenly felt really tired and he gave an enormous yawn. Mum said, "Come on, let's try out that bath, and then you can go straight to bed. I'll wrap your pyjamas round your hot water bottles and you'll be snug as two bugs in a rug."

"Aw, Mum!" complained Billy, "I don't have to go to bed yet, do I? I'm a lot bigger than Harry and there's no school tomorrow."

"You've had a very busy day, Billy, and I bet you'll be yawning too after a hot bath. Come on now, there'll be lots more for me to do after you're in bed."

The bath was so big that both boys could go in at once, and they were allowed to stay in there while mum went to finish making their bed. They had great splashing fun and the floorboards were wet when Mum came back. "I think we'll have to get some oilcloth for this floor," she said, "but you'll have to remember not to splash so much next time."

Billy was still complaining when they were dried and putting pyjamas on, but he got in bed and snuggled up with Harry, who could tell his brother was feeling sleepy too. "Night night, God bless," said Mum.

"Night night," the boys chorused.

After Mum had gone downstairs Billy said, "Shall we see how many trains we can count before we go to sleep?"

"Mmmm," replied Harry, sleepily.

They heard one train just then, but before another one came they were both sound asleep.

oOo

Harry was dreaming. He knew he was dreaming, but this dream felt real, although he knew that he'd never been to this place before. He was in an unfamiliar house, in someone's bedroom. There was a lady in the bed and she was crying out in pain. Another lady was talking to her, soothing her, he thought. Suddenly the helping lady went to the bottom of the bed and started doing something that Harry couldn't see, and then she was holding up a tiny baby, showing the lady in bed. The lady in the bed started laughing and crying at the same time and she held out her arms to take the baby. Harry moved nearer to look at the baby. It was beautiful, with lots of dark curly hair, and somehow he knew that the baby was a girl, and that she was important. There was an aura of love in the room, but there was also a great feeling of sadness that he couldn't understand. Harry moved away, and then he was back in his own bed, snuggled up to Billy, and there was light coming through the uncurtained window.

At breakfast Harry told his Mum about the dream, and how real it seemed. "How did you know the baby was a girl?" she asked.

"I don't know, I just knew," he replied. He looked at his mum and he could feel that she was, not upset, but the dream had affected her somehow. She put her hands down to her tummy and Harry noticed for the first time that his Mum's tummy seemed to be a lot fatter than usual.

2 EXPLORING

After breakfast Billy and Harry asked if they could go out to explore. Bill said that they could go out the front way and stick to the roads. The back was too muddy. There had been a lot of rain recently and the uncultivated gardens had been churned up into mud by the builders. It was dry now, anyway, so the boys could go out and give their parents time to put up curtains and get the furniture into place.

As Alice was seeing them off at the front door, they noticed Fred Kerr's lorry a few doors along. "That must be their house. I wonder if Joe and Bobby are there?" said Billy

"No, their Grandma is minding them today so that their mum and dad can get on with moving in. You'll likely see them tomorrow," said Alice.

The boys were a bit disappointed, but everything was so new and interesting they set off up the front garden path in good spirits. It looked strange, because the path led to two concrete gate posts, but there was no gate yet and no fence or hedge to the garden. All the other houses looked the same. At least the road had been surfaced and there was a pavement of stone slabs.

They walked down the road and met two other boys. "Have you just moved in?" the bigger boy, with a mop of ginger hair and bright blue eyes, asked them.

Billy answered for them. "Yes, just up there. I'm Billy and this is my little brother, Harry."

"I'm in the first house. It's the best one cos we're right next to the way into the Ollers," the boy answered. "I'm Malcolm and this is me mate Charlie. He lives there, the third house" Charlie gave them a gap toothed grin. He was smaller than Malcolm and had brown eyes and jet black hair.

"What's the Ollers?" said Harry.

"It's the best place to play cos it's all long grass with lumps and dips that you can hide in for hide an' seek. The way in is just here," said Malcolm. He was leading them round the corner into the next road, which ended in a dead end. On the left was a big gate into a field, but they didn't need to use the gate because the builders had done away with the boundaries on the side where the new houses were. They just went through the gap next to the gate, avoiding the mud, and they were on the Ollers.

"Why is it called the Ollers?" asked Harry.

"No idea. Everyone calls it that," said Malcolm, and he started to run through the long grass, with the other three following him. They stopped, breathless, at the top of a steep slope. At the bottom was a high wire fence and beyond that was the railway. They could hear a train coming, so they stood there waiting, and they were soon rewarded with the sight of a steam locomotive puffing its way along. The four boys waved madly at the men in the engine and whooped with delight when their waves were returned. They were so close to the railway that they could feel and smell the steam as it passed. "Wow!" breathed Harry. "That was great!"

They spent the rest of the morning exploring and playing hide and seek and tiggy it. Harry and Billy identified their own house from the back, but they didn't attempt to go home that way later, because they didn't want to wade through the mud. They did see Bill, who was out looking at his "garden" and they waved to him. But he didn't call them in yet, so they continued playing until they all agreed that they were "starving", and made their way home.

After dinner Billy and Harry went out again. Malcolm was just emerging from his house with a jam butty in his hand. "Hiya Billy," he called as they approached him. "Come 'ere Billy, I wanna tell you somethin'," he whispered, thinking Harry couldn't hear him, but Harry's hearing was acute, and he also could sense that Billy was feeling excited. "I wanna take you somewhere good, but your Harry is too little. He'll slow us down."

Billy was in two minds. He didn't want to abandon Harry, but he really wanted to see this good place. Harry, typically, said, "I don't really want to play out, Billy. Mum said she was going to do some baking. I'll go and help her." He felt Billy's relief and he even detected some feeling from Malcolm, who was a bit ashamed, but glad that they didn't have a four year old tagging along. "C'mon, Billy. We'll call for Charlie," he said.

Harry was quite happy to be going home. He loved being with Billy, but he loved being with his Mum even more. He skipped back to the house, thinking about apple pie and jam tarts.

Alice welcomed him back and stood him on a stool to wash his hands at the kitchen sink so he could help her. She made a bowl of pastry for apple pie and mince and onion pie. The latter would do for tea with spuds and carrots. The leftover pastry was made into jam tarts, and Harry used the cutter to make the shapes and was allowed to push the pastry shapes into the baking tray. Alice then supervised him spooning in the jam, so that he didn't put too much in. She also made some cake mixture and spooned this into two round tins.

Alice was trying out the back to back oven, which was heated from the living room fire. She wasn't sure about the temperature needed for pastry, so she was checking regularly. Soon the delicious smell of baking was filling the kitchen. Harry's mouth was watering, and he hoped he would be allowed a jam tart when they were ready. All the pies and the cake turned out well and Harry could tell that Alice was delighted with the result. "You see," she told Harry, "It doesn't cost anything to cook in this oven. We have to have the fire lit anyway, and it heats the water as well as the oven. We'll only have to use the gas oven when it's very hot in the summer, when we don't need the fire."

Harry suddenly realised that Bill wasn't there. "Where's Dad? Has he gone back to work?" he asked Alice.

"No, he's not back at work until Monday. He's gone to see where he can get wood for fencing off the back garden," she replied.

oOo

Alice and Harry were sitting at the kitchen table eating a jam tart and drinking tea, surrounded by pies and an iced cake, when Bill and Billy arrived within a minute of each other, and both wearing smug smiles. Though Billy was itching to tell about his adventure, he had to let his dad speak first.

"Well, I met Fred coming out of his new house, and he was going for fencing wood too. Not only that, he had been talking to some of the other blokes here and came up with the brilliant idea of us all going to the wood yard together and trying to get a job lot cheaper than usual. It worked too! Six of us went down to Evans's sawmill, off Oldham Road. They don't usually sell small lots of wood, but the wood man was pleased there were so many of us and he's going to deliver all the wood tomorrow. It was so cheap that we went on to the ironmongers to get nails, and hinges for the gates, and we got those at cut price too. We just need some good weather this weekend and we'll have the garden fenced in no time!"

Billy was hopping about now. "Dad, Dad! Can I tell you my adventure now?" he shouted.

"Go on son," Bill replied.

"We've been under the railway in a tunnel and we went right down to the Red River. It doesn't half go fast!"

Alice gasped, and Harry got a terrible feeling of foreboding. "You didn't go near the edge of the river, did you?" Alice asked, "And where is this tunnel under the railway?" she looked at her husband as she asked this. He worked on the railway lines, so he should know.

"He'll be ok Alice. The tunnel is just at the end of Culcheth Lane. I'll take you there tomorrow, after the wood man's been. It's just a bridge really and it's nice beyond that. I think they call it Clayton Valley or something like that, because Clayton's on the other side of it. Billy's sensible enough to stay away from the edge of the river, aren't you son?"

"Yes Dad," Billy replied, but Harry didn't think that Billy really meant what he said. He felt as if cold water had been poured down his back.

oOo

In bed that night, Harry said, "Billy, you won't go near that river will you?"

"Oh, it's ok," said Billy, "I know what I'm doing. You shouldn't go near, cos you're only little, but I'm ok." Harry wasn't convinced, but he said no more about it.

As Harry drifted into sleep he found himself in the strange bedroom again. The lady was asleep and so was the baby. She was wrapped up and lying in a big wooden drawer at the side of the bed. Harry looked closer at the beautiful face beneath the black curls. She looked very peaceful, but there was still a feeling of infinite sadness around her. He wondered about this.

oOo

The Geo Evans and Sons lorry arrived at 8.30 that Saturday morning. All six men came out to claim their timber. Billy and Harry were there too, along with several other children, all wanting to help. Each man received a stack of long thin timbers and a few shorter, thicker ones that were pointed at one end and smelled very strongly. Bill said the smell was creosote. They soon had the lorry unloaded. The delivery man was very happy and he told them to recommend the company to others who may be moving in. "As long as it's a bulk order like this, the boss will be well pleased," he said.

Harry and Billy were intrigued with the timber. "How can you make a fence with those long pieces, Dad?" asked Billy.

 "Get your wellies on and you can help, Billy, but Harry, didn't you want to go to the market with your Mum?" said Bill.

Harry looked at his dad, and he could feel that Dad would rather just have Billy there. He knew it was something to do with him being little, but there was something more that his dad wasn't saying. For a moment he felt disappointed that he wasn't included, but he did love shopping with Mum, so he just nodded and went inside.

Before they left home, Harry and Alice went out to the back door to say they were going. They watched Bill and Billy for a while. Fortunately the weather had been dry since they moved in and the mud had dried somewhat, into thick clods of heavy earth. Billy was having great fun stumbling up and down the lumps. Bill got one of the pointed pieces of wood – he called them stakes – and hammered it into the ground between their house and next door. He measured the distance for the next one with one of the longer, narrower pieces and hammered that one in too. With Billy bringing the stakes to him, he had a line of stakes along one side of the garden before Harry and Alice left.

Swinging the shopping basket between them, Alice and Harry made their way up Amos Avenue and along Culcheth Lane. They were soon past the church and on to Church Street, which was bustling with shoppers. Alice said that she was pleased with all the different shops. "It's as good as Cheetham Hill Road," she told Harry. They turned on to Silk Street, where they saw the entrance to the market. "We'll look at the market first and then we'll get some meat from that butchers on the corner," she said.

The market was a wonderland to Harry. So many colours and sounds and smells. It seemed like there was everything you could ever want here. He was most interested in the toy stall and the toffee stall, but Alice wanted greengroceries, bread and some curtain material for her kitchen. When her spud bag was loaded and she had two fresh loaves in her basket she chose some yellow gingham from the material stall. Harry liked the bright material, and he was rewarded for his patience with a penny and a visit to the toffee stall. He got two ounces of pear drops in a triangular white bag. Alice got some sherbet lemons for Billy too, "because he's been working hard with your dad," she said.

As they were leaving the market they saw a familiar figure coming towards them. "It's Mrs Kerr and Bobby," said Harry, and he ran up to the woman pushing her pram, with a small boy holding on to the handle. Sitting up in the pram was five month old Audrey.

"Hello Dorothy," said Alice.

"Hiya Bobby, where's your Joe?" asked Harry.

"He's helping Dad with the fence," said Bobby, "I was helping too, but Joe kept saying I was too little to help, even though Dad didn't mind me being slow, so I came out with Mum instead.

"Same here," said Harry. "Never mind, the market's good. D'you want a pear drop?"

"Ooh thanks," said Bobby, putting a sweet in his mouth and sucking with gusto. "Are you playing out after dinner?"

"No, we're going down to the river with Mum and Dad and our Billy. There's a tunnel under the railway," Said Harry; Bobby looked crestfallen.

"Would you like to come with us?" Alice said to Bobby. "Joe might want to come too, if he's had enough of fencing."

"Oh thanks Alice," said Dorothy, "I could do with a quiet afternoon to get the house straight. It's hard with three children to look after. You'll find out soon, won't you?" Alice blushed and Harry gave her a puzzled look. There was something his mum wasn't telling him. He didn't think it was a bad thing. He could always tell when she was upset, but he wondered what it was.

After ordering meat from the butchers, and flour, sugar and rice from the grocers, they made their way home. The meat and groceries would be delivered later, by a boy on a bike with a big basket in front. This free service was offered by a lot of the shops because competition was stiff. They needed as many customers as they could get.

When they got home Alice took a big dish of vegetable soup out of the back oven. Harry inhaled the delicious smell. Alice said, "It's just right; I'll call your dad in now."

They went out into the back garden and Harry was amazed at how much of the fence was already done. Both sides of the garden were enclosed and the stakes were in across the end. Bill and Billy were looking very proud. Harry stood by the fence. To him it seemed really high, just above his head. "It's a great fence Dad," he said. Bill gave him a rare smile.

"Hello Alice. What time is it?" said Bill.

"Quarter past twelve," she replied.

"Flipping 'eck. That morning's gone quickly," he said. "Billy, you better go in and have a wash if you want to go to the river after dinner." Billy didn't need telling twice. Leaving his wellies at the back door he shot through the house and up the stairs to the bathroom. The boys were already used to having a wash upstairs, though Billy was often sent back to do a proper job because he had a tide mark on his neck!

While Bill was collecting his tools Alice was admiring his work. "How did you know where to put the end fence?" she asked. "Did the council say how much garden we could have?"

"They didn't say anything about gardens, but I got together with the other men and we decided that, as the land beyond is wild, the council won't be bothered about the size of the back gardens, as long as we keep them tidy. So we worked out how long to make the side fences according to how much wood we had. It's a good size isn't it?" Alice agreed. Harry looked up at his dad in wonder, thinking how clever he was.

After their dinner of soup and fresh crusty bread, Bill and the boys set off. Alice had to stay at home to wait for the delivery boys. She said that she could see the river another time, probably in the summer. They called to collect Joe and Bobby Kerr. Fred decided to come too. It would be a break from building fences. They went up Amos Avenue and turned right on to Culcheth Lane. The lane became narrower as it went downhill and was bordered on the right by a high stone wall. "That's the Nunnery," said Bill, as they passed a big wooden door in the wall. They look after poor old people who haven't got any family. There was a slot in the door and some writing above it. "What does that say?" asked Harry.

"I can read it!" shouted Joe and Billy together, but Joe was quicker at reading, "Alms for the poor," he said, "Haven't the poor old people got any arms then?"

Bill and Fred laughed, "No, it's alms with an L. it means money. If you've got any spare coppers it's good to give some of them to people who've got nothing. The nuns need money to buy food for the poor old people," said Fred.

Billy and Joe were sucking sherbet lemons. "Shall we give them the rest of our toffees?" asked Billy, reluctantly.

"No, you're ok son. I'll put something in," Said Bill, and he fished a couple of pennies out of his pocket, giving them to the boys to push through the slot.

They continued down the steep, cobbled hill and came to the railway bridge. It wasn't really dark, because the sun was shining and they could see the other end. Still, Harry was glad the two men were with them. On the other side the cobbles continued for a while, with a building on the left, and then became a rough path that led down to the river. The older boys ran ahead, but Harry and Bobby stayed close to the men. The river really was red! It was lined with shiny red bricks and the fast flowing water was well below the banks. Harry didn't like it at all, but the older boys and Bobby were fascinated and stood for ages right on the edge.

"It's good, innit Dad?" said Billy.

"Yes, but your mother is right, you shouldn't go too near the edge, especially if we aren't with you. You'll remember that, won't you?"

"Yes Dad," Billy replied.

They explored the wild land around the area. Harry found some pussy willows that he thought his Mum would like, and Bill cut some twigs off for him with his penknife. The other boys weren't interested in trees and flowers, but they found some thick blades of grass that they could blow through to make a screeching noise. Bill and Fred laughed at their sons doing the same things that they themselves had done not so long ago.

oOo

It was nearly teatime when they got home. The delivery boys had been and Alice was putting the finishing touches to a shepherd's pie. Bill decided to leave the fencing for the day and settled in his chair by the fire to read his paper. Alice found a jam jar for Harry to put the pussy willows in. she said they looked lovely on the kitchen windowsill.

All too soon it was bedtime and Billy and Harry snuggled up to their hot water bottles in their cosy bed. "I like living here, do you?" said Billy.

"Mmmm," said Harry. He was already half asleep.

oOo

They awoke to the sound of Alice calling them to get up. "Breakfast's ready. You'll have to be quick. We're going to Church and Sunday School," she said. Billy groaned. Harry knew that Billy would much rather play on the Ollers than go to Sunday school. Harry quite liked going though. He had been big enough to go to their old Sunday school for about six months. He enjoyed the bible stories and loved singing hymns.

Faces and necks scrubbed and wearing their Sunday best, the two boys and Alice made their way to All Saints Church. Bill had decided to spend his Sunday morning finishing the fence. Harry knew that Alice would have liked Bill to go to church too, but he also knew that his dad wouldn't be swayed from acting as he pleased.

They met Dorothy Kerr with her children on the way. Billy and Joe exchanged a look that showed their disgust at having to go to Sunday school. Bobby hadn't been before so it was all new to him.

The Sunday school was in the hall of the primary school, just across from the church. Alice and Dorothy went in with the boys to introduce them to the teacher, who seemed very friendly. "Now, we are going into the church," said Alice, "If you get out before us, just wait in the yard until we come," the boys chorused, "Ok".

When the boys came out an hour later their mothers were just coming into the yard. "Did you enjoy the class?" asked Alice.

"Yes, we sang songs," said Harry, and Bobby smiled his agreement.

"No, it was boring!" complained Billy. Characteristically, Joe agreed with him. The two mothers laughed. "Well, it's just too bad. You'll be going every week and you'll learn a lot," said Dorothy. Billy was too polite to disagree, but his face said it all.

oOo

The rest of Sunday passed pleasantly, with a hearty dinner of roast lamb, potatoes and cabbage, generously covered with gravy. Bill had finished his fence and had made a gate leading to the Ollers. After dinner, the boys went out to admire it. "I just need some privet cuttings for the front now. I'll call on Farmer Richards in my dinner break tomorrow; find out when he's cutting his hedge."

The boys played out on the Ollers that afternoon, joined by several other children. Bill started digging over the back garden, and Harry noticed that most of the other men were out doing the same thing, all making the most of the dry weather.

After a pleasant evening listening to Billy reading while Alice knitted and Bill finished reading his Sunday paper, the boys were again snuggled up in bed. Harry fell asleep immediately and found himself in the dream that was becoming familiar. The lady and her baby were there again, but this time they weren't in the bedroom. The lady was pacing up and down a small sitting room, trying to calm the baby, who was crying. Although Harry was sure they couldn't see him, he started singing one of the hymns he had learned. The baby stopped crying and the lady looked down at her with tenderness. "At last," she whispered, and started to croon the same tune that Harry had been singing. There seemed to be a sense of peace in the room, though there was still the undercurrent of sadness that Harry couldn't understand. He puzzled about this as the dream faded.

3 AN INVITATION FOR GRANDMA

On Monday the boys were up early. Bill had already left for work and Alice had their breakfast ready. Billy was starting at the new school today and they set off in good time, Meeting up with Dorothy and her brood. Joe was starting at Brookdale Park School too. Alice would have liked Billy and Harry to go to All Saints School, but there weren't any places. Newton Heath was growing rapidly. There would soon be a need for another school.

Both the boys were a bit nervous, Harry could feel it, but they covered it up with bravado, keeping up the banter all the way up Daisy Bank and along Albert Street, where the red brick school was situated. The school and the yard looked enormous, compared with the one at All Saints, and there seemed to be hundreds of children running about. Alice and Dorothy found their way to the Headmaster's study. The older boys were soon escorted away to their classroom, and the Headmaster looked down at Harry and Bobby.

"So, Robert and Harry, you will be joining us in September, I believe?" the boys nodded nervously. "Well, I'm sure you will enjoy your time at our school. As long as you work hard and behave well, we will get along famously." His smile didn't reach his eyes. Harry thought that they would have to behave really well to avoid this man's wrath.

oOo

Alice and Harry arrived home after doing a bit of shopping. The house was already straight after the move. They didn't have many possessions and the bigger house had lots of storage, so everything had been put away. "I should do the washing, as its Monday," said Alice, "but I haven't got a washing line yet. I think I'll leave it till Wednesday, but don't tell your auntie Elsie. She'd be horrified!" She laughed, and Harry laughed too. Alice's sister in law was a stickler for doing everything on the right day: washing on Monday, ironing on Tuesday and so on.

"We'll do some more baking, and then give the house a good sweep through," said Alice.

They were interrupted during the morning, by two men from the council telling them they were fitting a front gate and a washing line pole. They soon had the gate fitted to the concrete posts. Harry watched them, fascinated. They were so quick, and he noticed that all the houses up to theirs now had gates.

The men drank the tea that Alice had made for them before they went round to inspect the back garden. "I see you've made a good start on the garden," one of them said. "Looks like everyone's been fencing and digging this weekend. Well, missus, we've been told to place your washing pole twenty yards from the house. I won't bother measuring. I can just put it level with the ones we've done," and he winked at Harry. They dug a hole just by the fence that Bill had erected at the end of the garden, and concreted a metal pole into it.

"Why did he wink, Mum?" whispered Harry.

"Well, I'm not that good at measuring, but I would guess that the garden is longer than twenty yards. He's giving us a good long washing line. We'll have to buy the rope ourselves though."

Before they left the men knocked a big hook into the house wall for the other end of the line. Harry and Alice noticed that the lady two doors down was already beginning to put her washing line up. "Oy, missus!" the men shouted, "Don't put your line up yet. The concrete won't have set properly. Leave it till tomorrow!" The lady looked abashed. "I've already told her that. Some people don't listen." the man complained.

They left early to collect Billy from school. Alice called on Dorothy and offered to bring Joe home too. "Thanks, I'll have the kettle on when you get back and we can have a chat," said Dorothy.

They made a detour to Church Street, so they could buy a length of rope from the hardware shop for the washing line. They got one for Dorothy too. Alice was grateful that Bill had a good job and was generous with housekeeping money. So many new things were needed.

The children piled out of the school, chattering noisily, glad to escape from the restrictions of the classroom. Billy and Joe were among the first ones out.

"Mum, Mum!" Billy shouted, "We've got a man teacher, Mr Smith. He shouts a lot, but we don't mind, do we, Joe?"

"No, we're not scared of him!" said Joe with bravado.

"I'm starving. Can I have a jam butty when we get home?" said Billy.

"Well, we're having a cuppa with Joe's mum first, but I don't see why not," Alice replied.

"My Mum'll give you a butty," said Joe.

"Well, only if she offers," said Alice, "You know it's rude to ask."

Dorothy did offer butties to all the children, and that kept them quiet while she and Alice chatted. Alice gave her the rope for her washing line and Dorothy paid her the few coppers it had cost. "I've missed doing my Monday wash," She said. "Fred had heard that they were coming today to fix the poles, so I thought I'd leave it till tomorrow, so I won't have wet washing all over the house."

"I'll have to leave mine till Wednesday. I'm going to see my mum tomorrow and I've promised to bring her back to see the house."

"How is she?"

"Physically, she's fine, but Elsie's got her sitting in a corner doing nothing. She's completely taken over the house, so Mum's just turning into an old lady. It worries me."

"Why don't you have her living with you?"

"Oh, Mum!" said Harry, who had been listening intently, "That'd be great. We could see Grandma every day!"

"I would love that," Alice agreed, smiling at Harry. "I don't know whether Grandma would want to leave her house though. I'll talk to Dad tonight".

oOo

On Tuesday, the journey to Grandma Davis's house was soon accomplished. As usual, Elsie answered the door and grandma was sitting in the corner, but she was wearing her best hat. "Are you having a cuppa?" asked Elsie. She already had the ironing blanket on the table and her irons were heating on the range.

"No thanks Elsie. I can see you're busy. We'll just get going. I promised

Mum we'd take her to see the new house. Maybe you can come over one day?" said Alice.

"Yes. I will, but I don't know when I'll get time," she replied.

They walked to the tram stop on Cheetham Hill Road, Harry skipping between the two women, holding their hands. He was bubbling with energy and excitement, but he had been told to say nothing about the possibility of Grandma coming to live with them. Alice had warned him that Grandma may not want to move, but Harry felt sure that she would.

They got the tram into town first; as Alice thought that the walk to Oldham Road might be a bit too much for Grandma. They changed trams in Piccadilly and were soon getting off at Church Street. The route was already becoming familiar. "Look Grandma," said Harry. "That's the big co op shop, and the canal's just up here. The Market's a bit further on. Oh, and that's the shop where we bought the washing line."

Grandma chuckled, "It's all lovely Harry."

Grandma was very impressed with the new house. "It's so clean and roomy," she said, "and aren't you lucky having two gardens?" Alice and Harry agreed.

Grandma sat in the rocking chair by the fire while Alice put the kettle on. Harry stood close to her so she could give him a cuddle. She was smiling, but he could sense that she was unhappy. "Are you ok Grandma?" he asked, and he was upset to see a tear roll down her cheek.

"I'm just happy that you all have this lovely house to live in. I wish you were nearer to me though."

Alice came in with the tea then. "I wanted to ask you, Mum. Would you like to come and live here with us? You could have the little front bedroom. It's lovely and warm with the airing cupboard being in there."

The tears really flowed then. Harry was alarmed! Through the tears she sobbed "They've taken my rent book away, Alice. It doesn't feel like my home any more"

"I know, Mum. Elsie told me. I think she talked Tom into it. It's not his fault. Anyway, we'd love to have you here."

"I'd love it but won't Bill mind?"

"We've already discussed it, and Bill thinks it's a good idea, especially as you can help when a certain thing happens." She looked down at her tummy. There it was again, Harry thought. It was something that the grownups knew, but they weren't telling Harry and Billy. He puzzled about it again and thought about asking, but he was so happy that Grandma was coming to live with them, he soon forgot.

The women carried on discussing the details of Grandma's move and Harry went off to play with his engine, content now that he could sense the happiness around him.

oOo

Bill and Alice lost no time organising Grandma Davis's move. On Saturday Bill and Fred went in the lorry to fetch grandma's belongings. They even managed to lift Grandma into the cab, and she enjoyed the novelty of the ride. She was leaving most of her household goods for Elsie and Tom, but Elsie still complained about her taking the treadle sewing machine and her button box and sewing basket. "You won't be doing much sewing will you? Alice has got a sewing kit, hasn't she?"

Bill told Alice what had been said when they got home. Harry was all ears, as usual.

"But your mum stood up for herself for once," he said "I was proud of you, Mum, when you told her that Alice hasn't got a sewing machine, and your basket was a present from Tom and Alice's Dad the first year you were married. She's a greedy c...!"

"Bill! Little ears present," warned Alice. Bill looked down at Harry with a frown.

"Where's your brother?" he said.

"He's playing on the Ollers with Joe and some other boys."

"Well, go and play with him. You're getting underfoot here!" Harry went off to get his coat. He knew that the older boys didn't want him messing up their games, but he didn't dare disobey his dad. Alice gave him an understanding smile, and Grandma hugged him.

As he went out of the back door he heard Bill say, "You spoil that boy, you know. He needs toughening up. He spends too much time with you women!"

"But he's only four, Bill," he heard Alice reply as he shut the door.

Harry traipsed up the flat area that was going to be a path. It was already partly covered with cinders from the fire. Bill had told the boys that cinders would make a good path that would keep dry in wet weather. They had been lucky up to now. The weather had been dry since they moved in and Bill had dug over the whole garden.

When he got to the gate he could see Billy and his friends in the distance. They were playing "tiggy it" and making a lot of noise. Harry stood by the gate for a while, and then he heard his name being called. He looked round and saw Bobby at his own back gate. "Come and play, Harry!" he called, and Harry ran over to him.

"I was playing tiggy it with our Joe and the others, but they're too quick. I was always "it" and I couldn't catch them, so I came back here. Look what my Dad has made for me. It's only for now, cos he'll need the wood sometime." Fred had made a small seesaw with a plank balanced on a log. "Dad was pushing the other end down for me, but he had to go in. Anyway, you can sit on the other end now." The two boys got on the seesaw and had a great time.

When Harry and Billy came in for tea they found grandma setting the table while Alice was getting ready to dish up. "Go up and wash your hands and faces, and you can have a quick look at Grandma's bedroom. Don't be long though."

Grandma's bedroom looked lovely, with her patchwork quilt making a splash of colour, and her picture of Grandad in its frame on the dresser. "Isn't it lovely having Grandma here?" said Billy. Harry smiled and nodded. He was brimming over with happiness.

After tea they all settled down to an evening that would soon become the routine for the family. Bill was sitting in his chair on one side of the fire and Grandma had the rocking chair on the other side. Alice made herself comfortable on the settee with the boys, the glow from the fire lighting up their faces. Both women were knitting while they listened to Billy reading from his school book. "You're getting to be a good reader, our Billy," said Bill proudly. "You'll soon be able to read as well as you play football."

"I'd rather play football though. It's much more fun," Billy replied.

4 Whit Walks and a New Baby

By Whitsun, Harry and his family felt as though they had always lived in Newton Heath. Bill had planted privet cuttings around the front garden and had dug, raked and seeded a lawn. The back garden was sectioned into vegetable plots and interesting looking shoots were already showing. Every fine Monday Alice and Grandma could be seen hanging out the washing and enjoying the feeling of space and fresh air that felt so much cleaner than it did in Collyhurst or Cheetham Hill.

Billy had made lots of friends and had explored all the fields and wild areas around. He had also learned not to go too near to Farmer Richards' yard. The gruff man wasn't fond of children and, though he tolerated them going through his pasture fields, he would threaten them with his dogs if they got too near his house.

Harry was happy and content in the company of his mum and grandma, and he often played with his friend, Bobby.

oOo

On Whit Sunday, 20th of May, they all set off early for church. Everyone was in their best clothes. The boys had new grey shorts and jackets, Alice and Grandma had new hats, and even Bill was in his Sunday best. They were going to join the rest of the church congregation for the Whit Walks. This would be the first time they had walked with their new church and the boys were jumping with excitement. They would be separated from their parents for the walk. The boys would be with their Sunday school class, walking in lines behind the girls. Harry didn't recognise most of the girls in their finery. They had frilly white dresses and flowers in their hair and little posies that they carried. Bill had the honour of carrying one of the poles that held the church banner, as he was one of the biggest and strongest men in the congregation. Alice and her Mum would walk at the back with the mothers' union. After reminding the boys to be on their best behaviour, Alice took her place just as the procession began.

Led by the local brass band, they left the church and progressed down Church Street through all the crowds, and turned left by the Duke of York pub, on to Oldham Road. The crowds were even greater here, and they joined other churches, making an enormous procession. Harry couldn't see a gap between the people on the pavements as he walked behind Billy and Joe. Suddenly he heard his name called. "There's our Harry and Billy! Cooee Billy, see you later!" It was Auntie Elsie and Uncle Tom with their two children. Billy waved, but Harry felt really shy, and he just smiled. He remembered then that the rest of the family was coming to tea after the walks, including Grandad and Grandma Roberts.

By the time they got back to the church and went over to the school for orange juice and buns, Harry's legs were aching. Billy, as usual, was full of bravado. "I could have walked another ten miles," he boasted, when Harry complained.

Joe piped up, "I bet you couldn't!" and an argument commenced.

Harry left them to it and went over to where Alice was sitting with Grandma. "Are your legs tired too, Mum?" he asked. She was looking very weary, and gratefully accepted the cup of tea that Dorothy brought.

"Yes, Harry. It was quite a long walk, but I was glad to do it."

"You shouldn't have, in your cond….!" Began Dorothy, but Alice silenced her with a glance.

"I'm fine, Dorothy, but thanks for your concern. I'll just have this cuppa and then we'll have to get home, before the family arrives."

"You're a glutton for punishment, Alice," said her friend, "It's a good job you've got your Mum."

"Yes, she's a godsend," Alice replied, smiling and grasping her Mum's hand fondly.

oOo

It was Grandad Roberts' first visit to the house, and he inspected everything minutely.

"It's not hygienic, having the lavvy in the house," he said, inspecting the sparklingly clean toilet by the back door, "and what's the idea of having the coal here? It should be outside if you haven't got a cellar. I bet you get beetles."

"Well, we haven't seen any, though we had plenty in Collyhurst," retorted Bill. The comments went on and on, but even Harry could see that Grandad was impressed with the house.

Elsie couldn't find anything to criticise either. She had visited before, and her envy was palpable, but Harry knew that Alice didn't worry about it.

They all sat around the big table in the living room for tea. Harry and Billy and their two cousins were sitting on a plank stretched between two chairs and there were just enough seats for the adults, using the bedroom chairs too. They had a ham salad with lots of bread and butter, followed by jelly and tinned peaches with evaporated milk and a piece of Grandma Davis's sponge cake to finish off.

After tea the men went out to the Culcheth Gates Pub "for a gill" and the children were asked to do a "Turn" for the women. Harry's five year old cousin Tilly recited "Twinkle Twinkle Little star" and her older brother, Walter, started to recite a poem, but forgot most of the words. The women applauded him anyway. Billy sang, raucously and out of tune, "What shall we do with the drunken Sailor", which made everyone laugh. Then it was Harry's turn. He sang his favourite hymn, "All things Bright and Beautiful." There were tears in Alice's eyes, and even stern Grandma Roberts commented, "That was sung lovely Harry," which was praise indeed!

The men came home and it was time for everyone to leave. It had been the best Whit Sunday ever, according to Billy.

oOo

The first of June started differently from the usual Friday mornings. Harry woke very early, just as the birds were starting to sing, and he knew immediately that there was something wrong with his mother. She was already up and in the bathroom and Bill was in there with her. He came out just as Harry emerged to see what was happening. "Go back to bed!" said Bill, roughly. "This is nothing to do with you."

"Is Mum alright?" ventured Harry.

"Of course she is. You're always asking questions!" and then Bill went into Grandma's room and Harry could hear them talking in low voices. He got back in bed, but he didn't try to sleep. He just sat there, listening to Billy's deep breathing and the adults' muted conversation

Eventually Grandma came to get the boys up. "Is Mum alright?" Harry asked again. This time he got an answer.

"Yes, she's just got a tummy ache. Get up and washed and you can see her. She's downstairs making toast for your breakfast.

Harry got dressed more quickly than he ever had and ran downstairs. Alice was in the kitchen, but she was in her nightie and dressing gown, which was very unusual, and she was sitting down to butter the toast. Harry felt a pain in his own tummy as he saw her wince.

 "Come on boys, eat up," said Grandma. "Billy, I want you to go and ask Mrs Kerr if she'll take you to school. Harry, I need some things from town, so you can come with me. Your Dad's gone to work early, so we can let your Mum have a nice quiet rest in bed and she'll soon be better." Harry wasn't sure if he wanted to leave his Mum when she was poorly, but he had no choice. Obedience to adults had been the norm for as long as he could remember.

Just as Harry and Grandma were ready to go out a lady came to the door. She was carrying a black bag and she came in and started talking to Alice. "It's just the nurse," said Grandma, "She'll help to get Mum's tummy better. By this time Harry was getting worse tummy pains, but he said nothing, and, as he and Grandma walked down to Oldham Road to get the tram, he started to feel better.

oOo

When they got off the tram in Piccadilly Grandma said, "Shall we go to Tib Street first, and see the puppies?"

"Ooh yes!" he replied. Harry loved all animals, especially dogs. He would have loved to have a dog, but he knew that Bill wouldn't let him have one.

They wandered up the little narrow street, passing all the barrows on Church Street and finally coming to the pet shops. There were all the puppies, all falling over each other to get attention. Harry could feel that the puppies were happy in each other's company and they were well fed, judging by their little round bellies. There were kittens and rabbits too, but Harry kept coming back to look at the puppies. It certainly took his mind off his Mum for a while.

Too soon they moved on. They got some apples, pears and peas in fat green pods, from the barrows and then went in Woolworths, where Grandma bought a few things. Among other things she bought knitting wool, very fine and soft and white. "You and Mum are always knitting, aren't you, Grandma? What are you going to knit now?"

"Oh, I'm not sure yet," she replied, "but I don't want to run out of wool." Again Harry thought she was holding something back, but that was adults, always keeping secrets.

They had a look round Lewis's, but didn't buy anything there. Grandma said everything was too dear, and then they went back to Woolworths to have fish and chips in the café. This was a real treat. Harry couldn't remember having been in a café before, though they often got fish and chips from the chippy on Culcheth Lane. He relished every bite. Then it was time to go home. "Do you think Mum will be better when we get home?" Harry asked Grandma.

"I think so. I hope so." She said.

oOo

When they got back home the nurse was still there. She was just putting something wrapped in newspaper into the fire. She smiled and nodded at Grandma, who breathed a sigh of relief. "You can go up now." The nurse said, and she winked at Harry, "There's a nice surprise upstairs".

Alice was sitting up in bed, looking very tired but very happy. "Come and see your new baby sister," she said, and Harry saw the bundle that she was holding. A tiny baby with a fine fuzz of blonde hair on her head was wrapped in a soft white blanket that he recognised as one his Grandma had been knitting for a few weeks.

"Did you know we were getting a new baby, Grandma?" he asked.

"Yes, but we wanted it to be a nice surprise for you and Billy."

"Where did she come from?"

"The nurse brought her in her bag," said Grandma. Harry looked at her quizzically, sure that this wasn't the full story, but he accepted it, as he accepted all the puzzling things that adults said and did. He was absolutely delighted with his new sister, and he couldn't wait for Billy to get home from school.

"Is this the baby girl you saw in your dream?" asked Alice.

"No Mum. That baby has black curly hair, and I saw her mum. She wasn't you, and I think she lives a long way away. I think I might meet her one day."

"But it was just a dream, lovey."

"It wasn't an ordinary dream. I think she's real." Harry gazed earnestly at Alice, willing her to believe him. She looked into his clear grey eyes, and nodded. She believed him.

They heard someone knocking at the door and Grandma went down to answer it, Harry rapidly following her. It was Billy, with Dorothy and her brood.

"Billy, we've got a new baby sister!" Harry could hardly contain his excitement. Billy's eyes were wide with wonder.

"You go up," said Grandma, "I'll make a brew and come up with Mrs Kerr later."

oOo

Billy and Harry stood as close to Alice's bed as they could get. They could hardly believe that this tiny bundle was their sister. "When will we be able to play with her?" asked Billy.

"Not for a few months," Alice replied. "She'll just sleep and drink milk while she is tiny."

"But Joe and Bobby play with Audrey." Billy insisted.

"Yes, but she is eight months old now, and big enough to sit on the floor with them. The time will soon pass, you'll see."

Grandma came in then, with a welcome cup of tea. "Are you ready for visitors?" she said, and Alice nodded. Dorothy and her boys came in and Billy proudly showed them his baby sister. He was already laying claim to her, and Alice smiled indulgently.

oOo

When Bill came home from work it was Billy who ran to the door to tell him of the new arrival. Bill seemed to be completely surprised about the new baby, but Harry could feel that his Dad knew something. Satisfaction and happiness was oozing out of him. He lost no time in going up to see his wife and baby, and, this time, Grandma kept the boys downstairs, to give the new parents a bit of privacy.

oOo

After tea – Grandma had made a big shepherd's pie and taken some up for Alice – they all went upstairs and sat around to discuss a name for the new baby.

"I think it should be something posh, like Esmerelda." Said Billy

"What!" roared Bill. Grandma and Alice burst out laughing.

"That's a bit too posh, Billy," said Alice. "I quite like Rose"

"Too plain," said Bill, "and remember that Rose Griffiths in Collyhurst? She was horrible!"

"Norma," said Harry. "Grandma, do you remember that book you read to us once? There was a very pretty girl called Norma in it. Our baby is very pretty."

"I like that name," said Alice.

"So do I," said Billy. "It's not as posh as Esmerelda, but it's quite posh, and I remember that story too."

"That's sorted then," said Bill. "Norma it is." He bent over the pretty baby, now slumbering in her wooden cradle. "Hello Norma Roberts. Welcome to our world." Harry had never seen his dad look so tender. The feeling of love in the room was palpable as everyone smiled at the new member of their family.

oOo

Harry and Billy fell asleep so quickly that night that they didn't hear even one train pass. Harry soon found himself in the familiar room. The black haired baby was now in a proper cot and she looked a lot bigger than Norma. He studied her face and he still thought that she was lovely, "but not as lovely as our Norma," he said to himself.

oOo

5 Picnics and School

Alice stayed in her bedroom for nearly two weeks. The nurse came every day and told her to stay in bed, but after she left, Alice would be pottering around, tidying the room, seeing to baby Norma or sitting in her chair, knitting. Harry and Billy never stopped to wonder why Alice had to stay in bed after the nurse had delivered Norma in her bag. It was just another of those inexplicable things that adults did.

Grandma proved her worth at this time. Her cooking was, obviously, as good as Alice's, as she had taught Alice everything she knew about keeping house. Grandma also seemed to have recovered the energy that she had lost when she lived with Elsie and Tom. Harry often joined in with her singing while he was helping her in the house. He was developing quite a good singing voice and he had an aptitude for remembering all the words to a song.

oOo

A wonderful summer followed for Harry and his family. Baby Norma thrived and it seemed no time before she was smiling and holding out her chubby little arms to her two big brothers. The boys couldn't do enough for her. Harry would even take her dirty nappy to the bucket in the kitchen. Though Billy drew the line at that, he would entertain her, playing peep-boo and shaking her rattle. His singing voice hadn't improved much, but Norma loved all his silly songs anyway. Harry could sing her to sleep with his sweet voice, singing all the lullabies that Alice and Grandma had taught him.

When Billy finished school for the summer, Alice or Grandma, or both, would often take them to Brookdale Park and they would have a picnic. Dorothy was usually with them. The two mums would be pushing their daughters in their prams, with the boys skipping alongside. The boys would have a football and play for ages on the grass. This idyllic time flew by, and it was soon September. Harry and Bobby were starting school.

oOo

Harry and Bobby were used to the playground by now, but they didn't know the teachers, except for second hand reports from Billy and Joe. Apparently the first year infants teacher was "ok", whatever that meant.

They didn't have to go to the headmaster's study this time, which was a relief. They had been told to wait in the playground until their name was called. A lady teacher came out and blew a whistle. All the older children immediately formed lines in their class groups and soon disappeared into the school. The new children stood in a close group, looking scared.

"When I call your name, line up in front of me and no talking!" the teacher spoke in a strong, clear voice. "James Bates!"

"Me name's Jimmy!" shouted a stocky, ginger haired boy. He had the cheekiest grin that Harry had ever seen.

"I said, no talking, James Bates. Stand there and don't speak!" He did as he was told, but looked round at the other children, grinning like a Cheshire cat. The teacher continued calling out names. When she got to "Robert Kerr," Bobby meekly joined the line. There was no way he was going to claim that he liked to be called Bobby.

Harry's name was one of the last to be called. Alfred Smith and Jean Winstanley were the last two.

"Now, you will follow me in a straight line, and no talking. That includes you, James Bates!" Jimmy Bates was already looking round and grinning. Harry thought that Jimmy Bates was going to be trouble.

When she had everyone settled in the classroom, the teacher addressed them all. "My name is Miss Williams. If you want to speak, you must first put your hand up and wait for me to tell you to speak. You will say, "please Miss" and then ask your question. If I ask you something, you say, "Yes Miss Williams". Do you all understand?"

"Yes Miss Williams," most of the children chorused. Jimmy Bates just grinned.

"James Bates. Do you understand what I am saying?"

"Yes," said Jimmy.

"Yes, Miss Williams!" she shouted. She was obviously getting annoyed.

Jimmy grinned again. "Yes ... Miss Williams," he finally said.

"I can see that I'll have to keep an eye on you, James Bates. Come and sit at the front." Jimmy shuffled to the front desk, scraping his boots along the floorboards. Yes, Harry thought that Jimmy Bates was going to be big trouble.

By the end of the day Jimmy Bates had been made to stand in the corner while the other children were painting. They had all been learning the alphabet and numbers. Jimmy seemed to be wilfully getting them wrong, and Miss Williams said he was preventing the other children from learning. Harry wasn't too worried. He already knew the alphabet, as it was something that he and Billy had chanted with Alice almost since they first learned to talk. He could count up to a hundred too.

It seemed a really long day, but, at last it was half past three. Alice was waiting in the yard with Norma in her pram when Harry and Bobby spilled out of the infant's door with all the other children.

Billy and Joe were now in the juniors, and they didn't finish until four o'clock. Alice wanted to wait for them, although Billy had insisted that he could come home without his Mum. After all, he was eight this week, he would be with Joe, and he knew the way. For this day at least she would wait for them, and Dorothy would have the kettle on when they got home.

"We'll just go to the bakers on Albert Street and get some bread while we're waiting," Alice said. The delicious smell of fresh bread was wafting out of the bakery door. Harry and Bobby sniffed appreciatively. Alice bought two loaves, one for Dorothy to make jam butties for all the children and one to take home. When they got back to the school yard the bell was ringing in the junior and senior departments. As usual, Billy and Joe were among the first out of the door, chattering like magpies.

"What's the juniors like, Joe," asked Bobby, when he could get a word in edgeways.

"We've got Miss Scott," his brother answered, "She's a lot nicer than Mr Smith, but she's got a slipper that she throws at anyone who's naughty, and she's a good aim!"

"Did she throw it at you, Billy?" asked Harry. He knew that Billy was an incurable chatterbox. Billy looked sideways at Alice. She was trying not to smile.

"Well, yes she did, but I had to tell Joe something and I would have forgot if I waited till playtime. I don't know how Miss Scott knew I was talking, cos I was very quiet and I had my hand in front of my mouth. D'you know what she said?"

"No," said Harry, all ears.

"She said, "I can hear every whisper that goes on in this class. I've got ears like an elephant." But she hasn't. Her ears are really small. I looked. So she told a lie, didn't she, Mum?" He turned his bright blue eyes to Alice, feigning innocence.

Alice struggled to keep a straight face. "I expect that she meant that she has very good hearing, like an elephant. But, Billy, you know that you shouldn't talk in class, and I don't suppose the slipper really hurt, did it?"

"No, it didn't. You won't tell Dad, will you?"

"I don't think he needs to know about this, but you will remember not to talk in class, won't you?"

"Yes, Mum. I'll try."

oOo

As they walked home they saw Jimmy Bates in the doorway of a house on Daisy Bank. He was standing with his legs splayed and his hands on his hips, looking like he thought he was king of the castle. He took in the sight of the four boys walking along with Alice and he sneered at them, but he just said, "Hiya." Harry thought that Jimmy would have said a lot more if Alice hadn't been with them.

oOo

At playtime the next day Jimmy Bates swaggered over to where Harry and Bobby were talking to some other children.

"You're big babies, aren't you? Going home with your Mam. Can't you find your own way home then?" he had to look up at Harry, who was tall, like his Dad and brother, but his whole attitude was intimidating.

"We're not babies. My Mum likes to come and meet us, and so does Bobby's Mum. They take turns."

"Well, you are a baby. I bet you couldn't fight me, could you?"

"I don't want to fight you. Why should I? There's no need to fight."

Jimmy grabbed at Harry's jumper and he raised his right hand in a fist. "You'll fight if I say so. Come on you big softy!" As Jimmy went to hit Harry his arm was suddenly grabbed from behind. Billy towered over him. Billy was nearly eight, but looked like a ten year old. He was strong too, from helping his Dad in the garden.

"Touch my brother and I'll bash you!" he warned, "Now, move!" Jimmy strode away, but the look he gave Harry was malevolent.

"Thanks Billy. I don't like fighting, but I would have had a go if you hadn't turned up."

"Don't fight in the playground if you can help it," said Billy, "You'll be sent to the Headmaster, even if you didn't start it. If that Jimmy starts anything, just run to find me, you too Bobby."

"Ok Billy," Harry replied.

oOo

Throughout that first term Jimmy Bates gathered together several boys and called them his gang. They intimidated anyone who didn't have a big brother or sister, and they were sent to the headmaster on a regular basis. This didn't seem to bother Jimmy, who would show off the weals on his hands as if they were battle scars to be proud of.

Harry kept out of Jimmy's way as much as possible, but there was a day, just before Christmas, when Harry couldn't ignore what Jimmy's gang were doing.

Alfred Smith was the smallest boy in the class. He was also painfully thin and his clothes were ragged. Jimmy and his gang had got Alfred in a corner and they were pushing him from one boy to another and taunting him, calling him "scruffy" and "smelly". The poor boy was sobbing pitifully.

Harry, as usual, was with his best friend Bobby when they saw this. "Come on Bobby, we've got to stop this!" said Harry.

"Oh, I don't know. Shouldn't we go and get our Joe and Billy?" said Bobby.

"They're not in the playground. I think they've been kept in, again!" Harry replied. "Well, I'm going to do something, anyway." Harry walked boldly up to the gang, with Bobby following at a distance.

"Leave him alone!" Harry shouted. The whole gang stopped in surprise and stared at him.

"Oh, look who it is, the big baby whose mummy takes him home!" jeered Jimmy. "How are you going to stop us?"

Harry could feel the waves of animosity coming from Jimmy, though he also detected that most of the other boys were feeling ashamed, and they just stood, waiting to see what would happen. Jimmy advanced on Harry.

Though he was frightened, Harry was determined that he wasn't going to back down. He stared into Jimmy's eyes, and in his mind he was saying, "You don't want to hit me, you don't want to hit me. You know it's wrong."

Amazingly, Jimmy stopped in his tracks, looking puzzled. "Oh, c'mon gang. They're not worth bothering with," and he strode off with his henchmen following in stunned silence.

Bobby was wiping Alfred's tears with his hankie – he always had a clean one. "How did you do that?" he looked amazed.

"I...I don't know. I think I just made him realise it was wrong." Harry was just as amazed as his friend. "Are you ok Alfred?"

"Yes, thanks. I like to be called Alf, but don't tell Miss Williams," he gave a weak laugh.

Harry and Bobby laughed too. "Ok Alf, you can be our friend. We'll stick together and guard each other. Where do you live?"

"Culcheth Lane, just near the pub," he replied.

"Oh, we go past there on our way home. We can all go together at home time," said Bobby. The three boys all smiled together. They didn't know then, but this was the start of a lifelong friendship.

oOo

Soon after this they had two weeks off school for the Christmas break. Harry and Billy were bubbling with excitement. Alice always made Christmas special, and this year grandma Davis would be with them for the whole time, and not just for Boxing Day. So it would be even more special. The Christmas cake and pudding had already been made. Harry and Billy had helped with stirring the pudding and putting a sixpence in the mixture. Each boy hoped he would be the one to get the lucky sixpence, but even if they weren't the lucky one, there would be so many more delightful things to enjoy.

A few days before Christmas they awoke to a world of whiteness. "Snow!" shouted Billy. "Let's get breakfast quick and then we can build a snowman."

They lost no time in having breakfast and donning wellies, coats, scarves and gloves. They were soon out of the front door and making for the Kerr's house. The door was opened as soon as they knocked. Joe and Bobby were already in their outdoor clothes. As they were debating the best place for a snowman, they saw a small figure coming down the road. "It's Alf!" shouted Bobby, "C'mon Alf, we're going to make a snowman. What have you got on your hands?"

"Socks, "said Alf, "I haven't got any gloves."

"Well, they should do for making a snowman," said Harry, philosophically.

"C'mon, we're going on the ollers," said Billy. They all trooped round the back of the house and up the back garden path, all delighting in the footprints they made in the snow.

The ground looked completely smooth on the ollers. The snow had filled in all the bumps and hollows, but the boys soon found them, falling into the snowdrifts and tripping over bumps. It was all the best of fun and they were soon laughing uncontrollably at each other. They were so covered in snow that they looked like snowmen themselves. They finally made a big snowman just outside Harry and Billy's back gate, where there was a level patch of ground.

Harry was just about to say that he was hungry when Alice appeared and shouted them all in for a hot drink. "Have you got wet gloves now?" she asked. All the boys held up their dripping hands. "Come on, I'll put them on the oven to dry." She pursed her lips when she saw the threadbare socks that Alf had on his hands, but said nothing.

"Ooh, my fingers are tingling now!" said Joe, rubbing his red hands against his rosy cheeks.

"Mine too, mine too!" everyone chorused.

They all sat on the rug in front of the fire, drinking hot cocoa and talking nineteen to the dozen. Grandma was in the rocking chair, knitting and laughing at their jokes. Norma was in her high chair next to Grandma. She was laughing too, as if she understood the jokes.

"Why don't you boys stay for dinner? I've got a big pan of tater ash on the stove, enough for everyone. You can make paper chains while you're waiting," said Alice.

"Ooh yes please! I'll go and tell my Mum where we are," said Joe. "What about your Mum, Alf?"

"Oh, she won't miss me till teatime. We don't have much for dinner," Alf replied.

Alice went over to Grandma and said something quietly, and she nodded, put her knitting away and got out some dark wool and different needles. Her fingers were soon a blur with the new knitting.

The boys all sat round the living room table making paper chains and blowing up balloons. Billy was so tall now that he was given the task of standing on a kitchen chair to put up the chains with drawing pins, a job that was usually done by Bill, when he came in from work. Billy was almost bursting with pride. They finished just in time to troop into the kitchen for the tater ash.

Alf tucked into it with relish and Alice gave him second helpings. "This is lovely!" Alf said. "Isn't your Mum kind? We don't get grub like this at home."

"What do you have at home then?" asked Billy.

"Oh, something like bread and dripping, or sometimes we have something like this, but it's mostly spuds and Mum doesn't call it tater ash. We don't get much of it either. The big lads get most of it, cos they're working."

Harry knew by now that Alf was one of eleven children. Three brothers and a sister were over school age, one sister was in the senior school, and then there was a gap between her and Alf. The five youngest consisted of two sets of twins and the youngest baby, a boy the same age as Norma. Harry had seen Alf's Mum, who was a frail, thin woman who always looked tired. He had never seen Alf's Dad, who seemed to be away a lot. Even though four of the children were working, there didn't seem to be much money for food.

When Alf was going home Alice gave him a parcel wrapped in brown paper. "Its, just a few sweets for Christmas. You can share them with your brothers and sisters." She said. "And here's a present from Harry's Grandma." She produced a pair of dark brown mittens. Grandma had knitted them that afternoon. He put them on and pushed the dry socks into his coat pocket.

"Ooh thanks Mrs Roberts," he replied. Alice had tears in her eyes as she watched him go up the road in the twilight. Harry, standing at her side, looked up into grey eyes the colour of his own, and he loved her more than ever.

oOo

Christmas Day finally arrived. Harry awoke from the familiar dream when Billy switched on the light and began rummaging in a lumpy sock. Harry's sock was also bulging at the bottom of the bed. Billy shouted, "Wow, Look what I've got, a mouth organ! Oh, and a paint box, lovely!" He lined up an apple, an orange, several nuts and a pink sugar mouse on the bed. "What have you got, Harry?"

"I got a paint box too, and a box of dominos. We can have a game after church."

"Oh yes, church," Billy groaned, "and it's not even Sunday!"

"It's the Birthday of Jesus though," said Harry, "We have to be glad for all the good things we get when it's not even our Birthday."

"I know," Billy replied, "but church is so boring!"

"It won't be boring today, cos we'll be singing carols."

"I suppose so," Billy grudgingly agreed.

"I wonder if it's time to get up yet?" said Harry.

"Well, we'd better not wake Dad up if it's not time. He won't be happy, and that'll spoil the day," Billy reminded him.

"Mmmm," Harry agreed. "Well, shall we play dominoes now? We can smooth the bed cover to use as a table."

Munching an apple each, they started playing dominoes, trying to keep quiet, but not really succeeding.

The door opened and they both held their breath, and breathed a sigh of relief when they realised it was Grandma."Come downstairs, quietly," she whispered. "It's only seven o'clock, so let's give your Mum and Dad a lie in. We'll surprise them with a nice breakfast."

Pleased with this idea, they crept down to the kitchen and shut the door so that they could talk. Billy and Harry set the table while Grandma got out bacon and eggs – a treat for Christmas - and cut generous slices off a loaf. "We'll have our breakfast first, and then it'll be a good time to get theirs ready."

While they were eating they heard Norma start to cry and Alice's gentle voice responding. "They'll be down as soon as Norma has been fed, so we'll be just in time with their breakfast," said Grandma.

Bill and Alice were all smiles when they came down and saw the delicious bacon and eggs and toast. "Merry Christmas!" they both said before they tucked in.

The boys had time for a game of dominoes before they had to put on their best clothes for church. Alice put a chicken in the back to back oven to start cooking while they were out and Grandma put the best tablecloth on the living room table and set out the cutlery. The vegetables had been prepared last night, so they were all soon ready to go out.

It was easy walking, as it hadn't snowed overnight and everyone had cleared their own bit of pavement. They met Fred and Dorothy and their children on the way and joined up with other families on the way to the church. They were quite a crowd by the time they arrived.

The church looked beautiful with all its decorations and the nativity scene at the front. The service, to Billy's relief, wasn't boring, and they sang all the favourite carols.

The crowd of happy people all made their way back to their homes, thinking of Christmas dinner and roaring fires. The smell of roast chicken was wafting through the house when they got back. Alice and Grandma went to put in the potatoes to roast and the vegetables on the stove. Bill was in such a good mood that he played two games of dominoes and then showed Billy how to play his mouth organ. Then he produced something from behind his chair.

"This is for both of you to share, but you'll have to wait until the snow goes," it was a beautiful scooter! Bill had made all the wooden parts himself and then attached metal wheels. It was painted bright red.

"Wow, Dad!" breathed Billy, "It's great. Thanks!"

Harry could hardly speak. They had never had such a smart toy. "Thanks Dad," he breathed. He wanted to give Bill a hug, but Bill was a big tough man and he didn't do hugs. Harry had to make do with a smile. He could feel that Bill was pleased with the effect his present had on his sons.

Dinner was as delicious as promised and Grandma got the sixpence in her bit of pudding. She got out her purse and changed it for two threepenny bits to give to the boys. Then she brought something out from behind her chair, two thick colouring books and a pair of mittens each. The red mittens were for Billy and blue for Harry. Then Alice produced scarves to match. The boys felt so lucky, they danced around the room. Norma, in her high chair was chuckling and clapping her hands. She wasn't left out either. There had been a teddy and a teething ring in her stocking, and she had mittens and a scarf in bright pink.

The boys spent the afternoon with colouring books and paints. Bill had a bottle of stout and the two women had a glass of sweet sherry, sitting round the fire chatting about past Christmases. At teatime they had ham sandwiches and Christmas cake with a nice pot of tea.

All too soon it was bedtime. Harry and Billy were tucked in with their hot water bottles and they were asleep in no time

oOo

The dream was so familiar to Harry by now that he usually knew which room he was in immediately. Most times he was in the bedroom, looking at the baby girl in her cot, but sometimes she was in the living room or kitchen. Tonight he found himself in a completely different room. A big table dominated the room, and there were several people sitting around it, obviously just finishing a meal. "They must have their Christmas dinner at night," he thought. The baby girl was in a high chair similar to Norma's, and there were five other children all sitting together on one side of the table. Harry realised that they were sitting on a plank in the same way that he, Billy and their cousins had, due to the lack of chairs. Everyone seemed happy, and the man at the head of the table began to sing. The tune was "Away in a manger" but the words were strange. Harry couldn't understand them. He had heard of

70

foreign languages – Bill had told them some French he'd learned from his time in the war – but he had never heard anything like this before. It was strange, because he had heard the mother speaking English. This was another mystery to puzzle over.

oOo

On Boxing Day morning Harry was in the kitchen, telling Alice about his latest dream when Bill came in. "What's this all about?" he asked. Harry looked at Alice, wondering how much to tell his Dad. He could feel the disapproval even before he said anything. Alice answered for him.

"Harry has a recurring dream about a little girl and her family. It seems that it isn't anyone we know, but the dreams seem real to him."

"They are real…!" began Harry, but Alice gave him the look that meant, *don't say any more.*

"What a load of rubbish!" Bill shouted. "I don't want to hear any more about these dreams, and don't tell your mother either. A dream's a dream, nothing more. Do you understand?"

"Yes Dad," Harry's answer was subdued. Head down, he went to get his outdoor clothes and then went to join Billy in the back garden. First, he went to the toilet, by the back door. He could hear everything that was said in the kitchen.

"There's something wrong with that boy, he's unnatural," said Bill, "and you encourage him, Alice. Why can't he be a normal boy like Billy?"

"He is normal. He's just different to Billy. He does a lot of thinking. I know, but he enjoys football and making snowmen, just like the others."

"Well, why does he leave the other boys and come in to help you with baking and such? You'll have him knitting next!"

"That's not fair Bill. He only comes in when Bobby isn't there. The bigger boys are too fast for him. Anyway, there's nothing wrong with a boy learning to cook. He might need to know that someday."

Harry quietly went out, hoping that his parents hadn't heard him. He was upset that Bill thought he was unnatural. He wasn't exactly sure what that meant, but he knew it wasn't anything good. "Is there something wrong with me?" he thought.

oOo

6 Clayton Vale

The next two years flew by. Harry found his feet at school and was soon reading and writing as well as Billy. He mostly managed to avoid Jimmy Bates and his gang, and when they did come face to face, Harry was very good at talking himself out of trouble. His friendship with Bobby and Alf continued, and they rarely disagreed.

Alf was looking a little less waiflike, partly due to the provision of free school meals and partly due to both Alice's and Dorothy's generosity. Alf's mother never seemed offended by the charity offered. Her younger children could often be seen wearing clothes that the Roberts and Kerr children had grown out of. It wasn't that either family were well off, but both Dads had good jobs and both Mums and Grandmas were very good at housekeeping, knitting and sewing.

oOo

By the time Harry was seven, in March 1926, he and his friends were allowed to go to places like Brookdale Park without adult supervision, and they had even been as far as Daisy Nook with the older boys. Easter was the best time at Daisy Nook, when the fair was on, but it was good at other times too. Fishing for sticklebacks with a net in Crime Lake would keep them amused for hours, and, if they had any spare coppers, there was a wooden shack that sold drinks and sweets. Hot Bovril was particularly good on a cold day. Blackberrying in September was another favourite pastime, despite the scratched arms and legs. Grandma's blackberry jam was delicious on fresh bread.

The only place Harry wouldn't go was Clayton Vale. He had a horror of the place. He had only ventured under the railway on odd occasions, and only when Bill or Fred took the boys there. Even then he wouldn't go anywhere near the river. No amount of taunting from Billy and his friends could induce him. They could call him coward and "yeller belly", but he wouldn't budge.

So, on the first fine Saturday in March, after what seemed like weeks of rain, Harry opted to stay with Alice and Grandma when Bobby and Alf joined the older boys for a trip to Clayton Vale. They had taken fishing nets, planning to catch tiddlers in the reservoirs next to the dye works, but Harry knew they would be drawn towards the hated Red River, particularly to see how high it could get when in flood. It was a big group of boys that trooped up Amos Avenue, including Malcolm and Charlie from down the road and a few others. Harry watched them from the front door, still glad that he wasn't going with them.

After a quick trip to the market, Alice, Grandma and Harry got back in time to check the soup for dinner. Bill had been digging in the back garden and came in to wash his hands. Harry was just setting the table when he suddenly felt a tightness in his chest. He dropped the cutlery with a clatter and sat on the floor, gasping.

"I can't breathe!" he gasped, as Alice and Grandma crouched down to grab him. "No, Billy can't breathe. He's in the river. The water's coming over his head! Dad, Dad! You've got to help him. Go to the river, please Dad!"

Bill glared at him."What sort of rubbish is this he's spouting now? Pull yourself together lad!"

"No, Dad. Billy's in trouble, please, please!" Harry was tearing at his chest, anguish in his face.

"Bill, please run down to the river and have a look," pleaded Alice, "give him the benefit of the doubt. You can punish him later if he's wrong."

Bill took one look at his wife's terrified face and he turned and ran.

Alice lifted Harry, still gasping, and took him into the living room, laying him gently on to the settee. Harry could almost see the river water pouring over his face. He tried to wipe it away, but his face was dry. Then he felt strangely calm and he heard Billy's voice, "I'm sorry Harry, sorry ...." the voice faded away and Harry's chest felt free.

"He's gone!" he cried, and then started sobbing uncontrollably. "Billy's gone. I can't feel him anymore. I could always feel him, wherever he was. He's gone, Mum!"

Alice then joined in with his sobbing, "No, no. It can't be true!"

Grandma was crying too, but she said, "Alice love, it may not be true. Wait and see. Wait until Bill gets back."

"No, Harry's right. I don't have whatever it is that Harry has, but I feel it too. I've always felt the presence of my children, from the day they were born. I can't feel Billy now." The two women embraced, with Harry between them, and they all just sat there, crying for what seemed like hours, until they heard the knock at the door.

Joe stood there with tears rolling down his face as he pointed up the street. Bill was carrying a dripping Billy, pain and anguish etched on his face. All the other boys were following, heads down and feet dragging.

Without a word Bill gently laid his son down on the settee. Alice threw herself on the still body, fresh tears pouring out. Bill just stood there; dry eyed, but obviously suffering. Harry tried to take his father's hand, but he was cruelly rebuffed. "Get away! Leave me alone!" Bill shouted, turned away and stormed upstairs. Harry was distraught.

"Did anyone call the doctor?" asked Grandma, looking at Joe.

"My dad phoned from the telephone box. He's gone to tell Mum," whispered Joe.

"The doctor's no use now!" cried Alice, bitterly.

"I know, love, but he needs to see him, to... you know?" Harry didn't know what Grandma meant, but he could see that Alice did, as she just nodded and continued to hold her firstborn, rocking him back and forth as if he was still her baby.

Alice only let go of Billy when the doctor came in. He listened with his stethoscope and then turned and shook his head. They already knew, but it elicited fresh tears from everyone. "What exactly happened?" he asked. They all turned to Joe, who was standing there, tears sending clean runnels down his grubby face. "Sit down lad," the doctor said, gently. "Can someone make tea?" grandma nodded and went into the kitchen.

"It was the Claytoners that started it," Joe sobbed.

"What, who are the Claytoners?" Alice asked.

"I can tell you who they are, and I'll kill them if I find the buggers!" Bill was standing at the living room door. Anger had temporarily taken over from grief on his face. "They're a gang of lads from Clayton who think they own the vale. I've told our lads to keep away from them, but I won't keep away if I can find them!"

"No, Mr Roberts," said the doctor, "That would only cause you more trouble. Let's get the full story first. Carry on Joe."

"Well, these three lads seemed friendly, though we knew they were from Clayton, and they were a lot bigger than us, probably about twelve or thirteen. We were throwing twigs into the river to see how fast they would go. They said that was for babies and why don't we see if we can jump across the river. One of them showed us that he could jump across and then the other two did the same. They could get a good run at it from our side. Then they went up the other side, to the bridge and came back. They bet us that we couldn't do it. I said that we were smaller than them, but they pointed at Billy and said he wasn't smaller. It's true; Billy is a lot bigger than the rest of us. I told him not to do it but, he wanted to prove that Newton Heathers are better than Claytoners. He nearly did it too. He did a massive jump, but he just reached the bricks on the other side, and they were too slippy. He slid down into the water and it was dead fast and dead deep. We ran alongside shouting at him to grab something, but there was nothing to grab. We were nearly at Philips Park before something stopped him, but we couldn't reach him, and he'd gone still. The big lads lay on the bank and tried to reach down, but when they saw Mr Roberts running up to us, they scarpered."

Everyone was quiet as Joe took a big gulp of the tea that Grandma gave him. "I told him not to, Mr Roberts. I told him!" He was shaking like a leaf. Grandma took the cup from him and put her arms round him.

"It's all right lad," said Bill, "it's not your fault.

Fred and Dorothy came in just then. "Oh, my God, my God!" cried Dorothy, when she saw the still figure on the settee. Joe ran to her and she hugged him tightly. Grandma gave her a cup of tea and went to put the kettle on again.

Harry was still standing in the same spot where Bill had rebuffed him. He had stopped crying, but he couldn't take his eyes off his beloved brother. He felt as though there was a great big hole inside him, a space that used to be filled with the knowledge that Billy would always be there for him. How could he carry on without his big brother?

"Harry, Harry, have this cup of tea lovey." Grandma pushed the cup into his hand, pulled him over to her chair and sat him on her knee. The tea was very sweet and it tasted funny. "I've put some brandy in it. It'll help." Harry didn't know how anything could help when the worst thing in the world had happened, but he drank it anyway. It made him feel a bit fuzzy, and it did seem to take the edge off the awful emptiness.

The doctor finished his cup of tea and gave Bill a piece of paper that he'd been writing on. "You'll need the death certificate for the undertaker and the registry office. Had you got him insured?" Bill was glaring at the certificate as if it alone was responsible for the loss of his son.

"Yes, we've got penny policies for all the children with the Prudential. Never thought we'd need them, though." Bill looked lost now that his anger had faded a little. Alice had resumed her place on the settee after the doctor had finished examining Billy. She didn't seem to notice, or care, how wet she was getting. Bill was wet too. He hadn't changed in the short time he'd been upstairs.

"Mr and Mrs Roberts, I've left you some sleeping tablets here. Take them for the next few nights; you can also give a half tablet to Harry if you think he needs it. Shall I ring the undertaker for you when I get home?"

"Yes, thank you doctor," said Bill.

"Now, you should both go and get dry clothes on. We don't want you going down with pneumonia, do we?" he added, in a vain attempt to lighten the moment.

Grandma saw the doctor out and Bill went upstairs to get changed. Harry heard Norma's little voice as Bill opened the bedroom door. She had been asleep in her cot since they came back from the market. They had all forgotten about her.

Dorothy spoke up. "I'll take Norma to our house, Alice. You won't want her to see this. She can play with Audrey. I need to get back to Bobby and Alf too. My Mum is looking after them. Thank goodness she was there!" Alice just nodded and continued rocking Billy.

"Harry, do you want to come with me too?" Dorothy asked. He shook his head. He just wanted to stay near his Mum and Grandma. He heard Dorothy go up the stairs and speak to Bill and then Norma's bright little voice. It was good that she was spared the anguish of the rest of the family, but Harry knew that she would be asking questions when she realised that Billy was no longer there.

Bill brought a big blanket and clothes for Billy. Alice had to be coaxed to let go of him, but she finally went upstairs to change. Bill folded the blanket under Billy and undressed him with a gentleness that Harry had rarely seen. With his clean clothes on and his hair combed, Billy just looked as if he was sleeping. Harry wished that was so, but the big empty feeling didn't go away.

oOo

It was in the evening, after the undertaker had taken Billy's body away, and Norma had been brought back home, that they realised they hadn't eaten since breakfast and the soup was dried up in the oven. Nobody was hungry anyway, and Norma had been fed at Dorothy's, so the adults just had more tea and Harry was given a cup of Ovaltine and half a sleeping tablet. He didn't want to go to bed without Billy, but obedience towards adults was ingrained in him, so he went upstairs with Grandma without complaint. She tucked him in with his hot water bottle, but the bed felt cold and empty. "Try to sleep lovey," said Grandma as she kissed him.

He didn't think he would be able to sleep, but he soon fell into a deep, dreamless sleep. When he awoke it was still very early and the house was quiet. He went over all the events of yesterday in his mind, and then started to cry again. He tried to be quiet, sobbing into his pillow.

He didn't want to wake his parents, but he heard the door open and looked up in alarm. It was Grandma. "Come on lovey," she said, and led him into her bedroom. He cuddled up with Grandma and cried his heart out. Eventually he fell asleep again.

When he awoke Grandma had gone, and he could hear sounds of activity downstairs. He dressed quickly and went down. Norma was sitting at the kitchen table; she had recently been promoted from her high chair, as she was now nearly three. "Arry!" she shouted, "Where's Billy?" Everyone went quiet.

"Billy's not here lovey," said Grandma, "He's in heaven with Jesus now." Bill made a strange noise in his throat and rushed out of the room.

"Norma go to heaven, too?" asked Norma.

"Not just yet, lovey, but you'll see Billy sometime." Norma seemed satisfied with that explanation for now. Harry was grateful for Grandma's common sense. Alice was at the sink. He could see her shoulders shaking with silent tears. He went up to her and put his arms round her. She didn't turn round, but he could feel that she was grateful for the hug.

They didn't go to church that Sunday. Bill spent most of the time alone in his garden. Harry offered to help in the garden, but Bill wouldn't even look at him. He just shook his head. Harry was heartbroken. Billy had always been the one to help in the garden and it seemed that Bill would now prefer to be alone rather than have Harry helping.

The women tried to keep busy. Norma had to be cared for, and her cheerful ignorance seemed to help them, and Harry, to cope with their grief a little.

Dorothy and Fred came round with their children. Joe and Bobby were still very subdued, but Audrey, in the same blissful ignorance as Norma, cheered them up a bit. In the afternoon Alf arrived with a little bunch of coltsfoot he had picked for Alice. "Thank you, Alf. They are lovely," she said, and found a jam jar for them.

oOo

The next two weeks were very difficult for the family. They had visitors almost every day, which mostly helped, but, when Grandad and Grandma Roberts came round, Bill was ready to throw them out.

"You know this wouldn't have happened if you'd stayed in Collyhurst," said Grandad."

With a wordless roar, Bill launched himself at his father, and was only stopped from hitting him by all three women intervening. Even Grandma Roberts looked outraged, although she didn't say a word against her husband. It was gentle Grandma Davis who managed to say the right thing.

"I'm sure he didn't mean it. We can't fall out at a time like this. Let's all sit down and have a cup of tea." Bill stormed upstairs. It seemed that he had spent a lot of time up there when he wasn't in his garden. Grandad had the grace to apologise.

"Sorry, Alice. I shouldn't have said that. I'm just missing the lad, that's all."

"Well, I think you should go up and say that to Bill." For once, Alice was brave enough to speak to her father in law.

"Aye, lass, I will," he said.

"Here, take him a cuppa," said Grandma Roberts. He took two cups and went upstairs.

Grandma Roberts ventured a question. "Do you think you'll stay here after this?"

Harry was alarmed. He looked imploringly at Alice. He didn't want to move. His friends were here and he liked his school. Yes, he would never go to the other side of the railway again, but he loved this house and garden, as had Billy, and he knew his Mum and Dad loved it too.

"No, we won't move from here," Alice replied, "We all love this house, and what happened to Billy wasn't a fault of the area. He was very adventurous. He could have got into trouble in so many different ways. Also, I think what has happened might stop all the other boys from getting into similar trouble." Grandma Davis and Harry nodded in agreement.

oOo

Harry wasn't allowed to go to the funeral. Bill said it wasn't a place for children, but, a week later, Alice took him down to Philips Park cemetery to visit Billy's grave. There wasn't a headstone yet, but there were lots of flowers on the mound. "It'll look a lot better when they put the headstone in, and we'll plant some crocuses and daffodils," said Alice. "We'll come often, and Billy will know we are thinking about him."

"Are you sure, Mum?"

"Yes, as long as we remember him he'll always know, and he'll be there in heaven to meet us when our turn comes. That won't be for many years though."

"I miss him so much, Mum. Will I always feel this sad?"

"You'll be very sad for a while, and there'll be times when you'll think of him and be sad again, but there'll be happy times too, and Billy would want you to be happy. Play with your friends and look after your little sister. That's the best thing you can do. Enjoy life, but it's ok to be sad at times. You know I lost two brothers in the war?" Harry nodded. "I still miss them and I feel sad for them, but I remember all the happy times we had growing up, and that makes me feel better. I'll remember happy times with Billy too, and that will also make me feel better. Best of all I've got you and Norma, and you make me very happy." She gave Harry a big hug, and, although there were tears in her eyes, she was smiling. He felt glad that he had such a lovely, loving, Mum.

oOo

Harry hadn't dreamed about the girl for a few weeks, but that night he was there again, in the familiar house. The girl was three years old now, and her black curls were shoulder length. He noticed too, for the first time, that her eyes were very dark brown, almost black. Those eyes were full of mischief tonight. She was in her nightgown and was running round the living room, being chased by her mother. "Come on, cariad. You know its bedtime. Behave yourself!" Harry wondered if the girl's name was cariad, but somehow it didn't seem like a name. It sounded more like when Grandma called him lovey. Perhaps that was a word they used where she lived.

Eventually she was caught and her mum carried her up to bed. Harry followed. She was now in a different bedroom and she was in a bed, not a cot. He noticed another bed besides hers. He wondered if it belonged to one of the other children he had seen there.

The scene faded and he woke up in his own bed, which felt very empty without Billy, but he looked across at Norma, now in her own little bed, sleeping peacefully. Bill had brought the new bed home only yesterday. Alice had suggested that the two children would be company for each other, and Norma was getting a bit big for her cot. Harry was glad to see her there.

7 THE DOG

As the weeks passed Harry began to get used to the empty feeling, although he didn't believe that it would ever go away. He took Alice's advice, playing with Bobby and Alf, even when he didn't really feel like it.

It was a beautiful May Saturday when Bobby and Alf called for Harry and they decided to play on the ollers. There was a smooth place where they liked to play marbles, or alleys, as most of the boys called them. They scraped a depression in the soil and dug into their pockets for the alleys. They were engrossed in the game when Harry felt a strange sensation. "Somebody's in trouble," he said, "I can feel that somebody's in pain, but where are they?"

The other two boys were used to Harry's "Feelings" now, and they always believed him, especially since the tragedy. They all looked around but they couldn't see anyone. Harry started walking towards the gate that led on to Scotland Hall Road. Malcolm's dad had planted a privet hedge that came right up to the gate, and, under the hedge, Harry found a pathetically thin dog, not much more than a puppy. It was whimpering in pain and it gave a weak yelp as Harry picked it up. He sat down with his back to the gate, cradling the poor thing, and his friends hunkered down to look.

"Oh, you poor thing, what happened to you?" asked Harry, as though the dog could answer. He was amazed when he got an image in his mind of a man beating the dog with a stick, and then the dog running away. He got the impression that the dog had travelled a long way since escaping from the man. "She was beaten by a man and she ran away. She just got under Malcolm's hedge when she couldn't go any further. I don't think she's got any broken bones," he said, feeling all her limbs, "it's just bruising and tiredness."

"How do you know it's a girl?" said Bobby.

"I don't know how, I just know, and she's called Bess."

"So you're calling her Bess?" said Alf.

"No, she told me she's called Bess, well, the name came into my head, and it feels right. I think we should take her to my Mum and get her some food."

They all agreed this was a good idea. They collected their alleys and trooped through the back garden to Harry's back door.

Alice was in the kitchen with Grandma and Norma and there was a delicious smell of tater ash. "Just in time. Are you staying for dinner boys? There's plenty," said Alice. Then she noticed the dog. "Who's this?" she asked.

"Aw, doggy!" said Norma.

"This is Bess, and she needs looking after," said Harry. "Can I keep her? She was beaten by a man and ran away. I don't think he wants her."

Alice didn't bother asking how Harry knew this. Like Bobby and Alf, she knew that Harry was no ordinary boy, and she accepted this.

"Well, we'll have to ask your Dad, and we'll have to put a note in the paper shop window, just in case someone is looking for her, but I think it will be ok."

Harry felt happy for the first time since he lost his brother. "Oh thanks Mum. I think Bess was meant to find me."

"Well, first of all I think she needs a wash. We can't tell what colour she is. Then we'll cool some of this tater ash for her. Dogs don't like hot food."

The boys all wanted to help. They got the green fairy soap out and put a few inches of warm water in the sink. Harry lifted Bess into the water and she only whimpered slightly as he massaged the soap into her coat. The water was filthy when they finished, and they had to get more clean water to rinse her. Grandma produced an old towel to dry her. "I think she's got some golden retriever in her. Look at her lovely coat!" she said.

Now that she was clean she really did look lovely, with a shiny golden coat. She looked up at Harry with adoring brown eyes. He put her down by the dish of tater ash and she wolfed it down as though she hadn't eaten for weeks. Her little tail started wagging.

"She looks happy now, but she's still too thin," said Alf.

"Yes, but we can soon remedy that," said Alice. When we've had dinner you three can go up to the pet shop and get some dog food. You'd better get a collar and lead too, and take a note to the paper shop."

"Yes!" they all chorused enthusiastically. Harry was happy that Alice seemed to think that Bess would be staying. He knew that Bill wouldn't want to keep the dog, but he was confident in Alice's ability to talk him round. She always could when it really mattered.

Grandma had found an old piece of blanket and made a bed for Bess in the corner of the kitchen. The dog seemed to know it was for her. She got on the blanket, turned round three times and settled herself to sleep. Norma sat on the floor, stroking her. The boys tiptoed out so as not to disturb her.

oOo

When the boys got back they went round to the back door and they could hear Bill's voice. "Oh, my Dad's home." Said Harry, "you two better go. I'll see you at Sunday school tomorrow." Bobby and Alf nodded and they were soon gone, leaving Harry with the shopping bag. He opened the back door quietly. The kitchen door was shut, so he waited and listened. He knew that Bill would be angry. He had been constantly angry since they had lost Billy, and his anger was often directed at Harry. It was as if he blamed Harry for his loss, as if telling his parents that Billy was in trouble had somehow made it happen.

Bill's voice was raised now. "A bloody dog, why would we want another mouth to feed, especially now, just after the general strike? Who's going to look after it, take it for walks, and clean up after it?"

Harry knew that Bill had been on strike just a week ago, supporting the coal miners, but he also knew that they had managed a lot better than other people. Alice had explained it all to him.

"She won't be much trouble, and Harry will look after her and take her for walks. She'll be good for all of us. Look, Norma loves her already." Harry heard Norma's little voice agreeing.

"It's a bitch too. That'll mean unwanted puppies. No, we're not keeping it!"

"Bill, think about it, a dog is just what we need to take our minds off – other things. Let's give it a go. Someone might claim her anyway, and if not, let's have a trial period. I'm sure Harry will look after her well."

Harry felt that this was a good time to make his presence known. He opened the kitchen door and Bess ran straight to him, wagging her tail. He put the shopping bag down and picked her up. He looked imploringly at Bill, who, as usual, didn't look directly at Harry, but stared at the wall behind him.

"Well, your mother thinks this dog will be a good thing, so you are going to have to show me how responsible you are looking after it. If it makes a mess, or chews anything, it will have to go. Do you understand?!"

"Yes Dad," Harry replied. He didn't say anything else because he didn't want Bill to change his mind. He looked at Alice and she was smiling, a natural smile that he hadn't seen for a long time.

oOo

When he met his friends at Sunday school the next day, Harry's smile told them all they wanted to know. "So your dad has let you keep Bess?" asked Bobby.

"Yes, as long as she doesn't make a mess or chew anything, and I know she won't do that. She's a good dog. Shall we start to train her this afternoon?"

"Ooh yes!" his friends were delighted to be included. Harry invited Joe too, he was still looking lost after losing his best friend, but he declined, saying that he was going to call for Malcolm and Charlie after dinner.

Alf came for Sunday dinner and, before they had finished, Bobby was back at Harry's house. It was another lovely day, so they took Bess out to the ollers. She was looking better already and her tail was constantly wagging.

The flat area that they used for alleys was perfect for training Bess. The boys sat cross legged in front of the dog. She stood looking at them expectantly, her head on one side. "Bess sit!" said Harry, pushing her bottom down to a sitting position. She stayed sitting, looking up as if to say, done that, what next? "Good girl, now up!" Harry gestured with his hand and Bess stood up. "Good girl!" All three boys laughed with delight. "Now, let's see if she will sit again, without me touching her. Bess, sit!" She sat.

"Wow that's amazing!" said Alf. "You only showed her once. How did you do that?"

"I'm not sure, but I am sure that she's a clever dog. She's already clean in the house and she didn't cry during the night. She went out for a wee in the garden last night and when I got up this morning she cried at the back door and had another wee. Course, she might have been taught that before, but I don't think she lived in a house with that nasty man, and I don't think she'd been told to sit before." Alf and Bobby looked impressed.

They all took turns telling Bess to sit, and saying "up" to get her to stand. Next, she learned to shake hands, lifting her right paw every time after being shown just once. By the time they were feeling hungry and thought it was teatime, Bess had learned to stay, to roll over and to fetch a stick. For a little thin dog she was very enthusiastic, but she was obviously very tired, because she just flopped onto her blanket when they got back in the house.

When the family settled down in front of the fire after tea, Bess was allowed into the living room. She went from one family member to another, wagging her tail and being petted. She even went to Bill, who was reading his paper. He patted her head and said, "Go and sit down now," not unkindly, and she went over to where Harry was sitting on the settee and lay at his feet.

After Norma was put to bed, Harry went for his Sunday night bath. He was allowed to stay up for half an hour after this, and went down in his pyjamas. He was amazed to see that Bess was now sitting by Bill's chair and he was absentmindedly stroking her head while reading his paper. Harry's heart soared. He knew that Bess was now a member of the family.

oOo

Over the months Harry and Bess became inseparable. She seemed to love all the family, but if Harry was in the house she would be by his side, and it was Harry who fed her and took her out for walks. He got into the habit of getting up early so that he could take her out before school, and the first thing he did after school was take her out on the ollers. Alf and Bobby were often with him and Bess accepted them as members of her "pack".

Bess filled out and grew rapidly. By Christmas she looked like a fully grown golden retriever. Nobody had claimed her and Harry felt that the "nasty man", as he thought of him, lived a long way from Newton Heath, possibly in Clayton or even further afield. He reasoned that the man would have come looking for her if he really wanted her back.

oOo

Christmas was a very subdued affair that year. They all felt the loss of Billy acutely. They tried to make it a good time for Norma, however. She and Harry got their stockings from Father Christmas, and Norma also got a little tin doll's pram, complete with pillow and blankets knitted by Alice and Grandma. She was delighted, and spent all of Christmas Day pushing the little pram round the house, her dolly sitting proudly against the pillow.

Norma, thankfully, didn't seem to miss Billy as much as the rest of the family, but she did ask if Father Christmas went to the children in Heaven too, and was reassured that Billy would get his presents too.

Harry was in the kitchen helping to wash up after dinner when Norma shouted, "Harry, look what Bess can do!" Alice and Grandma joined

Harry at the kitchen door to watch.

"Bess, push the pram," said Norma. Bess took the handle of the doll's pram in her teeth and pushed it towards Norma. "Good girl!" said Norma, as Bess sat back on her haunches, looking very pleased with herself.

"That dog is so clever!" said Alice. "She never ceases to amaze me".

Shortly after this Bill said, "Alice, I've got a present for you." Harry was intrigued. The adults didn't usually give each other presents. Alice was wide eyed as Bill went out to the coal store at the back of the kitchen and came back with a large cardboard box. "Mum, I'll have to ask you to move for a minute," said Bill. Grandma got up and he moved the rocking chair aside and unpacked the box on top of the sewing machine. He produced a wireless, plugged it in the socket by the fireplace and turned a knob on the front of it. Everyone waited with bated breath.

 Nothing happened for a minute and then music started to come from the speaker. They all smiled. "It has to warm up first, so you need to turn it on a few minutes early if you want to hear the beginning of the news, or a programme. You can find out what's on in here." He produced a magazine called, "Radio times".

Wirelesses had become more popular since the general strike in May, when the BBC covered all the news, but Bill had been reluctant to get one at first, saying that his newspaper was good enough for him, and why would they want a lot of noise in the house? Harry didn't know why Bill had changed his mind, but he was glad that he had.

oOo

The wireless made a big difference to their evenings. Alice and Grandma still did their knitting and sewing, and Harry was often reading a book that he'd brought home from school. The wireless was always on though. They listened to plays and music and the news, and had lively discussions about what they heard. They didn't grieve any less, but it helped them all to bear it.

The programme that Harry and Norma liked best was "Children's Hour" at five o'clock every night. They were usually in the kitchen having tea at this time, but Alice allowed them to listen with the sound turned up. Bill usually didn't get home until after six, so he couldn't complain about the noise.

oOo

Back at school Harry was doing well. His favourite subject was English, though he was reasonably good at most other subjects. He loved music and was in the school choir, as was Alf, who had developed a sweet voice as he grew. Bobby was tone deaf, but he tolerated his friends chat about music as long as they didn't go on for too long. He would much rather talk about football or cricket, as he was on both teams.

Jimmy Bates continued to hassle them in the playground, when they couldn't avoid him. He never hit them, contenting himself with kicking their ball away or knocking caps off their heads and then striding away with his henchmen following.

It was Easter time when an incident occurred that Harry and his friends couldn't avoid.

It was the first time that they had been to Daisy Nook since they had been with Billy and Joe a year ago. Joe still didn't want to go, but Harry, Bobby and Alf wanted to go to the fair. All three boys were now eight years old and they felt that they were big enough to go without the older boys. Alice and Dorothy and Alf's mum agreed to let them go, as long as Bess was with them. "We wouldn't go without Bess, anyway," said Harry.

They set off with butties wrapped in greaseproof paper and a pop bottle full of water. They had their picnic at the side of Crime Lake before they went to the fair, which was in a field at the bottom of the hill. They had just enough money to go on the chairaplanes. Bess was glad to welcome them back after this. She didn't like seeing them up in the air, and she didn't really like sitting and waiting for them either. They had a few pennies over to have a go at roll a penny. If the penny went all the way down the board without touching the black lines, they would win a prize. It was designed to make it almost impossible to do, though, and they gave up after losing tuppence each.

They wandered around enjoying all the sights, and were just admiring the gaily painted caravans when they heard a girl scream. It came from behind the caravans. They started towards the sound, and heard a girl shout, "No, no, I won't!" and then they heard a familiar voice.

"Give us yer money, I said!" It was Jimmy Bates, and they saw him as they rounded a corner. As usual he was surrounded by three of his gang and they were menacing a group of girls, about the same age as themselves. It looked like a couple of the girls had already given up their precious coppers, but one girl, obviously braver than the rest, was refusing. Jimmy had his face inches from hers and he had grasped a handful of her hair.

"Hey!" shouted Harry, "leave her alone!" Jimmy spun round.

"Well, if it isn't mammy's little treasure! No big brother any more, is there?" he sneered. "And these two tiddlers can't do anything."

Harry was absolutely furious at the mention of his lost brother. He drew himself up to his full height, which was a good two inches taller than Jimmy, although he was much slimmer, and he projected all of his anger at Jimmy's eyes. Bess picked up on his emotions and advanced on Jimmy, snarling and baring all her teeth. Alf and Bobby came up beside them to give support. Jimmy blanched and took a step backwards. His mates moved even further back.

"Look, this hasn't got owt to do with you," said Jimmy, "We was just having a bit of fun. You can go now."

"They pinched my friend's money!" said the brave girl, "And they tried to pinch mine too!"

"We was only kiddin'. Here's your money." Jimmy threw the coins at their feet.

"See, 'Arry, everything's alright. Anyway, we've got to go now. See yer!"

The bullies didn't run away, but they walked very fast, and didn't look back until they were at the field gate. Bess gave one sharp bark as if to say, "good riddance."

All the girls thanked them profusely. Harry asked them where they lived. "Newton Heath," they answered.

"So do we, but you don't go to Brookdale Park school, do you?" asked Bobby.

"No, we all go to St Ann's on Oldham road. We live down that way,"

"Well, we can walk back with you as far as Church Street if you like, just in case Jimmy Bates turns up again." Said Bobby, "Alf here lives on Culcheth Lane, and we both live in the new houses on Amos Avenue.

"Ooh, posh aren't you?" Said the brave girl.

Harry was a bit taken aback by this, but the girl quickly said, "I'm only kidding. I'm Susan Dickson, by the way." They all exchanged names as they emerged from the caravans back into the fair proper.

The girls had enough money to buy candy floss for everyone. They bought some for the boys too, as a thank you.

It was a happy group of children who walked through Woodhouses and down Bunkers Hill, munching candyfloss and exchanging information about their respective schools. Bobby was walking in front with Susan, deep in conversation. The others caught up with them just as they reached the level crossing at Pot Brew. There was a train coming, so the gates were shut. "What have you two been talking about, Bobby?"

"Cricket," said Bobby, "I've never met a girl who likes cricket before."

"I'm a good cricketer, too," replied Susan. "D'you fancy a match? We could meet in Brookdale Park. What about next Saturday, if its fine?" the other girls groaned, but agreed to meet anyway. Some of their brothers would come to make up numbers.

oOo

For once, Joe was persuaded to join in the cricket game, and Malcolm and Charlie came too. It was one of those beautiful clear warm days that you get in the early spring. Alice and Dorothy decided to make up a picnic and bring the girls. Bess, of course, was included in the outing.

Bill said he would stay at home; there was a lot to do in the garden. Harry thought that it had more to do with Billy not being there to play cricket, rather than a need to dig the garden. He was sad for his dad but couldn't do anything about it.

Susan and her friends arrived with various brothers and mates in tow. They had a real cricket ball, but nobody had any stumps. They found some likely looking sticks that they stuck in the ground. The women settled on a nearby bench to watch the game and look after the food that everyone had brought.

Susan was as good as her word. Her bowling was good, but she was an amazing batter, hitting several sixes, although this was disputed, due to nobody being sure exactly where the boundaries were. Bobby had to concede that she was a better cricketer than him, and agreed that her team had won by a narrow margin. It was great fun, and everyone agreed that they would play again whenever possible. It became a regular event that summer and continued for several years.

oOo

The day after the cricket match Harry woke with a sore throat and no appetite. Alice decided that they wouldn't go to church. Bill had stopped attending church since losing Billy anyway, and Norma hadn't started Sunday school, so Alice felt that she could miss church for once. She made Harry comfortable on the settee and gave him an aspirin and a honey and hot water drink. Eventually Harry fell asleep and he was immediately in the familiar dream. This time it was a sunny day, and the girl was on a beach, playing with several other children. Her black curls were flying in the breeze as she chased after a ball. She looked very happy and Harry felt happy for her.

He woke up, still feeling poorly, and lay on the settee just thinking. He realised something about his recurring dream. He was dreaming what the girl was doing at that particular time. That's why he usually saw her in her bedroom or getting ready for bed. If he'd had the words for it, he would have said the dream was happening in real time. "It's strange," he thought, "it's like I am travelling in my sleep to wherever she is." It didn't worry him at all, he was sure that he was intended to meet this girl at some time in the future, so he stored up all that he learned about her in his brain, so that he would know her when he met her. He didn't tell Alice about his dreams any more. Although she accepted that there was something different about Harry, he knew that she sometimes worried about this, so he spared her the worry whenever he could.

8 ANOTHER BABY

It was shortly after Harry's ninth birthday that he realised that Alice wasn't well. She seemed very tired and he noticed that Grandma was often looking concerned, and was taking on more of the housework. She was always encouraging Alice to sit down with her knitting. The worrying thing was that Alice didn't complain about this, but seemed glad to sit down. Harry started helping Grandma with the Saturday shopping on the market. He was big and strong for his age and it was no problem to him to carry two heavy shopping bags. Grandma could carry the lighter things in her basket, and Norma often came with them, carrying her own little basket.

Harry started watching Alice closely. As well as being tired and listless, she seemed to be putting on weight, despite not eating an awful lot. He remembered the rumours that had been circulating the playground about how babies were born, and he began to think there was some truth in what had been said.

His suspicions were confirmed when he overheard his parents talking one evening. Harry was finishing drying the dishes and Grandma had gone up to put Norma to bed. The kitchen door wasn't completely shut.

"I think this baby will be a boy," said Bill, "It'll make up for losing Billy. We could call him William!"

Alice gave a weary sigh, "Bill, we can't replace Billy! It would be unfair to a new child to compare him with Billy. He, or she, will be a completely different person and should have a name that suits him, or her."

"Well, it was just a thought. I'm sure it will be a boy though."

"Don't build your hopes up, Bill. It could equally be a girl." Alice sounded exhausted, and Harry decided to end the conversation by going in and saying, "Mum, shall I put the kettle on for a brew?"

"That'd be lovely. Thanks Harry," she replied.

Grandma came down and they all had a cup of tea while listening to the radio. Harry could tell that Bill was disgruntled. Even Bess couldn't do right when she went over and put her head on his knee. "Go and lie down, girl," was all he said. Bess's ears flattened and she went over to Harry. She knew that she was always welcome there. Her love for Harry was almost palpable. He gave her a big cuddle that set her tail wagging again.

oOo

During the next few months Alice seemed to have less and less energy and she always looked pale. Though, when asked, she always said that she was fine. Harry worried anyway because he could feel that Alice was worried too. He didn't remember anything like this in the months before Norma was born. Alice had been full of energy all the time then.

It was almost a relief to go to school every day. Norma was at school now, and Harry had the responsibility for her on the way to school, although they generally joined Dorothy and her family. Audrey was in

98

the same class as Norma and they continued to be best friends, as they had been since they were babies, and Norma would go home with Dorothy and Audrey in the afternoon. Joe, now aged twelve, preferred to go to school with his friends, but Bobby and Harry were inseparable, and Alf invariably joined them when they got to Culcheth Lane, usually with his younger siblings tagging along. They made quite a crowd going up Daisy Bank.

There was always something new to learn at school, so Harry's mind was kept off the problems at home. As soon as he saw Alice sitting in the rocking chair though, while Grandma got tea ready, all his worries came flooding back. "Are you ok Mum?" he would ask, and she would reply.

"Yes lovey, I'm fine,"

Bill had taken to going to the pub two or three times a week, so Harry took the opportunity one evening when Grandma was putting Norma to bed, to talk to Alice.

"Mum, I know that you're expecting a baby. " Alice looked shocked!

"People at school have been talking about it," he said, "so I know, but really, Mum, are you ok? You don't seem like you did before Norma was born."

"I'm fine, lovey. It's just that I'm older now, so it makes me more tired. You and Grandma and your Dad help a lot. I'm a lot luckier than some mothers. I'll be fine. You'll see," and she kissed him.

oOo

It was two weeks after Norma's Birthday that Harry woke in the early hours with the uneasy feeling that something was wrong. He soon realised that it was similar to the feeling that he'd had the day Norma was born. He got up and dressed quietly, Norma was blissfully asleep.

He hovered outside his parents' door, wondering whether to risk Bill's wrath by going in. Alice made a noise and he heard Bill talking quietly to her, so he knocked and went in. "You're butting in where you're not wanted lad!" said Bill roughly. "Get back to bed!"

"No, Bill, it's alright. Harry, you could help by going down and making me a cup of tea. Your Dad'll have one too." Bill looked as though he didn't really want a cuppa, but he said nothing, so Harry went downstairs.

While he was waiting for the kettle to boil Grandma came down. "You can make one for me too," she said. "It looks like we're up for the day now. Your Mum tells me that you know all about babies now, is that right?"

"Well, I don't know that much, but I know they grow in your Mum's tummy and it's a lot of pain when they come out."

"That's true, though there's a lot more to it than that. It's enough for you to know now, anyway. I'll tell you more when you're older. Now, let's get this tea made."

Grandma took the tea up and left Harry drinking his in the kitchen. It was just getting light and he could hear the birds singing. They sounded so beautiful; he hoped the sound was helping his Mum.

Bill came down and put his empty cup on the table. "I'm going to get the nurse," he said, and rushed out without saying anything else.

Grandma didn't come back down and Harry didn't want to go up and disturb whatever was happening. He just sat at the table with Bess at his side. Bess also knew that something was wrong. She sat with her head in Harry's lap and whimpered. Stroking her head was very calming for both of them. Bill soon returned with the nurse, and she went upstairs, leaving Bill in the kitchen with his son.

Bill was still ill at ease with Harry, and he didn't look directly at him as

100

he said, "Having babies is women's work. We men are not allowed near." It was the nearest to a conversation that Harry had had with Bill for a very long time. Harry was gratified, and he groped for something to say in return.

"Does it take very long to have a baby, Dad?" he finally asked.

"They are all different, lad. You were the quickest, and even that seemed to go on for hours. It's better if the man can go to work and come back when it's all over and done with." Harry hoped that he wouldn't be sent to school today. He wanted to stay just there and wait to see if everything was alright. He was beginning to get pains in his stomach and he knew now that they were sympathy pains for Alice.

Bill was ready for work now. He went upstairs to say goodbye and then came back into the kitchen. "The best thing you can do is to take your dog out for a run and then you can help by getting Norma up and dressed for school." Bill didn't say whether Harry had to go to school, so he said nothing, determined to stay at home for the day, and just nodded to his dad.

The early morning air was invigorating. The sky was a deep, cloudless blue and the green of the ollers was dotted with wild flowers. Bess ran the full length of the field to the gate at one end, and then back the other way to the walls of the nunnery. Harry laughed at her antics despite his anxiety. His beloved dog could always make him feel better when he was upset. Eventually they went back through the back garden. Harry looked up at the window of Alice's bedroom and wondered how things were going.

It was eight o'clock and Grandma and the nurse were still upstairs. Harry went up to call Norma and found that she was awake, but still in bed. "Where's Mum, Harry?" she asked when she saw him getting her clothes ready.

"She's got a tummy ache," he replied, remembering what Grandma had told him when Norma was born, "So she's staying in bed today. The nurse and Grandma are looking after her, so I'll get your breakfast and take you to Mrs, Kerr's. She can take you to school."

"Aren't you going to school, Harry?" She asked.

"No, I might be needed to run an errand. It won't matter if I don't go for once."

Blissfully unaware, Norma accepted everything that Harry told her. He was her clever big brother who always had answers to her questions.

Harry boiled eggs and made toast for himself and Norma. Grandma came down while they were eating. "How is Mum?" asked Harry.

"Not too bad lovey, but it will be some time yet. I'm just making tea for us. The nurse could do with one." Grandma looked weary, but Harry didn't comment.

After Grandma had gone back upstairs Harry took Norma to Dorothy's house. Bobby answered the door, looking surprised. "Bobby, I'm not coming to school today. Can you tell Mr Smith that I've got a bad stomach ache?" Bobby knew this was a downright lie, but Harry was never off school, so he knew that there would be a good reason. Norma had gone into the house to find Audrey, so Harry whispered, "Mum is having a baby. The nurse and Grandma are there, but I want to stay in case I can help." Bobby was in on the secret of the baby, as he, Alf and Harry told each other everything, so he nodded and whispered back, "Good luck, Harry, I hope your Mum's ok," and he patted him on the shoulder. Dorothy came to the door then.

"Is it the....?"

"Yes," said Harry.

"Ok, I'll take the girls to school and then come round to see if I can help." She replied. She didn't ask why Harry wasn't going to school. Harry knew that she understood why he wouldn't want to be far from Alice today.

oOo

The day dragged on for Harry. There were intermittent sounds of activity upstairs, and, now and again, one of the women would come down and put the kettle on. Occasionally he would hear Alice moan, but. On the whole, she seemed to be quiet. Bess was constantly at his side and, every time he winced with a pain in his belly, she whined and reached up to lick his face. She was a great comfort. He took her out again when there seemed to be a lull in the activity, but they didn't stay out long.

It was early afternoon when the activity increased and Grandma rushed down the stairs. "Harry, you know how to use the telephone, don't you?" Harry nodded, yes.

"Go to the phone box and ring the doctor. Just tell him that your Mum needs him. He'll understand. Here's the number and some pennies."

Harry felt panicky, "Is it bad?" he gasped.

"Don't worry lovey. It's just a precaution, but be quick" Harry grabbed the pennies and ran for all he was worth up the street to the phone box. The doctor himself answered the phone. Harry was glad it wasn't the doctor's wife, who was known to ask a lot of questions. "I'm on my way, Harry. Don't worry," the doctor said, and the phone went dead.

Harry ran back down the avenue and left the front door open. The doctor was there within five minutes. "Good job surgery had finished, Harry," he said, "I didn't have to throw anyone out!" Harry was glad for the doctor's jovial manner, but still worried as the doctor bounded up the stairs.

Another hour passed with Harry listening to the activity and murmur of conversation, and then he heard a wonderful sound; a baby crying!

Another agonising half hour, and then Grandma came downstairs carrying the precious bundle. "A baby sister for you Harry and she's a big baby. That's why she took so long to be born."

The baby looked tiny to Harry, and she had red marks on both sides of her head. "What are these marks?" he asked.

"The doctor had to use an instrument to help her to be born, but don't worry. The marks will be gone in a few days."

"What about mum, how is she?" Harry almost shouted.

"Your Mum is very, very tired, so she'll have to have lots of rest, but she will be fine in time."

"Can I go and see her now?" he asked.

"In a while. The doctor and nurse are still seeing to her. When they come down you can go and see her. Meanwhile, sit down and you can hold your sister." Harry sat in Grandma's rocking chair and she gently laid the baby in his arms. The baby opened her eyes and looked straight at Harry. She had the dark blue eyes that most new babies have, but otherwise her eyes were the image of Billy's. Harry had no doubt that her eyes would be the same bright blue that Billy's eyes had been and she already had the same dark hair. Harry wondered if she would be just as bright and happy and fearless as Billy had been. One thing was for sure, Harry would never let her go near the river! Bess moved as close as she could to get a good look and a sniff at the creature in Harry's arms. As she smelled the baby, Harry got a picture in his mind of Alice smiling down at the dog. Bess knew that the baby was part of Alice, and therefore one of the family. She gave the baby's cheek a small lick and then looked up to Harry as if to say, "Yes, she'll do!"

Harry had kept the fire built up, despite the warmth of the day, and it was cosy in the living room. He started to doze, still holding the baby, and he felt Grandma gently take her away as he drifted into sleep.

He was back in the dream. Annoyed with himself for falling asleep he tried to wake up, but it seemed he had no control over it. He was in a classroom, but it was smaller than the classrooms at Brookdale Park and the children seemed to be all different ages. He saw the girl, sitting at the front. Her black curls were tied back in a pony tail and her dark eyes were alert as she listened to the teacher. It was English, Harry's favourite subject, and it seemed to be hers too, as she nearly jumped out of her seat when she raised her hand to answer a question. The teacher seemed pleased at her enthusiasm.

Harry didn't have time to observe any more, as he jerked awake to the sound of voices. The doctor was talking to Grandma and they didn't notice that Harry was awake. "Can you ask Mr Roberts to come to my surgery tomorrow?" The doctor spoke quietly. "I need to advise him that there mustn't be any more children. We nearly lost your daughter today, and she'll take a long time to recover. I think he'll take it better from me."

"Yes, of course you're right, doctor. I'll tell him," said Grandma. Harry kept his eyes closed until the doctor left. He didn't want them to know that he had heard. Oh, Bill was going to be upset that the baby was another girl. There would be no chance of having another son now. Harry knew that he was a disappointment to his Dad, though he wasn't completely sure why. He had tried to talk to him about football and railways like Billy used to, but Bill didn't seem to want to talk to him at all nowadays. Harry didn't know how he could make things better for his Dad.

He opened his eyes and looked across at Grandma, who was rocking the baby in her arms. "Can I go up and see Mum yet?" The nurse came in just then and answered for her.

"Yes, you can go up now Harry, but not for long. Your mum needs lots of sleep." He bounded up the stairs, three at a time, but slowed as he went into the room, so as not to startle Alice.

She was lying back with her eyes closed and her face was as white as the pillow. "Mum?" he whispered. She opened her eyes and smiled at him.

"How do you like your new sister?" she asked.

"She's lovely, and she's got eyes like Billy's." Harry gulped as he said this.

"Yes, I noticed that," said Alice, "we'll have to tell her all about him when she's older." Harry nodded. He saw Alice's eyes begin to close again, and remembered what the nurse had said. "I'll go down now, Mum. Then you can get some sleep."

"Ok, night night lovey," she murmured.

oOo

Norma was absolutely delighted with her new baby sister. She was not curious at all about where the baby had come from, and Harry remembered being the same when Norma was born. She sat next to Harry on the settee and Grandma gave her the baby to hold. "She's lovely, Grandma. What shall we call her?" she asked.

"Well, when you were born we all decided together, so why don't we wait for your Dad to come home and for Mum to have a good sleep, and then we'll decide. Have a think about names while I get tea ready." Norma's old pram had miraculously appeared and the sleeping baby was put in it. Harry and Norma set the table while Grandma was busy. Bill arrived home just as tea was ready.

"Dad, we've got a new baby sister. Isn't she lovely?" shouted Norma. Bill's disappointment was obvious to Harry, but Norma was oblivious. "Look at her tiny hands and feet, Dad. Isn't she lovely?" she said again. Bill glanced into the pram and just said, "Yes," and then went upstairs to wash his hands and see Alice. Grandma hadn't had time to tell him how poorly Alice was, so his face was a picture of shock when he came down. "Has the doctor been?" he asked Grandma.

"Yes, he wants to see you tomorrow," she replied. He didn't ask why. Harry thought that Bill had a very good idea what the doctor wanted to talk about, and it didn't make him look any happier. It was a good job that Norma was so happy and excited, because she was the only one talking at teatime and she didn't notice that everyone else was quiet.

After tea they all sat around Alice's bed while she held the baby. She looked slightly better after her sleep, but she was still extremely pale. "What shall we call her?" asked Alice, looking at Norma.

"Well, Harry chose Norma's name, so I think Norma should choose first, and if we all like it, then it's decided," said Grandma. Bill said nothing but just looked at the floor. Alice and Harry agreed with Grandma.

"Can we call her Jennifer?" Norma looked expectantly at everyone.

"Yes, that's really pretty," said Alice

"Yes, and Jenny for short," said Grandma. Harry smiled and nodded agreement. Bill still said nothing, but as they all looked at him, he also nodded, but he didn't give the baby the same welcome that he had for Norma. Harry hoped that Bill would get over his disappointment and eventually love Jenny as he loved Norma. If he didn't, Harry determined that he would make up for it.

9 LEAVING SCHOOL

Over the months Alice slowly improved, but she didn't get back her former energy for a long time. Jenny was a strong, bonny baby and she soon captured the heart of everyone. Even Bill was finally captivated by her. She was so like his lost son, in both looks and personality, he couldn't help but love her.

Harry was relieved to see Bill's love for Jenny, but sad that Bill was still distant towards him, Harry.

oOo

There followed four years of relative harmony for the Roberts family, though this wasn't the case for many working class families. As the 1930s approached work became harder to find, and the Wall Street crash of 1929 tolled a death knell for many businesses. Geo Evans and Sons' sawmill continued to do well though, and, in 1931, they amalgamated with Bellhouse Brothers, who had moved from central Manchester to Miles Platting. They preferred the Newton Heath site, and so closed the Miles Platting mill, and changed the name to Evans Bellhouse, a name that was to be synonymous with Newton Heath for many years. However, they were unable to take on any extra staff at first, which didn't bode well for the boys leaving the local schools.

Joe Kerr left school in 1930 and was lucky to be able to work with his Dad, Fred, whose removal business was doing reasonably well, particularly as building work was beginning on a second phase of Newton Heath Estate, to the west of Scotland Hall Road, taking away all the farmland between there and Ten Acres Lane. Farmer Richards was left with just his farmhouse and yard in the middle of the new houses, but he was happy with this. The sale of the land had made him a gentleman of leisure.

Joe's friends, Malcolm and Charlie were also lucky to get apprenticeships on the building site. Other boys were not so lucky, and those families with a coal miner at the head were really struggling, as the miners had taken a cut in wages after the general strike.

Work on the railways was steady and Bill, as a charge hand, was bringing home a reasonable wage. Grandma Roberts helped by contributing a good part of her pension. Though Alice had argued against this, Grandma got her way. They had plenty of fresh vegetables from the garden and eggs from their hens, so they never went hungry. Clothes were a different matter, they had to make everything last as long as possible. Socks were darned until there was more darn than sock, and shirt collars were turned when they frayed. Alice and Grandma got cheap material from the market to make frocks for the girls. The treadle sewing machine was kept busy, as it was also used by Dorothy, and Alf's Mum, Mary, who had become a good friend, now that her younger children were at school and she had more time.

Alf's Dad had finally disappeared for good. In fact he hadn't been seen since the year Alf became friends with Harry and Bobby. Alf had confided to his friends that his Dad had been in prison, but when he was due to be released in 1927, he hadn't returned home. Alf didn't seem at all bothered about this, and neither did his mother. "At least there'll be no more babies," he said, grinning. "We'll be happy if he never comes home," Alf's family struggled on with handouts from friends and the wages of the five eldest children, who, thankfully, hadn't been laid off yet. The younger children also got free school meals, so that was a big help.

Harry continued to do well at school, especially in English, his favourite subject. When he was eleven his teacher suggested he could probably get a scholarship to Manchester Grammar school. She thought that he would make a good teacher. He was always helping the less able pupils with their work. He took a note home and Alice seemed in favour of his trying for the scholarship, but Bill was dead set against it.

"No! You're not spending an extra two years at school. What about the tram fares and all the extra things you'll need, uniforms and such?"

"He'll get a grant..." began Alice, but she was interrupted.

"I know about these grants. They're not nearly enough. No, he'll stay at Brookdale and leave when he's fourteen like his friends. Likely I'll be able to get him on at the railway. He could work his way up to be an engine driver." He was adamant, and this time Alice couldn't change his mind.

Harry was in two minds anyway. He didn't want to leave his friends and start at a new school, and the thought of being able to contribute to the family coffers, however little, was at the forefront of his mind. Also, although he had little interest in the railway, he thought that, if he could go to work with his Dad every day, it might bring them closer together. So, even though he liked the thought of being a teacher, he quietly accepted Bill's decision.

oOo

Outside of school Harry's main interest was the wireless. He had been fascinated with the mystery of radio waves since they had got theirs, and had read everything he could get hold of on the subject. When the wireless broke, one summer Saturday in 1931, he borrowed a handcart and took it to a shop in Moston, just off Lightbowne Road, that specialised in repairing wireless. Bess trotted along at his side, enjoying this trip with lots of new smells.

Mr Marshall was the proprietor of the shop on Hugo Street. It was a combined hardware and electrical shop, selling everything from nails to light bulbs, and Mr Marshall knew everything there was to know about wireless. Harry was enthralled.

Mr Marshall was also a dog lover. "Come here lass" he said to Bess, "You look like you need a drink of water." Bess recognised a kindred spirit and followed him, tail wagging, into the back of the shop. "Come through lad," he said to Harry, who followed him into a room that served as kitchen, sitting room and workshop. Every surface was cluttered with wirelesses and parts, valves, wires and solder. It was like an Aladdin's cave to Harry. He would love to have a go at repairing his own wireless.

"My dog died a few months ago, I might get another one, as I'm on my own here since my wife died. In the meantime this lass can use his water bowl." Bess was already enthusiastically lapping up the water, splashing and dripping. Mr Marshall didn't seem to mind.

Mr Marshall had brought Harry's wireless through. "I wonder, lad, as you've got that there handcart, if you could do me a favour?"

"Yes, if I can," said Harry.

"Can you take this wireless I've repaired to a lady on Attleboro Road? And I'll have a look at yours while you're doing that."

"Yes, no bother. Where's Attleboro Rd?" Harry replied.

"Straight down Hugo Street to the end. That's Attleboro, then turn left and go up to number three. Mrs Hewitt. Tell her it's one and six and she can give you the money or bring it in when she's passing."

Harry put the wireless into the hand cart and was soon knocking on Mrs Hewitt's door. "Aw lovely, I can listen to the band show tonight. Tell Mr Marshall thanks. The wireless is me company since Mr Hewitt passed. Here'yar lad," and she gave him threepence for himself in addition to the one and six. Harry was delighted.

Mr Marshall was also delighted, as he didn't have to carry the heavy wireless, and he had good news for Harry. "Yours is just a valve lad, and I've got the right one in, so it'll just be a few minutes. I won't charge you after you doing me that favour, but can you just put the kettle on for a brew. I'm spittin' feathers!" Harry soon made the tea and they both had a cup, while Mr Marshall was asking him where he lived and how old he was.

"Is that your handcart?" he asked.

"No, I've just borrowed it," was the reply.

"Oh, that's a shame; I was going to ask you if you wanted a Saturday job as errand boy, but I haven't got a bike or a cart."

"Well..." said Harry, "I might be able to borrow it on a Saturday. It belongs to a friend's Dad, and he mainly uses it on weekdays. There might be the odd Saturday I can't have it though."

"Well we can cross that bridge when we come to it. There's always going to be odd jobs you can do round the shop, and, if business picks up, I might be able to get you a bike. How does half a crown sound for a wage?" Harry thought of how happy Bill would be that he'd be bringing in a wage, albeit small. He agreed immediately. "Right lad, I'll see you next Saturday, nine o'clock, and you can bring Bess too. She's a fine, clever dog." Bess wagged her tail and looked up at Mr Marshall as if she knew what he was saying.

Harry couldn't wait to get home and tell his parents and Grandma about the job. He skipped along, pushing the handcart, and he didn't slow down, even going uphill to the railway bridge on Thorpe Road. Bess bounded along at his side. She never needed a lead, even when crossing Oldham Road. She responded obediently to Harry's every word.

oOo

Harry could sense that Bill was pleased about the job, though he didn't say much, except, "That was handy, not having to pay for the valve."

Alice was more appreciative. "It was good of you to do that favour for Mr Marshall, and that lady will be glad to get her wireless back. Keep that threepence," she said, when Harry tried to offer it to her, "and you can keep your wages too. We're not that short of money, yet." Bill looked as if he was going to object, but she gave him that 'look' that meant she was adamant.

"I won't need all my wages, Mum. I wish you'd have some of it," said Harry.

"I'll tell you what," she replied, "put some of it in Parr's Bank, on the corner of Dean Lane. You can save up that way. You might need it when you're older."

"Ok Mum, but if you ever need it I want you to have it." She smiled fondly at him.

Grandma said, "Just think Harry, You'll have money for the fair at Easter, and you can treat your friends when you go."

"Oh yes, I never thought of that, and I can buy toffees for Norma and Jenny too."

"Ooh yes!" cried Norma and Jenny, avidly. They had been listening with interest, although three year old Jenny didn't understand all that was being said, she certainly knew what toffees were.

"I'll tell you what," said Harry, "after Sunday school tomorrow we'll go and spend this threepence in the toffee shop."

"Yes!" the girls shouted and the adults laughed. Even Bill had a smile on his face.

oOo

Bobby and Alf were pleased for Harry, and a little envious. Alf especially would love to have a Saturday job. Bobby often helped his dad and brother in the removal firm when he wasn't at school, but he didn't get paid any more than his spends. Alf didn't get any spends, though he sometimes got a penny off one of his older brothers for doing odd jobs. They were such good friends, though, that a piece of luck for one was enjoyed by all three. Harry determined that he would keep his eyes and ears open for work for his friends. He felt sure that there would be lots of opportunity when he was out delivering for Mr Marshall.

Charlie's dad, who owned the handcart, was happy to let Harry use it on Saturdays, as long as he looked after it and it wasn't needed for Charlie's family. He knew that Harry would take care of it. Harry came from a well liked family, who were always helping out neighbours.

oOo

Harry and Bess arrived on time the next Saturday. Harry was eager to get to know the work and Bess just loved to be with him. When she saw Mr Marshall, Bess gave him such a greeting of tail wagging and licks that he couldn't stop laughing.

"Right lad," he said when Bess had calmed down, "there's a couple of deliveries to do, but it's a bit early yet, and I've had a couple of ideas during the week. I think we'll advertise our delivery service. What's your writing and drawing like?"

Well, I think its ok," said Harry, modestly. "I like writing at school, and we do drawing in art."

"Ok, this is my idea; I've written this leaflet to put in shop windows on Moston Lane and Oldham Road, but I'm not that good at writing. I'm better at mechanical things. Can you write it neatly and make a few copies?"

Harry looked at the pencilled writing and was sure he could make it neater, and improve on the grammar. He filled Mr Marshall's fountain pen with ink and got to work immediately. The end product was pleasing to both of them:

Marshall's Hardware and Electrics.

Wireless sales and repairs.

Batteries Recharged.

Too Heavy? Don't worry.

Our Saturday delivery service is second to none.

Collection can also be arranged.

Corner of Hugo Street and Adrian Street,

Lightbowne Road, Moston.

Harry had his neat copy done in no time and Mr Marshall was so impressed that he made the tea while Harry did six copies.

As they were finishing their tea the shop bell rang and Mr Marshall went to serve a local man who wanted a tin of white gloss paint and several other items. "Would you like these delivered Ted? The lad is just on his way out now," said Mr Marshall, proudly.

"Oh, I didn't know you delivered. That'd be a help because I've got to visit my mum before I go home."

"It's a new service. Don't forget to tell your friends. It's only on a Saturday, mind."

The man gave his address and Harry loaded the order into his handcart and added two wirelesses that had been repaired. Mr Marshall gave him three of the leaflets and told him which shops on Moston Lane to take them to. The other three he could take to Oldham Road on his way home. He set off with Bess at his side and he soon had everything delivered. Everyone was appreciative, and Bess got a lot of attention too. Several people asked what he was doing while they petted the dog and Harry was pleased to generate more interest for Mr Marshall's business.

The afternoon was spent tidying the shop and workshop and watching Mr Marshall repairing wirelesses, in between serving customers. Harry was allowed to undertake a few simple sales and he started to memorise prices. It was a busy little shop and Harry understood why Mr Marshall had wanted his help. Tired and happy, he made his way home, jiggling his half crown against a penny tip he had been given in his pocket. He planned to go to the bank on Monday after school and open a savings account with two bob. The other sevenpence he was going to share with his sisters and friends to buy toffees.

He had news for Alf too. When Harry was taking a leaflet to a newsagent on Oldham Road, he met Susan Dickson. She was just going into the shop to tell the owner that her brother couldn't deliver papers any more. He'd just left school and had gone over to Liverpool to work with his uncle. It was short notice, but he couldn't turn down the job.

"My friend can deliver your papers," said Harry.

"Right lad, I'll give him a chance, seeing as you're a friend of young Susan here. Tell him to be here at seven on the dot tomorrow morning. If he can turn up every day, he's got the job." Harry ran up Church Street to Culcheth Lane to tell Alf the good news. Thankfully Alf was in and he was delighted. "Wow thanks, Harry, I'll definitely be there. I'll tell you all about it after church tomorrow."

When Bobby heard about Alf's paper job it gave him an idea. He went round every newsagent in the area to ask if they needed a paper boy. He was rewarded for his persistence a couple of weeks later when he went back for the third time to a shop on Church Street. One of their paper boys had just left and Bobby got the job.

oOo

When Harry went to get the handcart the next Saturday Bess started wagging her tail vigorously. As she looked into Harry's eyes he got a vision of Mr Marshall petting the dog. "Yes, we're going to work, Bess," Harry was used to getting these visions projected from the dog and he didn't find them unusual. He didn't realise that other people would have found it extremely strange if he told them, but he didn't tell anyone about this, or about his ability to detect other people's feelings. He simply didn't think it worth talking about. So it was only his closest family and his two best friends who were aware, though some people marvelled at his uncanny rapport with his dog.

Harry and Bess became a common sight on Saturdays around Moston and Newton Heath. They soon got to know all the streets, and Harry's mental map meant that he was very quick when delivering.

Mr Marshall was really pleased with his work. Harry also became adept at weighing out nails by the pound and discussing the merits of different types of screws, hinges and staples. His favourite work, though, was repairing wirelesses. Mr Marshall taught him to take the back off the set and look for anything obvious first, like a loose wire that could be soldered back to the baseboard. Failing that, the wireless would be plugged in and all the valves checked. If one wasn't lit up, then that was usually the problem. Harry never tired of this work.

The fact that Harry was so pleasant and helpful when out on his deliveries had a beneficial effect on the business. More and more people were coming into the shop, and Mr Marshall began to stock more variety, and he could keep his prices down to match bigger shops. This was very important at that time, when so many men were losing their jobs. By the time Harry was due to leave school, in 1933, the papers were calling that period the "Great Depression"

oOo

After Harry had been working there for a year Mr Marshall surprised him one Saturday by saying, "Don't bring the handcart next week lad, you won't need it."

Harry looked up at him in surprise; "Is there anything wrong, Mr Marshall?" he was anxious. He didn't want to lose the job that he loved.

"No lad, nothing wrong. I won't tell you anything else, but it's nothing bad. See you next week lad."

Reassured but very curious, Harry said goodbye.

Bess couldn't understand why they didn't go to Charlie's for the handcart the following Saturday. She hesitated at the gate until Harry said, "C'mon Bess, we'll be late for work." Bess knew the word "work" meant going to see Mr Marshall, so she caught up with Harry, tail wagging furiously.

As soon as they got there Mr Marshall said, "Can you go out to the yard, lad, and bring in those sacks of nails?"

Harry opened the back door, and there was a black bike with a big basket on the front. A panel under the crossbar that should have had the name of a business on it was freshly painted with black gloss. "Surprise!" said Mr Marshall, "It's second hand, but in working order. Good brakes and that. You just need to write our name on it. That black gloss should be dry now. I did it last night, but I knew you would be better at the writing."

Harry was overwhelmed. Mr Marshall had mentioned getting a bike once or twice, but he hadn't thought it would ever happen. "It's a great bike Mr Marshall. I'll be able to get round quicker now, thanks"

"It's me should thank you lad. You've brought most of the business that's made it possible. Shall we have a brew before you start painting?"

"I think I should do the deliveries before I paint it or it won't be dry in time."

"Oh yes, good thinking lad. Right, well you make us a brew and after that you can get going."

Bess thought it was great fun running at the side of the bike. Harry could feel her pleasure. They got the deliveries done in half the time it took with the handcart, despite all the interest that the bike generated among their customers.

When they got back Harry set to with the white gloss paint and made a neat job of writing the business name on the bike. "It looks right posh lad!" said Mr Marshall.

From that time Harry did two delivery runs every Saturday. The Moston deliveries were done in the morning and then Harry would leave early enough in the afternoon to do the Newton Heath deliveries on his way home. He kept the bike in the back garden under a tarpaulin to protect it from the weather. The bike generated more interest, and Harry often stopped to tell people where they could get their wireless repaired. Despite the Depression Mr Marshall's business was thriving.

oOo

New Year 1933 brought a new interest for Harry and his two friends. They would soon be leaving school. Alf was fourteen in February and both Bobby and Harry had their birthday in March. They would leave school at Easter, so they would have to think about getting a job. Thinking about jobs was the easy part. Actually getting a job, when there were fifty applicants for every vacancy, was much harder. Two of Alf's brothers had been laid off at the factory, with no promise of going back, and his eldest brother had left home to work away, so there were only two sisters bringing in small wages, and Alf gave most of his paper round money to his mum.

 Bobby's dad said that he could work with him and Joe, but Bobby would really rather try and get an apprenticeship if he possibly could. Apprenticeships were slightly easier to get than fully paid jobs, as the apprentices were paid so little. Twelve and sixpence a week was the average rate, compared with a man's wage of six or seven pounds.

On a chilly Sunday afternoon it was too cold for sitting in their favourite clearing on the ollers so they were walking about and throwing the ball for Bess, while talking about jobs. "My Dad thinks he can get me an apprenticeship in the railway sheds," said Harry.

"Oh, I'd love to do that," said Alf, "You know, I've never been on a train, but I love watching them. Such power!"

"You don't need to tell us that," laughed Bobby, "You're always going on about trains." Harry laughed too.

"I'd like to be an apprentice at Evans Bellhouse," said Bobby, who loved working with wood.

"Why don't you ask your dad if you can apply? You never know, you might be lucky," said Harry. "I would really like to work with wireless, but I know that's not going to happen. I should be grateful to get any work, and I will be. Of course it's not definite that I will get the apprenticeship"

"At least you've got a dad. I've got nobody to speak for me," said Alf glumly. Harry looked at him in surprise. It was unlike Alf to moan about his lack of a dad. Of the three boys, he was normally the most optimistic. It made Harry think deeply about his own situation. Ever since Billy died there had been a coolness between Bill and Harry. Harry sometimes compared his relationship with his dad unfavourably with that of Bobby and Fred. Fred's pride in both his sons was obvious, and he would do anything for them. Bill's reserve had made Harry think that he didn't care, but he now realised that wasn't true. Bill did have his best interests at heart; he just didn't know how to show it.

Harry was deep in thought when Bobby threw the ball vigorously and Bess gave chase as it soared towards the railway line. "Oops, I hope it doesn't go over the fence!" said Bobby, "We've lost it if it does."

Bess disappeared down the steep slope and the boys ran after her. While she was still out of sight, Bess began barking excitedly. This was unusual, as she rarely barked. Harry knew there was something wrong. As they reached the top of the slope they saw Bess dragging something up the slope. "It looks like a sack," said Alf. They all reached down and pulled the sack up to the top.

"Ew, it's wet and filthy! What have you brought this for Bess?" said Harry. Bess stared earnestly at him, and he got an image of a cat in his mind. "She thinks it's a cat," he told the others.

They struggled to get the sack opened. The top was tied with string. They finally got it open and tipped out the contents. "Oh no, dead kittens!" Bobby cried. There were six wet newborn kittens, obviously drowned.

"Bess, they're dead," said Harry. "We can't do anything for them." He had a massive lump in his throat and tears were forming in his eyes. He could feel that his friends were also fighting back tears. Bess wouldn't give up though. She grabbed one of the kittens by the scruff of its neck and carried it away from the others. She then started to lick its face, over and over, she wouldn't stop. The boys just watched, unsure of what to do. Suddenly the kitten gave a tiny cry. They all heard it. "It's alive! Bess must have known all along. Come on, we'll take it home," said Harry.

"What about the others, we can't just leave them here?" Alf was obviously distressed. He and Bobby put all the tiny bodies back into the sack, while Harry put the live kitten under his shirt and jumper to keep it warm.

"We'll bury them in the garden," said Harry. They left the sack by the chicken run and continued into the house.

Alice was as upset as the boys. "How could anybody do such a cruel thing?"

Bill was more matter of fact about it. "They probably couldn't afford to feed their kids, never mind a cat and six kittens. They should have buried them though. That's just lazy and callous, throwing them on the ollers."

Alice found a clean rag and dipped it in milk. The kitten made a feeble effort to suckle the cloth, but it didn't seem to be getting much. "I'm sorry, boys, this kitten might die after all. It needs to be fed by a mother cat." She explained.

"I know," said Alf. "Our next door neighbour, Mrs Ridley's cat has just had kittens. I bet she would feed it."

"Well, you could ask Mrs Ridley. She's a nice old lady, so I think she would help if she could," replied Alice. "Let's all have a hot drink before you go. You'd best wash your hands boys, after handling those kittens" She put the ginger kitten next to Bess, who was lying on her blanket. Bess immediately began to lick the kitten and pull it towards her warm body.

"I think Bess would feed it if she could," said Harry.

oOo

Mrs Ridley was kindness itself. She invited the boys into her tiny kitchen and showed them the cat and four black and white kittens in a box in the corner. "Now, we'll have to trick her into thinking this is one of hers," she said. She enticed the mother cat into the front room with a piece of liver. "Tibby loves liver," she said, and she shut the door on the cat. She picked up one of the kittens in one hand and held the ginger one in the other. Then she rubbed the two kittens together, making sure she rubbed the orphan under the tail of the other. "I'm putting the familiar scent on the new kit," she said, and then she placed the orphan into the middle of the others, and they all instinctively cuddled together.

The mother cat came back in. She nuzzled each kitten, and at first seemed a bit confused, as if to say, "I'm sure there were only four!" She settled down, though, and didn't seem to be bothered. The kittens immediately found their way to the teats, despite their eyes still being shut, and the ginger one latched on as if this was its own mother. Everyone breathed a sigh of relief.

"There you go. That's nature for you. Mother animals will invariably look after an orphan." Mrs Ridley was proud to be proved right. Now, you boys, I want a favour in return. Can you bring in a bucket of coal from the yard?" The boys were eager to help, and soon shovelled some coal into the bucket and put it next to the fire. "Also, in eight weeks time I'll need homes for these little ones. Start asking people, you get around more than I do." The boys promised that they would.

Alf said, "I'm going to ask Mum if I can keep Ginger. I can buy his food out of my paper round money."

oOo

When he got to work on the following Saturday, Harry was still thinking about jobs, and he was unusually quiet in the shop. "Cat got your tongue?" Mr Marshall said, in a lull between customers, "You're not usually so quiet."

"I've just been thinking about what I'll do when I finish school," Harry replied.

"Oh, I'm glad you've brought that up. I've been thinking too." Mr Marshall seemed a bit hesitant, which was unlike him. Harry waited for him to go on.

"I, erm, wondered if you would like to work full time here. I couldn't pay much, say, thirteen bob a week to start with, and it wouldn't be a proper apprenticeship. In any case, you already know as much about wireless as I do, and you don't need an apprenticeship to sell hardware. The business is doing well though, and I thought we might get a van in a couple of year's time and you could learn to drive. We could branch out too. There's a market for renting out wirelesses. We could rearrange the shop to make more space. What do you think?" He looked anxiously at Harry.

It was what Harry would love to do. He enjoyed the work and he was very fond of Mr Marshall. Would his dad let him do it though?

"I'll have to talk it over with Mum and Dad, but yes, I would like to work here full time."

Mr Marshall was beaming. "That's right. You need to ask your parents, of course. Let's hope they say yes. Let's celebrate with a cuppa. Go and put the kettle on lad."

oOo

Harry thought he would broach the subject with Alice first. He waited until Bill went out to the pub, and Grandma, as usual, was getting the girls ready for bed.

"Mr Marshall has offered me a full time job." Harry was immediately aware of Alice's reaction. She was pleased for Harry, knowing how much he loved the work, but she worried that Bill wouldn't allow it.

"That's good news Harry. What will your long term prospects be?"

"Well, the business is doing well, and Mr Marshall likes my work and my ideas. He's never going to sack me. He thinks we will be able to get a van in a couple of years and I can learn to drive it. We might branch out into renting out wirelesses. The wage is thirteen bob to start with. That's the same as some apprentices and more than most. Even if I got an apprenticeship, there's no guarantee of a job at the end of it, the way things are going."

"Your Dad will be disappointed if you don't work in the railway sheds, but I'll talk to him." She smiled fondly.

"About the railway, Mum. You know Alf would really like to work there, and he hasn't got a dad to speak for him. If Dad lets me take the job with Mr Marshall, do you think he'd put in a word for Alf? He knows him well."

"That's a good thought Harry. I think you should bring that up yourself though, after I've spoken to your Dad. I'll leave it until after church tomorrow."

Harry was on tenterhooks that evening. He didn't want to see Bill until the next morning, so he went to bed early, despite feeling that he wouldn't sleep. However, his young body demanded the sleep that his active mind was denying him, and he was soon in the familiar dream.

The mystery girl was now nearly ten years old and she was more beautiful than ever. Her black curls were cascading around her shoulders and her dark brown eyes were full of life as she started to sing.

She was in the small school that he'd seen her in before and he could see a colourful banner on the wall above her head. There was one word on it – Eisteddfod. He wondered what this strange word meant, but he didn't think about it for long because he was captivated by the girl's beautiful voice. He couldn't understand a word of the song, but the tune had a haunting quality about it that had him mesmerised. She finished singing to rapturous applause by the audience of children and parents. Harry was clapping too, although he was sure that nobody was aware of him. He recognised the girl's mother when she came forward and hugged her daughter. Harry could sense the pride she felt. She was crying tears of joy.

The scene faded and he didn't remember any more dreams until he awoke on Sunday morning.

After Sunday dinner Grandma suggested that she and Harry should take the girls to Brookdale Park. She gave Harry a knowing look and he realised that Alice had told her about the job offer. It would be easier for Alice and Bill to talk without anyone else in the house.

It was too early in the year for cricket, but they found a few of Harry and Norma's friends kicking a football about. Audrey was cheering for Bobby and Alf. She didn't like playing football but loved watching it. Susan Dickson was in the thick of it. Cricket was her favourite sport but she would join in with anything. "C'mon Harry and Norma, You can be on our team. They've got one more than us and they're bigger!" Susan shouted. Harry noticed that the other team was made up of various members of Alf's and Susan's families. Bobby, Alf and Susan were teamed up with two girls and a boy, all Susan's friends.

Grandma and Jenny sat on a bench with Audrey and settled down to watch the fun. Grandma had bought toffees on the way and she gave one to each of the girls. The match lasted about half an hour and it was agreed that it was a draw. Harry thought it was amusing that all their matches usually ended in a draw, after quite a lot of argument though. They all congregated around the bench and grandma shared her toffees with everyone. They were all thirsty too. It was a good job the drinking fountain was nearby.

Audrey made a space for Harry at her side and Harry was uncomfortably aware that she was gazing up into his eyes and drinking in every word that he said. Audrey had been like a third sister to him for years and he was very fond of her, but her recent hero worship was a bit embarrassing. He didn't know what to do about it, except to treat her like a little sister as he always had. She stayed by his side as they walked home, linking her arm through his. Audrey had turned ten the previous September and Harry couldn't help comparing her smooth brown hair and hazel eyes with the dark beauty of the ten year old in his dreams.

oOo

There was still a good hour of light left when they got home and Bill asked Harry to help him in the garden. Harry knew this was Bill's way of getting him alone to talk.

At first they just worked in silence on the rows of early potatoes and it gave Harry the chance to probe Bill's feelings. He was surprised to feel that Bill wasn't angry. The undercurrent of grief was there. Harry thought that would never go away for any of them, but there was also a different kind of sadness, and guilt. What did Bill have to feel guilty about? Harry began to realise that his Dad felt guilty for pushing Harry away after Billy died, and this was the reason for the new sadness. Bill was worried that he was losing his younger son too.

Eventually Bill spoke. "Your mother tells me that you want to work in Mr Marshall's shop. Are you absolutely sure this is what you want? You might have better prospects as an apprentice."

"I've thought about it a lot. I really enjoy mending wirelesses and I'm interested in hardware too. If an apprenticeship would definitely lead to a job I suppose that's what I would want. But there's no guarantee of anything in this depression, so, yes, this is what I want."

"Well, I can't say I'm not disappointed, but your arguments are sound. I can't even guarantee that you would get the apprenticeship on my say so, but I would have tried."

"Thanks, Dad," Harry gave him a grateful smile.

Harry felt that he wouldn't get Bill in a better mood than now, so he decided to broach the subject of Alf wanting to work for the railway. "Dad, you know that Alf is mad about trains. I don't suppose you'd put in a word for him?"

"Alf's a good lad and his family have had bad luck," Bill mused. "Yes, I'll do my best for him. You can tell him I'll put in a word for him, but not to get his hopes up."

"Thanks Dad. He'll be delighted." Harry was overjoyed.

oOo

Part Two

Dreams Can Come True

1 BAD THINGS COME IN THREES

In the summer of 1939 Harry was driving his van around North Manchester, with Bess in the passenger seat. He always thought of it as "his" van, though his boss, Mr Marshall had bought it for the business, which was still very busy. It turned out that Mr Marshall couldn't drive and wasn't interested in learning, but he was an astute business man and realised the advantage of having good transport. On Harry's seventeenth birthday he rewarded Harry's hard work with the van and a few lessons from the car salesman. Harry then had to apply for a driving test, which had become compulsory in 1935. The driving examiner arranged to meet him at Newton Heath town hall and he easily passed the test. Mr Marshall paid the 7/6d for the test and bought the Highway Code, which cost a penny. Harry could then get a full driving licence for the sum of five shillings.

The van was well known in the area. The sign on the side read, "Marshall's Wireless and Hardware." This, and the golden dog in the seat, was difficult to miss and lots of people waved to Harry as he passed.

Today he was hoping to see his two best friends. He was taking a valve to the railway yard at Dean Lane. It was for the men's wireless in the canteen and he should be just in time for Alf's break. Alf was well on his way to becoming a top mechanic. He still loved the trains and, when he wasn't riding on them, he was maintaining them.

Alf saw Harry as soon as he came in and shouted him over. "Are we on for the pictures on Saturday?" He asked.

"Of course, it's The Flying Deuces, Laurel and Hardy," Harry replied, "Norma wants to come too." He tried to ignore Alf's blush. He knew that Alf was sweet on Norma, but she was only sixteen and Bill wouldn't allow her to have a boyfriend. Going out as a group was a good way of getting around the problem.

After a cuppa with the railway men, he made his way round to where Bobby worked, on Great Ancoats Street. He had quite a big order for Mr Fink, Bobby's boss. Mr Fink was a cabinet maker and, since Bobby had become his apprentice, he ordered all his fixings from Marshall's. He got special rates because of Bobby and Harry's friendship and he liked the fact that whatever he ordered was delivered promptly.

"Hiya Harry, how's it going?" said Bobby

"Busy as usual. Are you coming to the pictures on Saturday?" Harry replied.

"Yes, Susan's coming of course, and Audrey will be coming with Norma."

Bobby's long term friendship with Susan Dickson had blossomed into romance in the past year. Nobody, except Bobby, was surprised. He still hadn't got over Alf and Harry laughing when he told them that he and Susan were courting. He had thought that they would be as astounded as he was when he realised that he was in love with one of his best friends. He forgave them eventually though. They never stayed annoyed with each other for long.

The rest of the day passed uneventfully and Harry got back to the shop just before closing time. The business had grown so much that most of Harry's time was spent driving, and Ted, Alf's youngest brother, now worked full time in the shop. Mr Marshall spent most of his time mending wirelesses. He seemed to have got slower in the eight years that Harry had known him, and he left most of the running of the business to Harry now.

Harry and Bess arrived home to be greeted by the delicious smell of tater ash. Bess sniffed ecstatically. She gave Harry a vision of the time he rescued her, when she was starving. Alice had given her some tater ash and she had never forgotten. She usually just had dog food but, occasionally, Alice would cool a little tater ash for her, just for a treat. Harry laughed. "I'll save a bit for you," he promised. Bess's tail went into overdrive!

"Good day?" asked Alice, as he washed his hands at the kitchen sink.

"Yes. I saw Alf and Bobby. We're all going to the pictures on Saturday."

"Norma tells me Audrey is going too."

"Well, they're best friends. They're always together." Harry said this defensively. He was well aware that Audrey felt more for him than sisterly affection, and he also knew that Alice was aware of this. He had such a rapport with his Mum that he almost always knew what she was thinking. He knew that Alice would be pleased if he and Audrey started courting, even though Audrey wouldn't be seventeen until next month, September. He hadn't told Alice that he was still having dreams about the mystery girl, but he knew that she suspected as much. He also knew that he would never be able to think of another girl "in that way" until he met the mystery girl and found out how true his feelings were. He was absolutely certain that he would meet her one day. He just couldn't explain, even to himself, why he was so certain.

It was a shame about Audrey. She was the sweetest, kindest girl that he knew. If he could have offered her more he would, but he couldn't pretend feelings that he didn't have.

Alice sighed and smiled fondly at her son.

oOo

After tea on Saturday Harry and Norma walked up to collect Audrey. Bobby was down at Susan's house for tea. They would meet up at the Pavilion picture house. Alf joined them at Culcheth Lane and immediately joined Norma, leaving Harry and Audrey walking behind them. Audrey companionably tucked her arm into Harry's. The conversation was all about work. Audrey had recently been upgraded to the typing pool in her office and she was really enjoying the work. Harry felt comfortable. He wished that he could always feel this comfortable with Audrey, being the friends that they were as children. Maybe it would happen one day.

There was a queue outside the Pavilion as usual. Bobby and Susan were already there and the others joined them, despite complaints of jumping the queue from one or two disgruntled people. One of these was immediately behind them and Harry recognised the voice that he hadn't heard since he left school. It was none other than Jimmy Bates saying, "Oy, we were 'ere before you?" Harry turned and looked down at him. Jimmy hadn't grown tall. He was still stocky and at least four inches shorter than Harry. "Oh, hiya, Harry. Didn't realise it was you. How are you doing? Still with Marshall's?" Harry was taken aback by Jimmy's pleasant demeanour. In the last two years of school Jimmy had left Harry and his friends alone, on the whole, but he had never been particularly friendly. This new Jimmy was a bit unnerving, but Harry was always ready to be friendly with anyone, so he replied.

"Hiya Jimmy. We've not seen you for a long while. Have you been working away?"

"Er, yes, I have, but I've got a job at the gas works now, down Hulme Hall Lane, stoking the boiler."

"Oh, I bet that's heavy work," Harry replied.

"It bloody is! Oh, sorry love," He turned to Audrey, who was drinking in every word. "Are you Audrey Kerr?" Jimmy asked. He looked admiringly at her. Harry wasn't sure he liked that look. Audrey was like one of his sisters and he felt protective, knowing what a bully Jimmy used to be. He tightened his grip on Audrey's arm and she looked up at him in surprise.

"Yes, I am," she replied, shyly, "I remember you from school, though you'd left before I was in the seniors."

"I remember you too, but you've grown up a lot since then." His smile was genuine. Harry wondered if Jimmy had turned over a new leaf. He wasn't with any of his old gang. The lad he was with looked older, and he introduced him as his brother, Jack. Harry vaguely remembered him as being several years ahead of them at school.

The queue was moving now and it stopped any further conversation.

oOo

The film was good and they spilled out of the Pavilion laughing. "Fish and Chips now," Said Alf, and they all piled into the chippy on Culcheth Lane. Harry got chips for Alice, Grandma and Jenny, but when they got home Grandma had already gone to bed. Harry was concerned, because Grandma loved to hear about the films when they got back, and she loved chips too.

"She was tired," said Alice, "so she said that you can tell her about the film in the morning." Alice didn't seem too worried, so Harry relaxed. Bill came home from the pub just then, so he ate Grandma's chips. They all went to bed, laughing about the antics of Laurel and Hardy. It was the last time that Harry laughed for a long time.

He was awoken from a familiar dream by a severe headache. Harry never had headaches and he realised that he was experiencing someone else's pain. He sat up in bed and looked across at his sisters. They still shared a bedroom even though Grandma had offered to move in with the girls so that Harry could have his own room. They were comfortable with each other and Harry respected the girls' privacy when they were changing, so they didn't see any need for change.

The girls were fast asleep and obviously comfortable. Harry quested out mentally and realised that it was Grandma who was in pain. He got up and went into her room. She was awake and staring at him as he entered. She looked terrified! She said something that sounded like his name, but her words were slurred and her face looked lopsided.

"Grandma, what's wrong?" he knelt down at the side of her bed and tried to understand what she was saying, but he couldn't. "I'll get Mum," he said. His heart was pounding as he knocked on his parent's door and went in. Alice woke immediately. "There's something really wrong with Grandma. She can't speak and she's got a terrible headache," he said. Alice was up and out of bed in no time. She didn't stop to put on her dressing gown but rushed into Grandma's room.

"Mum!" Alice cried, "Oh Harry, I think she's had a stroke. Can you get dressed and go and phone the doctor, love?" Harry nodded and quickly went to get dressed. Thankfully his sisters were still fast asleep. He left Alice quietly sobbing, holding her Mum's hand. Bill appeared, already dressed. "You go on lad. I'll put the kettle on for a brew," he said.

The doctor arrived minutes after Harry got back in the house. Bill and Harry stayed in the kitchen, nursing mugs of tea, while the doctor went upstairs. Bess sat with her head in Harry's lap, quietly whining. She knew that something was wrong.

Eventually the doctor came down. "Alice is just getting dressed," he said. "I'm sorry to have to tell you that Mrs Davies is now in a coma and it's only a matter of time before she passes away. She has had a massive stroke. There's nothing I can do, I'm so sorry."

Harry was distraught. "Can't you do anything? She was fine yesterday. Are you sure there's nothing?"

"I'm sorry Harry. These things come on so suddenly. We don't know enough about it yet. Maybe in the future, but that's no help to you, I know."

"Can I go up?" asked Harry.

"Yes, of course. I don't think she will know that you're there, but she shouldn't be alone at this time."

Harry went up and pulled the chair up to the side of the bed so that he could hold Grandma's hand. He couldn't believe this was happening. Why was his gentle grandma being taken from them? She didn't deserve this. *They* didn't deserve it. The tears flowed freely down his face. He was a man now, but he cried as he hadn't cried since he lost his brother.

After a while, he didn't know how long but it was now daylight, Norma and Jenny came in. Alice or Bill had obviously told them, because they were already sobbing. Norma just stood, allowing the tears to flow down her face, but Jenny threw herself across Grandma. "Wake up, wake up, Grandma! You've got to get better. We need you!"

Harry gently lifted his little sister and sat her on his knee. "It's no use Jenny. The doctor has said we have to let her go. There's nothing he can do." Comforting his sister seemed to help Harry to come to terms with the awful truth. Grandma had been there his whole life, supporting him when his brother died, and taking his side when Bill was harsh. Now it was his turn to support his family. He reached for Norma and the three of them clung together, mingling their tears.

Bill and Alice came in, Alice quietly weeping and Bill looking stern. Harry knew that his father wouldn't show any emotion, but he could sense the grief. Grandma Davies had been more of a mother to him in recent years than his own mother had been. They had lost both Grandma and Grandad Roberts within a few months f each other, three years ago. Grandad had lung cancer and Harry suspected it was due to his heavy smoking. It was the reason Harry had decided not to smoke. Grandma Roberts just died in her sleep one night. The doctor said it was pneumonia. Bill had taken it all in his stride at the time.

They all sat around the bed, not speaking, just watching the slight rise and fall of grandma's chest. Then she suddenly gave a deep gasp, and then didn't breathe again. The girls and Alice broke out into fresh sobbing, but Harry felt as though he had no more tears. "I'll go and phone the doctor," he said.

"No, I'll go," said Bill, "I need the fresh air anyway. You put the kettle on, son"

Harry looked up in surprise. Bill hadn't called him "son" for many years, though he had taken to calling him "lad" in recent years which, he supposed, was a term of endearment. Harry felt slightly comforted as he followed his Dad down the stairs.

Bess gazed up at Harry questioningly. She projected an image of Grandma to him. "Yes, Bess, we've lost her," he told the dog. She then gave an agonizing howl and leaned against his leg. Harry didn't wonder how the dog understood so much; he just accepted the connection that he had with her.

oOo

For two weeks the family went through the household routines mechanically. The funeral came and went and they tried to get back to some normality. Harry knew that everyone felt as weary and washed out as he did and he noticed that Bess seemed as tired and depressed as the human members of the family.

She was now over thirteen years old which, he supposed, was quite old for a dog. She was slowing down and she didn't seem as keen on going out for walks. She would go out on the ollers, do her business, and then make her way back to the house. Gone were the days when she would run the whole length of the ground, from Scotland Hall Road to the nunnery and back again. Then came the Saturday morning when she didn't want to go to work with Harry. "Come on Bess, it's time for work," He tried to encourage her, but she gave him an image of her bed in the kitchen, the same old blanket that grandma had given her thirteen years ago. Harry let her go back to her bed. Alice was washing up the breakfast pots.

"I'll keep an eye on her lovey. I'm not going out today," said Alice.

"Thanks Mum," he replied. It seemed so strange, getting into the van without Bess at his side. He missed her terribly, and Mr Marshall was upset when Harry came into the back of the shop alone.

"Where's our lovely lass?" he asked.

Harry tried to swallow the lump that stuck in his throat. "She didn't want to come out. She's not been right since my Grandma passed away," he explained.

"I know, lad. I noticed that she wasn't her old lively self. Everything seems to be going wrong, doesn't it? What with the news about that madman, Hitler. He's invaded Poland now; did you hear it on the news?"

"No, I didn't," said Harry. He had been so wrapped up in his grief that he hadn't been taking notice of the news from Europe. "That's bad, isn't it?"

"Yes lad, it could mean war."

Harry pushed this piece of news to the back of his mind. He was more worried about Bess. He got through the busy Saturday somehow, and Mr Marshall sent him home as soon as all the deliveries were done. He drove as fast as he could and rushed round to the back door when he got home. He opened the kitchen door and his eyes went automatically to the dog's bed. Jenny was sitting on the floor with her arms round the dog, sobbing. Alice turned to him, "Harry ...." She couldn't say any more.

"No!" he cried, "No, not Bess too?" He knelt down beside Jenny and stroked the dog's head. She was still warm, but he could tell she was dead. He could feel the same kind of emptiness that he had felt at the loss of Billy and his Grandma. He felt as though his heart could break in two.

"She passed away in her sleep about fifteen minutes ago. She's been in her bed all afternoon. Jenny took her out on the ollers at dinner time, but she just had a wee and came back. Jenny has been sitting with her the whole time," said Alice.

"I didn't want to leave her. I thought she might get better if I stayed with her," Jenny sobbed.

"I should have taken her to the PDSA instead of going to work this morning," said Harry, "They might have been able to do something."

"I don't think so lovey, she was quite old. I think her heart just gave out. Just think of all the love you've given her over the years and be glad you found her. She's had a good life."

Harry knew that Alice spoke sense, but he still felt remorse for going to work instead of staying with his beloved dog. He went up to the bedroom and sat, staring out of the window, tears pouring down his face. Men weren't supposed to cry, but he felt that he had never stopped crying these past two weeks. What more could go wrong?

oOo

That evening Harry and Bill dug a grave in the back garden and they laid the dog in there, wrapped in her blanket. There was quite a crowd around the little grave. Bobby and Alf had foregone their trip to the pictures and they were joined by Susan and Audrey. Everyone had loved Bess and they all shed tears for her, even the young men. The only one not crying was Bill. Harry had never known him to cry, though he often felt his dad's grief. Bill just said, "Goodbye old girl," as he shovelled soil over the blanket-wrapped body. They all went in to drink tea and talk about the good times with Bess.

oOo

That wasn't the end of the bad things that happened in those weeks. The third thing affected the whole world though.

Only the next day, 3rd of September 1939, the Prime Minister spoke to the nation on the wireless.

The whole family, including Alf, were sitting around the wireless at 11.15 when the news came on. They listened in horror to what Neville Chamberlain had to say.

"This morning the British Ambassador in Berlin handed the German Government a final Note stating that, unless we heard from them by 11 o'clock that they were prepared at once to withdraw their troops from Poland, a state of war would exist between us. I have to tell you now that no such undertaking has been received, and that consequently this country is at war with Germany."

A stunned silence followed, and then Harry saw that Alice and his sisters were crying. Alf had his arms round both girls.
Bill was the first to speak. "Well, we knew it was coming. We'll just have to get on with it. We can't let that maniac take over

Europe. Anyway, I'm going to put the kettle on. We all need a cuppa after that."

Alice dried her eyes and said, "Its strange how bad things always come in threes."

oOo

2 Changes

In the week after the loss of Bess and the devastating news of war, Harry went through each day in a daze. He missed Bess dreadfully. Every time he looked at the empty passenger seat he felt an enormous lump in his throat. It didn't help that people kept asking where she was and he had to tell the bad news over and over again. The odd times when he wasn't thinking about Bess he was worrying about the war, what it would mean to his family and whether he should enlist in the forces before he was called up.

He was twenty, so it was only a matter of time before the inevitable happened. Of course it could be months, or a year, and he could remain doing the job that he loved in the meantime. On the other hand he had heard that he could choose which area of the forces he joined if he volunteered, and driving around without Bess was heartbreaking. His mind went from one to the other and back again, until he felt dizzy.

Eventually he decided to talk it over with his friends.

On Sunday after church Harry, Bobby and Alf, along with Susan, who was always with Bobby now, made their way to their favourite spot on the ollers. Even as young adults they still made for this spot when they had anything to discuss. They sat in a circle so that they could all face each other. The war was at the forefront of all their minds, so the others knew straight away what Harry was thinking as soon as he spoke.

"I'm thinking of volunteering. There's lots of reasons that I shouldn't, not least that my Mum will be devastated, but I want to ask you all what you think."

"Well, why don't you start by giving the reasons why you shouldn't," said Bobby.

Harry noticed that no-one had exclaimed against his thinking. "Apart from thinking of my Mum and sisters, I have a good job that I love. Also, the war could be over before I get called up, though nobody believes that it'll be over soon. If I give up my job, I may not get it back after the war, and what will Mr Marshall do? He is getting older and he doesn't drive, and Ted is only sixteen. He's needed in the shop anyway."

"And the reasons why you should?" asked Alf.

"If I volunteer, I've heard that I can choose which area of the forces I join. You all know of my, er, gift, though sometimes it's more of a curse. I couldn't cope in the infantry where I'd be expected to come face to face with the enemy. I couldn't cause direct pain to anyone, because I'd feel that pain too. For the same reason I couldn't be a stretcher bearer or medical orderly. I think I could work on an anti aircraft gun though. It sounds horrible, but the enemy would be far enough away, and I'd still be fighting for my country. Also, I may be lucky enough to stay in Britain, as they'll need protection from air raids in lots of places. My other reason is purely selfish. I hate driving the van without Bess at my side. It's a constant reminder that I've lost her. When I'm at home it's also the loss of my Grandma. I feel that I want to get away from all the grief. Lastly, my Dad would be proud of me."

Susan spoke next. "You know that none of us can make the decision for you Harry, but, regarding your job, I wouldn't mind taking over." There were gasps from all three young men. Harry stared open-mouthed at her.

"Well, I hate working at Tootal's and I'd love to be out and about like you Harry. You know I can drive because you taught me, and I've already got my provisional licence." That was true; Harry had taught all of them to drive.

"What about the lifting? Some of those wirelesses are heavy, and some of the other deliveries can be heavy too. What do you know about hardware?" asked Harry.

"I'm strong, for a girl. You all know that, and I know what a screw and a nail and a hinge look like. For the rest, I'm a very quick learner," The others all nodded their agreement. Susan was brighter than any of them. "Also, when the war's over, you can have your job back, Harry. I might be wanting to get married then, anyway." She smiled across at Bobby, and they both blushed.

"That's right; we discussed getting engaged just yesterday, but decided not to get married until after the war," said Bobby. Harry and Alf, beaming, thumped him on the back and gave Susan a big hug.

"That's great news Bobby. When were you going to tell us?" said Alf.

Susan laughed, "That was going to be next on this meeting's agenda." Everyone laughed, and it diffused the tense situation.

"Regarding your worries about your Mum and sisters," said Alf. "I think that my job will be a reserved occupation. They'll need train mechanics, and I'm hoping to become a driver eventually. So I'll be around to support the girls, though I can't stop them worrying about you. The government haven't made it clear yet, but that's what I think and hope."

"What about you, Bobby?" asked Harry.

"I think I might volunteer too, for the same reasons. Susan and I have already discussed it. I can't see my job as a carpenter being reserved. I hadn't got as far as deciding what service I'd like, but now that you have mentioned anti aircraft, I think that's what I'd like to do too, if we can choose."

Harry took a deep breath. "I've made my mind up then. If Mr Marshall is happy with Susan taking over and my Mum doesn't lock me up and throw away the key, I'm going to volunteer."

"And I'm coming with you," said Bobby. Susan had tears in her eyes, but she agreed with Bobby's decision."

oOo

Mr Marshall was in agreement with Harry. "I've been thinking about it too," he said, "and I had an idea that you would volunteer, lad. Susan is a good girl, and if you think she's up to the job I'm ok with that. What about your parents, are they ok with it?"

Harry looked sheepish. "I haven't told them yet. I was thinking of signing up first and then telling them. Give them a fait accompli."

"I wouldn't do that lad. Give them a chance to put forward their arguments and then they'll know they tried their best when you show them how determined you are."

"Of course, you're right. I'll tell them tonight. Bobby and I are planning to go to the recruitment office tomorrow in our dinner break."

"Good luck lad. I hope you get what you want."

oOo

Alice's reaction to the news was predictable. In floods of tears she tried to change his mind. "I shan't let you go!" she cried. "You might not have to go at all, if the war's over quickly." Norma agreed with her, but the arguments were all the same and Harry had an answer to each one. Bill agreed with Harry that it made sense to choose what war work he did, and Harry knew that his Dad was proud.

Surprisingly, eleven year old Jenny agreed with the men. "I think it's your patriotic duty," she said, eyes bright with fervour. She looked more like Billy than ever as they all stared at her, open-mouthed. "I wish I could volunteer. I bet it'll be all over before I'm old enough. It's not fair!"

"Jenny!" Alice was appalled. "Why would you want to fight?"

"I wouldn't want to be on the front line, but I'd want to do something that makes a difference. Maybe they'll have girls on the anti aircraft guns later on when they run out of boys." Everyone looked at her in shock at this outburst. "Oh, sorry, I didn't mean ..... Oh, you know what I mean. All the women helped in the last war." She looked down, abashed.

"She's right though," said Bill. "The women worked in munitions and all sorts. I hope it's over before you are old enough though, Jenny."

oOo

Harry arranged his deliveries so that he could pick up Bobby in the van at dinner time and they went round to the recruiting office. They had no idea how long it would take but both their bosses were aware of this and told them to make sure they got something to eat too.

It was remarkably easy. After giving details and showing their birth certificates they had to sign a form and they were given a date for a medical. Harry asked whether they could choose which regiment they wanted.

"Why is that, do you have family in the army?" the sergeant asked.

"No sir, but I would like to join the Royal Artillery. In particular I am interested in anti aircraft guns."

"I would like Royal Artillery too, sir," said Bobby

"Well, we'll put you down for RA then. It shouldn't be a problem, but which type of artillery you will end up on will depend on what they need at the time. You'll have extensive training first anyway."

"Thank you sir," they both replied.

As they were leaving the office they bumped into Jimmy Bates. "Hiya lads, we don't meet for years, and then it's twice in a couple of weeks. Have you been signing up?" They nodded. "Me too, I'm sick of stoking that bloody boiler! Did it take long?"

"No, we've only been here half an hour. We have to come back for a medical on Thursday," said Harry. "We're going to Woolworth's cafe for fish and chips now, before we go back to work."

"That sounds good. I might join you if I'm out of here quick. They know at work where I am, so I don't need to rush. See yer later."

As they walked along, Bobby said, "Why did you tell him where we're going? We don't want to mix with the likes of him!"

"I don't know, there's something kind of pathetic about him nowadays. I felt sorry for him," Harry replied.

"Oh, you and your "feelings" Harry. You're too nice for your own good, but, actually, I think I know what you mean this time. He does seem to have changed since we were at school."

oOo

They had finished their fish and chips and were enjoying a mug of tea when Jimmy joined them. "I'm glad you're still here lads. I hate eating alone," he said. He made short work of his fish and chips and breathed a sigh of pleasure as he sat back with his mug.

Harry was intensely curious about Jimmy's apparent change of demeanour, so he decided to broach the subject. "Jimmy, I can't help noticing that you aren't as aggressive as you were at school. If you don't mind us asking, what caused the change?"

Jimmy looked embarrassed. He looked around to see if anyone nearby was listening. "Well, you see, I've been in prison." He took a huge gulp of his tea and continued. "My Dad and one of my other brothers are still in prison, for armed robbery. They took me with them you see, but I got off with a shorter sentence, cos it was my first offence and I was only charged with abetting. I was lucky that I wasn't sent to the same prison, and while I was in there I started to think about how stupid I'd been. The prison padre helped, and my older brother, Jack, who you met at the pictures, visited me regular. He's the only one, apart from my Mum, who's any good in the family. He got me the job at the gas works and I'm determined to turn over a new leaf. That's why I'm joining up. I want to be far from here when my Dad gets out." He looked earnestly at Harry as he finished his story.

"What I can't understand is that you were always the ringleader at school, inciting other boys to trouble. Why did you do that?" Jimmy was quiet and Harry gazed into his eyes. He wasn't that surprised when he got an image in his mind of a young Jimmy cowering before his dad's raised arm, and a leather belt coming down across his back.

"I had to show my dad that I was tough. That was the only way I knew how. If I was the leader of the gang I thought my dad would be proud of me. It was you I thought of though, Harry, when I was in prison. Somehow you could always make me feel ashamed of what I was doing. Remember that time at the fair? You know, I never stole off anyone after that."

Harry and Bobby were lost for words. The three of them finished their tea in silence, until Bobby said, "Look at the time, I'll have to get back to work!"

oOo

That evening Harry and Bobby, along with Susan, went round to Alf's to tell him about signing up, and, of course, about Jimmy Bates.

As they all piled into the tiny front room Ginger, the rescued cat, came to join them. He sniffed at Harry's legs and then searched all round the room. "He's looking for Bess. This is the first time you've been here without her," said Alf. Harry didn't reply, he was too choked up, so he just nodded. He knew that Ginger and Bess had been good friends ever since the rescue. He picked up the cat and stroked him, and Ginger settled on his lap, purring.

Alf was amazed when they told him about Jimmy. "Never in a million years would I have believed he could change. Are you sure he wasn't joking?"

"He was sincere, I could feel it," said Harry, I can't see us ever becoming great friends, but I think I could tolerate him now."

oOo

Harry and Bobby passed their medicals as A1 fit and they were accepted into the Royal Artillery. They got rail passes for the second of October, which meant that they would still be home to celebrate Audrey's seventeenth birthday on 23rd September, which was a Saturday. The parents of both families decided to have a party on that day, as a send off for the boys as well. It would be in the Kerr house, as they had a piano and everyone loved a sing song.

Harry was helping with the washing up when Alice and Dorothy discussed the food.

"I think we should do sandwiches and cake, so that we don't have to crowd round the table," said Dorothy. "We don't have any little ones anymore to make a mess. I think Jenny's big enough to be tidy, isn't she?"

"Oh yes, but I can't vouch for her being quiet," joked Alice, though she didn't really feel like joking.

"I think some noisy singing will do us all good. I hope it takes our minds off this dreadful war!" Dorothy replied.

"Is it ok to invite Alf?" asked Harry.

"Of course, he's almost one of the family," said Alice, "and he's sweet on Norma," she added, quietly, because Bill was in the living room.

"Don't let on to Alf that you've noticed, though. He's a bit sensitive about it," said Harry.

"I wouldn't dream of it. He's such a gentle soul. I think he must take after his Mum. Though I must admit I never met his Dad, but, by all accounts, he was a violent man."

"Hopefully none of the boys take after him, then," said Dorothy.

Alice agreed, "Mary has made a marvellous job of bringing up all those children on her own. Shall we invite her too?"

"That's a good idea," said Dorothy, "she deserves a bit of R and R."

Jenny came in just then. "What's R and R?" she asked.

"It stands for rest and repair. They say it in the forces when the troops need a break from war," said Harry.

"But Mrs Smith hasn't been in a war."

Dorothy laughed, "You don't think bringing up eleven children singlehandedly is a war? It seems like it to me!"

"Well, I'm never going to have that many children. I'd rather be a soldier anyway!" Jenny retorted. The ensuing laughter made them all feel better.

oOo

Harry was with Bobby on Saturday afternoon when Audrey came back from the market. Alf was working until six o'clock, so he'd be coming along later.

"Er, I've invited someone else to the party," Audrey ventured. They looked up, surprised.

"Who?" said Bobby.

"Now don't moan – Jimmy Bates."

"What, oh no, why?" shouted Bobby.

"I said don't moan! I met him on the market and he told me that he's going in the army on the second too. He hasn't got anyone to see him off. His brother has gone in the navy and his Mum doesn't seem interested in anything. She was with him on the market. He was carrying her shopping and she never spoke a word. I felt sorry for him. It's my party too, so I can invite who I like!"

"Okay, okay, I get your point!" Bobby was disgruntled, but Harry gave

Audrey a hug.

"That was really nice of you Audrey. I probably would have done the same. I just hope he's not aiming for anti aircraft too."

"He didn't say, I got the impression that he doesn't mind what he does as long as he's away from here.

"Well, good luck to him anyway," said Harry.

oOo

The party was in full swing when Jimmy came in, looking shyly around. Harry was amused, remembering the cocky five year old who answered back when the teacher told him off. But then Harry was at ease with everyone in the room, even his own Dad. He took pity on Jimmy and went forward to speak to him.

"Do you fancy a drink, Jimmy? There's lemonade or beer, or, if you fancy it, the ladies are drinking port and lemon." He laughed and Jimmy joined in.

"A beer would be great, thanks," he replied.

Audrey was playing the piano and Jenny was singing, "Roll out the Barrel". As well as looking like Billy, she also sang like him, raucously! But she enjoyed herself so much that nobody minded and most people were joining in. Bill was looking down at her with pride. When the song finished Audrey looked round and saw Jimmy.

"Hiya Jimmy, do you like to sing?" she asked.

"Well, I don't know many songs, but there is one that I like, if you know the tune, Ole Man River?"

Bobby, Alf and Harry were flabbergasted! They didn't remember Jimmy singing at school at all. He started to sing and everyone went quiet. He sounded just like Paul Robeson in Showboat! The applause was spontaneous when he finished.

"That's the only one I can do, cos my voice is too deep," he said, modestly.

"It was wonderful!" said Audrey. Jimmy blushed with pleasure.

They all sang a few more popular songs and then they had a break for food. The three mothers had made such a mound of sandwiches that there was ample for everyone. Then Dorothy came out of the kitchen carrying a big iced cake with one candle on the top.

"Happy birthday Audrey. We pooled our ingredients to make this fruit cake. Goodness knows when we'll be able to make another, so make the most of it."

They all sang Happy Birthday while Audrey blew out the candle and the cake was cut into generous slices. It was very quiet while everyone devoured the delicious cake. Fred picked at the last few crumbs on the plate. "That was a very tasty cake," he said, and everyone agreed with him.

"Would you ladies mind if we men go up to the Culcheth for a pint? I'd like to have a drink with the boys before they go away," said Fred.

Alice and Dorothy said it would be alright, but Susan, Audrey and Joe's girlfriend, Meg, looked as though they wanted to object. Jenny, typically, wanted to know why the girls couldn't go to the pub too.

"I think I'll stay here with the girls," said Harry. He didn't drink much anyway, but now Bill looked disappointed.

"Come with us, son, just for a half. We won't be long."

Susan, the most vocal of the girls then piped up, "Right Bobby, You must go, but I want you back here by ten o'clock to walk me home." That seemed to make the decision for them all. The men trooped out into the blackout.

Harry walked alongside Bill. There were no street lights, but he could see his Dad's face quite clearly. "Just over a week before I go away, it'll be strange." He could feel Bill's sadness, but he could also tell that his dad was proud of him.

"We'll miss you, lad, especially your Mum. She's relied on you a lot in recent years. You'll write often, won't you?"

"Of course, and I'll probably be home fairly often at first, while I'm training."

Jimmy Bates was walking in front with Bobby and Alf; they were having quite a conversation. The old animosity between them seemed to have thawed considerably. Harry supposed that this war would bring a lot of people closer together.

They reached the pub and were welcomed into the smoky atmosphere. All the men knew Bill and Fred. A lively debate about the war started when they heard that three of the lads were going into the army. A lot of the older men had been in the first war and everyone had some advice to give. Harry had soon had enough of the war talk and Alf was of the same mind. Thankfully it was a quarter to ten. "Bobby, we need to be going," he said.

Bobby was on his second pint of bitter. "Ok, I'll just finish this and then I'm ready." He looked across at Bill, Fred and Joe. They were deep in conversation, and didn't look like they were leaving any time soon, so he just gave them a wave, and Joe detached himself from the older men. Bobby turned to Jimmy. "Are you coming back with us, Jimmy?"

"Do you think your Mum will mind?" asked Jimmy. "I wouldn't mind coming back for a cuppa. I've got nothing to go home early for. My Mum goes to bed about eight o'clock so she won't miss me."

"No, Mum won't mind. She'll have the kettle on before we get through the door."

This was true, as Bobby led them in, Dorothy said, "I'll just put the kettle on. Do you all want a cuppa?" They all laughed.

"Mum thinks a cuppa tea is the answer to everything," said Bobby.

Norma and Susan were on the settee with Jenny, who was desperately trying to keep her eyes open. Meg had her coat on, ready to go, so Joe left with her. Audrey was sitting on a dining chair by the table. Harry and Jimmy joined her there. "Harry is it ok if I write to you?" she asked.

"Yes, I'd like that, and I'll try and reply whenever I have the time."

"Er, Audrey," ventured Jimmy, "I don't suppose you'd write to me too? My Mum's not much of a writer, and my brother's at sea, so I don't expect to hear from him much."

"Ok, yes, I don't see why not. I do like writing letters."

Harry wasn't sure if he liked the idea of Audrey and Jimmy writing to each other. It still didn't seem such a long time ago that Jimmy was their enemy, but he did seem genuine, so he supposed that it couldn't do any harm. He realised that he still thought of Audrey as one of his sisters and he wanted to protect her.

Bobby and Susan left soon after, but Harry and Jimmy stayed chatting to Audrey until the older men came back. Alf had been sitting with Norma, but he jumped up quickly, glancing guiltily at Bill. "We'd better be going Mum," he said to Mary. Bill was beaming around at everyone. He'd obviously had a lot more than one pint, but Harry was glad to see his Dad so relaxed.

They all left together, Harry with his arms round his two sleepy sisters. It had been a wonderful party.

oOo

Harry now slept in what he still thought of as Grandma's room. Alice had finally convinced him that it was unnecessary to share a room with his sisters when there was a perfectly good room lying empty. He and Bill had repainted the walls and moved his bed in. Grandma's bed had been given to a needy neighbour. Harry had kept the patchwork quilt that grandma had made though. It made him feel close to her and he felt that she would be pleased.

He sank wearily into bed after the party and he was soon asleep. He hadn't dreamed about the mystery girl for a while, but he was unsurprised to find himself in the familiar house. It seemed that they were having a party too. There were a lot of people in the house, but then he realised that they were all wearing black and the atmosphere was subdued. It was obviously a funeral party. He wondered who had died. The girl was there, looking as beautiful as ever, and her mother was there. After a while he noticed that the man wasn't there, the one he had always thought might be her father. He was saddened to think that her father may have died. The man had looked no older than Harry's parents the last time he had seen him, but then he hadn't seen the man in his dreams for, possibly, two or three years. He hadn't noticed him much, of course. The girl was the focus of his dreams. He understood her grief.

oOo

Harry spent the next week teaching Susan his delivery rounds and introducing her to as many of their regular customers as possible. She was well received everywhere and she got on well with Ted and Mr Marshall. It was a very emotional time for Harry, with everyone wishing him well in his army career. It was with mixed feelings that he said goodbye to Mr Marshall at the end of the working week and then prepared for his journey. He wondered, on more than one occasion, if he had made the right decision in volunteering. Well, it was too late now. He was committed.

He called for Bobby on the morning of their departure. They had asked their respective mothers to not see them off at the railway station, though Susan had insisted on taking them there in the van, having asked Mr Marshall for permission. At the last minute Audrey also decided to join them, so they drove off, with Alice and Dorothy and Harry's sisters, tearfully waving from the gate. The men had already left for work and had said their goodbyes earlier.

They met Jimmy at Victoria Station, as he was joining the Royal Artillery too. They had only found out at the last minute where they were actually going to for their basic training. The main RA base was at Woolwich, down south, but there were so many men starting training that the army had set up training camps all over the country. They were going to a place in Lancashire where Nissen Huts had been recently erected. The train would take them to Preston and then they would be taken by lorry to the camp.

oOo

3 TRAINING AND POSTINGS

Several lorry loads of men arrived at the camp, which was in a large open area enclosed by barbed wire fencing. The whole area was surrounded by forest. There was a guard hut at the gate. They could see several wooden huts with corrugated iron roofs and a large concrete yard dominated the area immediately beyond the gate.

"You'll come to know this yard well," said the sergeant. "You'll do your square bashing and PT here, every day." There were quiet murmurings from the men. "Right men, when I call out your name, you answer, "yes sergeant" and form an orderly line here. Ashton?" one of the men responded and stood where the sergeant had indicated. "Arnold, Bates, Brendan, Cutler ...." He continued until there were twenty men lined up in front of him. Jimmy and Bobby were in this group, but Harry wasn't. "You men will be in hut number one. Now let's see what your marching is like. Proceed in line to the hut marked "Quartermaster's Stores" to collect your kit. They'll tell you in there where to go to next." He then continued calling out names until another twenty men were lined up. Harry was in the last group, who were allocated to hut number three. He wondered how much he would see of his friends. He was beginning to feel quite lonely.

Once they had collected their kit, been seen by the medical officer and had their hair cut, they were finally shown to the hut. They were carrying their bedding as well as their uniform and sundry other articles. It took some time to dress in their uniform, stow everything in their lockers and make their beds to the satisfaction of the corporal in charge of the hut. Harry was famished by this time and thankful that the next trip was to the mess hall for dinner. The food was plain but tasty and plentiful. Harry was pleased to see Bobby and, the atmosphere being quite relaxed, was able to talk to him for a while.

"Jimmy's latched on to me," Bobby whispered, "He's in the next bed. I hope he doesn't snore!"

"I should imagine that we'll be so tired that we'll sleep through anything. I'm exhausted already, and we've only made our beds!" Harry replied. Bobby laughed.

"I've already got a nickname," said Bobby, "Gripper. The lads picked up on my name, Kerr, changed it to Kirby grip, hence, Gripper. Jimmy is just Batesy."

"Me too, they've decided to call me Robbie, short for Roberts. It seems strange but I expect I'll get used to it. We've got a Tug Wilson and a Chalky White in our hut too. Chalky is from Manchester too. It seems everybody has to have a nickname in the army."

oOo

Six weeks of intense training followed. Every day there was marching, saluting, kit inspection, target practice and physical training, known as PT. Sometimes it was exercises in the yard but, just as often, they went out into the forest and over the hills, wearing full kit and carrying heavy packs. By the end of this time they were all very fit.

They were delighted, after all this, to be given fourteen days leave for Christmas. The men were in high spirits as the lorries took them to Preston to get the train home. Harry had made new friends in his hut, but he was pleased to be with his old friend, Bobby on the way home. Jimmy was with them too. They were quite used to having him along now.

When they got to Manchester they were met by Susan and Audrey, who were overjoyed to see them. Audrey had written every week to both Harry and Jimmy, and Harry had replied as often, as well as writing to his Mum. He had also found time to write to Mr Marshall once or twice. Harry recognised the bad spelling and grammar when he got a reply, and he remembered how Mr Marshall depended on him to do all that kind of work. He was sure that Susan would be making a good job of it.

Susan had picked them up in the van. She went by Daisy Bank first to drop off Jimmy, who had to get his key out to let himself in. It looked like his mother wasn't home, though Jimmy had said on the train that he had written to tell her what time they would arrive. Harry felt sorry for Jimmy, and decided then to call round in a couple of days and invite him, and maybe his mother too, for tea.

When they got to Amos Avenue, Harry's Mum and sisters were waiting with Dorothy at her front door. Alice couldn't wait for Harry to come down the path. She threw herself at him and hugged him fiercely. It seemed as though she wouldn't let him go, until Jenny pulled her away to get her share of the hugs. There were hugs all round and then, typically, the first thing Dorothy said was, "come in, come in, I've got the kettle on!" Fred and Joe were at home, but Bill and Alf were still at work. They would be along later. As it was, the house seemed full to bursting and everyone was asking questions at the same time. Harry felt cocooned in the love of his family and friends. He looked across at Bobby and they both smiled. It was good to be home.

Harry had never known fourteen days to pass so quickly. Every day was filled with activity; Christmas shopping, putting up decorations and talking, talking, talking. Everyone wanted to know the details of their training, particularly the young men who would soon be following in their footsteps. Harry tried to play down the intensity of it and the sheer, hard, physical work. Bobby was a bit of a joker, though, and thoroughly enjoyed alarming them with, almost true, tales of bullying sergeants and the size of the packs that they had to carry on route marches.

Harry kept his unspoken promise to invite Jimmy for tea. He discussed it with Alice first. "I didn't think you liked him," she said

"I didn't when we were at school, but I've since realised why he was like that. His dad was mentally and physically abusive, to all the family, I think. Jimmy became a bully to copy him, in an effort to gain his dad's approval. He only realised his mistake after he had grown up and saw his dad in a different light. His dad and his brother are now in prison and his other brother is in the navy. His mum seems to have completely withdrawn into herself. I thought that inviting them both to tea might help."

"You're right of course, lovey, and I'm proud of you for thinking about it. Why don't you invite them round for Christmas Eve? We'll be having the usual ham tea. I'll get some extra ham and we've got lots of piccalilli and bread and butter. With peaches and Carnation and mince pies, it'll be plenty."

In the event, Jimmy's mother refused to come, but she told Jimmy to accept. "Mum said she'd rather stay quietly at home, but she said thank you for the invite," said Jimmy when he arrived. Alice told Harry later that she would call on Mrs Bates after New Year, to see if there was anything she could do to cheer her up.

Norma had invited Audrey too. Harry was still uncomfortably aware of Audrey's feelings for him, and he felt guilty that he couldn't return them. So he tried to make it up to her by being as naturally friendly as he could, though he realised that this could make things worse. What else could he do though? He was relieved when Jimmy sat with her and monopolised the conversation. Jimmy obviously admired Audrey. Harry's misgivings about this weren't as acute as they were, now that he knew Jimmy better, and that Bobby was friendly with him. After all, it was Bobby who was Audrey's brother, not Harry.

oOo

Before they knew it, the three young men were back on the train to Preston. They already knew that they would be moving again within the week. They would be going on to their specific training areas, to learn about the particular type of artillery they would use, and from there they would be posted to wherever they were most needed. Jimmy couldn't wait to see some action, but Bobby was hoping to be near to Susan and Harry just wanted to do a good job and not show himself up by getting too emotional.

Two days later they were all marched out for inspection by the senior officer. He seemed to be satisfied. "Thank you, men, for all your hard work. The Royal Artillery is highly regarded and I expect you to keep up the high standard that we have started, wherever you are posted. Sergeant Jones will now inform you of your postings for the next part of your training." He then saluted and left the sergeant to carry on.

"Right then," Sergeant Jones bellowed, "The following men will become anti tank gunners. Gunner Ashton, Gunner Bates, Gunner Carter ..." he continued until he had called out roughly half of the names on his list. Harry and Bobby were not on that list. Harry was hopeful that he and Bobby would be going to the same camp. He was rewarded with the knowledge that all the other gunners were to be trained on anti aircraft guns and they were being posted to a camp in the Midlands.

The next day found them again on a train, but this time Jimmy wasn't with them. He was on his way to Aldershot with the anti tank gunners.

When they arrived the camp looked very much like the one they had left, except that they could see several lethal looking guns. "They're a lot bigger than I expected," Bobby said.

"Oh I've seen bigger!" boasted Nobby Clarke, who was a notorious 'know it all'.

Harry backed up his friend. "They certainly look very big to me. I expect we'll soon get used to them. They got used to them very quickly. In addition to the now familiar marching, PT and route marches they had to dismantle, clean and grease the gun, identify all the parts and put it together again and load it. When they became familiar with this each gun crew would compete with the others to see which crew was the fastest.

oOo

They soon settled into the routine of training and became expert gunners, and very fit from all the physical work.

In March, when it was Harry's twenty first birthday, He went with a crowd to the local pub to celebrate. He got drunk for the first time in his life and, when he woke with a hangover the next morning, he determined that it would be the last time too. He enjoyed all the presents and cards from home though.

The gunners began to wonder if they would be sent overseas when, in April, they heard that Jimmy Bates had gone with his anti tank gun crew, presumably to France. They heard nothing, though. Their training just continued.

The shocking news that the British Expeditionary Force were in retreat came in June. Harry and his friends waited in anguish, listening to every news bulletin. Everyone knew someone who had gone overseas.

Thousands of men had been ordered to leave any heavy armour and transport and most of them ended up on Dunkirk beach, being regularly bombed and suffering lack of food and water. The British people came to the rescue, taking every seaworthy boat of any size across the channel to help ferry the men to the big ships anchored offshore. They turned the retreat into a dramatic rescue, saving thousands of men who would have otherwise perished.

It was several weeks before Harry and Bobby found out that Jimmy Bates had been one of the lucky ones. He had been given some leave and he enclosed a note in Audrey's weekly letter to Harry: "*We had to leave our AT guns behind, but we made sure that Jerry couldn't use them. It broke my heart to destroy that gun.*" They were relieved to hear from him but at the same time they wondered what their own next move would be.

They soon found out, anti aircraft guns were now needed at home, particularly in the port towns and cities, when the Germans began to blitz the docks. Bobby and his team were sent back to Manchester in August. He was delighted as it meant that he could see his family and Susan every time he got a few hours leave. Harry was sorry to part with him, but he had known that they would probably be posted to different places, so he wasn't surprised when he found that his gun crew was being posted to Swansea, in South Wales. The port was receiving Atlantic Convoys from America and began to be a regular target for the Luftwaffe.

Harry found himself on a train again, this time with Chalky White and Tug Wilson, amongst others. They left the train at the small town of Neath, where a lorry was waiting to take them to the camp.

They were dropped off at a field containing several conical tents. "Welcome to Jersey Marine Camp!" said the guard on the gate. It looked very rural.

"Is this where the AA guns are?" asked Harry.

"No, this is the hotel where you sleep," he laughed, "There are several AA sites around Swansea and Neath. You'll soon find out which one you're allocated. Meanwhile, report to the officers' tent over there." He also pointed out the mess tent and the quartermaster's tent.

They were only given a few hours to settle in before they were taken to their gun site. The Germans didn't raid Swansea for a few weeks after that. So their training continued and they were all given additional duties. Harry found that his interest in cooking came in useful, as he often helped the cook in the mess tent. Driving was another of his duties. Although he had only driven a small van previously, he was soon able to drive the jeeps and military lorries and he became familiar with the area around Swansea.

It was late summer when the raids started. German planes came over as soon as it was dark. The gun crew had no time to be afraid, they just got to their positions and began to plot the range and timing of the gun as they had been trained. It was only after the raid had finished that Harry realised he was shaking and sweating. He was glad of the mug of sweet tea that was pushed into his hands. He looked at Chalky and Tug and gave a nervous laugh. They all breathed a sigh of relief. They hadn't let themselves or their officers down.

The German planes had dropped flares that lit up the sky for miles around. This was supposed to show them the targets, the docks and the oil works, but Harry found out the next day that the docks were largely untouched while the centre of Swansea had suffered a lot of damage and loss of life. His heart went out to the victims. This was the reality of war.

They found that the raids came at night, roughly three times a week, though the guns were manned during the day too, so at least they had some respite from the noise, the dust and the smell of explosives, not to mention the stress.

When they were off duty they could go into the surrounding villages and towns, to the pubs and dance halls. It was a welcome relief.

It was two weeks before Christmas, in the village of Skewen, close to Jersey Marine that Harry had an encounter that made his heart turn a somersault.

oOo

4 The Dream Girl

There was a Saturday night dance in the village of Skewen. A small band was playing when Harry, Chalky and Tug entered. They were just finishing a tune and then the compere made an introduction in his lilting Welsh accent.

"We have a treat tonight everybody. Our own Bronwen Evans will sing a new Welsh song, 'We'll keep a welcome in the Hillside'!" The crowd broke out into enthusiastic applause as a lovely girl walked on to the stage.

Harry could hardly breathe and his heart was threatening to jump right out of his chest! It was the girl he had been dreaming about for eighteen years! She was even more beautiful than she had appeared in his dreams. She was wearing a white dress decorated with red flowers, belted at her slim waist. Her shining black curls danced around her shoulders as she sang and her eyes, so dark that they looked black, were sparkling with emotion as she began her song:

Far away a voice is calling
Bells of memory chime
Come home again, come home again
They call through the oceans of time
We'll keep a welcome in the hillside
We'll keep a welcome in the Vales
This land you knew will still be singing
When you come home again to Wales
This land of song will keep a welcome
And with a love that never fails
We'll kiss away each hour of hiraeth
When you come home again to Wales

When she finished there was complete silence, and, despite his pounding heart, Harry noticed several people with tears in their eyes, and then the whole place erupted with cheers and applause. Harry's own eyes were wet as he clapped. Chalky slapped him on his back. "Go on you daft sod! What's up with you?"

"Leave him alone," said Tug, "I feel a bit that way meself. It's a grand song and she's a lovely singer."

"She certainly is," said Harry. He couldn't take his eyes off her as she began singing the dance tunes and everyone took to the dance floor. Chalky and Tug soon had a partner each, but Harry went over to the bar and bought a half of shandy. Oblivious to everyone else in the room, he just stood there gazing at her the whole time that she was singing.

When the band stopped for a break Harry made his way over to Bronwen. She was surrounded by people who obviously knew her, so he stood on the edge of the crowd.

She suddenly looked across at him, and he felt as though she was looking directly into his soul. His heart in his mouth, he smiled at her and she made her way to him. She looked puzzled. "I'm sorry, do I know you? I feel as though I've seen you before." Her smile was dazzling.

How could he tell her that he'd known her since the day she was born?

"No, I don't think so," he replied, "I've only been in the area a few months." He held out his hand. "Harry Roberts, I'm very pleased to meet you. I'm based at Jersey Marine, working on the anti aircraft guns."

"So you are one of the boys protecting us from those horrible Germans?"

"Well, we do our best," he said, modestly. He couldn't tear his gaze away from her eyes, until he heard a familiar voice.

"Hey, Robbie, trust you to find the most beautiful girl in the place!" Chalky was making his way through the crowd, with a lovely blonde girl on his arm. She looked a bit annoyed at his remark, but she still clung on to his arm.

Chalky was grinning from ear to ear. "This is er, what did you say your name is, love?"

"Rhiannon," she replied, "hello, Bronwen. I enjoyed your singing."

"Thanks Rhiannon. I love that new song, 'We'll Keep a Welcome'." She turned to Harry, "I thought you said your name is Harry?"

"Yes it is, but the blokes all call me Robbie, for my surname, Roberts. Everyone in the army has to have a nickname. This is Chalky, because his surname is White, and my other friend over there is called Tug Wilson. Apparently there was a famous tugboat captain called Wilson, so anyone with that surname is always called Tug. I don't know what we'll do if we get another Wilson in our unit."

"Well, I'll call you Harry, if you don't mind. I think it's a lovely name."

"Would you like a drink?" Harry offered.

"I'd love an orange juice, thanks. I'm parched after all that singing. The band is going to play without me later, so that I can dance. I'll just sing 'God save The King' at the end."

"In that case, can I have the next dance?" Harry couldn't believe how bold he was being. He had always been tongue tied in the presence of girls, apart from Audrey, Susan and his sisters. He realised that it was because he felt that he knew Bronwen already, he had seen her so many times in his dreams.

"That'd be lovely!" she replied.

Bronwen danced with Harry all evening, much to the disgust of all the other girls, and some of the men. There were many more girls than men, so none of the men went without a partner, but there were some locals who resented Harry's monopoly of such a popular girl. Bronwen obviously wasn't bothered by the dark looks, so Harry didn't worry about it either.

After Bronwen had sung the national anthem Harry offered to walk her home. He was delighted when she accepted. Chalky was still with Rhiannon, who lived on the same road as Bronwen, and Tug was also walking a girl home, so they all set off together.

Harry didn't want to lose Bronwen, now that he had found her, so he asked her if he could see her again.

"Yes, that'd be nice," she said.

"Are you free tomorrow? I'm off duty until evening," said Harry.

"Well, I go to chapel in the morning, but I'll be free in the afternoon. Would you like to go for a walk? I can show you the area if you like."

"I'd love that. I'll be at church parade in the morning anyway. I promised my Mum that I'd go whenever I could."

They had reached her house by this time. Harry didn't know whether to shake her hand or just say goodbye and walk away. They hadn't held hands on the way. He looked further up the road, where Chalky was enthusiastically kissing Rhiannon. Harry wasn't a prude, but he felt that it was too soon for kissing, despite the fact that there was nothing he'd like better than to kiss Bronwen. The mere thought of kissing her made him weak at the knees. What should he do?

Bronwen helped him out by taking his hand and, shaking it gently, she said, "I've had a lovely evening, Harry. Shall we meet here at one o'clock tomorrow?"

"Yes, but it's you who made it a lovely evening for me. Goodnight Bronwen."

"Goodnight Harry. See you tomorrow."

Harry hardly spoke to Chalky on the walk back to camp. He felt as though he was walking on a cloud. For the first time since losing his grandma and his dog, he felt happy.

oOo

There was a light dusting of snow on Sunday, but it didn't deter Harry and Bronwen. His greatcoat was very warm and she was wrapped up well too. They walked from her home on Bethlehem Road down the Old road to Neath Abbey. They wandered through the ruins chatting. There was nobody else around.

"Will you be going back to Manchester when you get leave?" asked Bronwen.

"Yes, I've got seven days at Christmas," he said, reluctantly. He realised that he wasn't as eager to get home as usual. He wished that he could take Bronwen with him, but he knew that it was far too early for that. He felt that he had known her all his life. In fact, he had known *of* her for most of his life, but there was no way of explaining that to her. Most likely it would scare her away. He changed the subject.

"Do you have brothers or sisters?"

"Yes, my older sister, Dilys, is a staff nurse at the hospital in Swansea, and my brother, Dai has just joined the Welsh Fusiliers. He's nineteen. Dilys lives in at the hospital but she comes home as often as she can when she's off duty, because my mother is not well. I look after her but Dilys takes over whenever she can, so that I get a break."

"What about your father?" Harry knew that her father had died, but he waited for her to tell him. He wondered if the aura of sadness that seemed to surround Bronwen was due to losing her father and having a sick mother.

"Daddy died just over a year ago." She swallowed before going on, and her eyes were bright with tears. "He was only forty two, but he had been ill for a long time. The doctor said that it was Parkinson's disease, but only old people get that, don't they?"

"I don't know. I've heard of it but I've not known anybody affected by it," Harry replied. Bronwen looked up at him and the tears spilled over. He took both her hands in his. He wanted to take her into his arms but he didn't want to alarm her.

"I'm so sorry. You cry if you want to. It may help." He led her to an alcove in the ruins and sat her down on a large stone. He handed her his handkerchief, glad that he always had a clean one. This made him think of his Grandma, who always made sure he had a clean hankie, and he almost joined in with her tears. She gradually stopped sobbing and offered the hankie back.

"I'm sorry," she said, "You must think me a big softy, breaking down like this."

"No, I understand. You should have seen me blubber when my dog died. It's natural to cry. It helps you to heal."

"You are so lovely," she smiled up at him, and her smile made him feel warm all over. "I loved my Daddy so much. He was a singer too. He taught me all his favourite songs when I was little and we would sing together at family gatherings. The last two years he couldn't sing though. He would have been so proud if he could have seen me singing with the band."

"He would be right to feel proud. Your singing is beautiful," Harry replied. He realised that he was holding her hand again, but she hadn't pulled away, so he kept hold of it. It was a lovely feeling.

It had started to snow again so they got up and began to make their way back to Bronwen's home, still holding hands.

"Would you think me very forward if I invited you in for a cup of tea?" she asked. "I feel as though I've known you for a lot longer than one day. Does that seem strange?"

"No, I feel the same way. But will your mother not mind?"

"No, she won't mind. She's always glad to meet new people, especially now she doesn't get out much, and you can meet Dilys before she has to go back to the hospital."

Bronwen let him into the hallway of a neat terraced house. Bypassing the first door, she said, "That's Mother's bedroom, but she'll be in the living room just now."

The second door opened into a cosy room. A tiny, frail lady was sitting in the corner by the fire. Harry recognised Bronwen's mother from his dreams, but he was appalled by how much she had changed. She was obviously ill and her once black hair was now pure white.

"Hello Bronwen. You're soon back, cariad. Was it too cold for you?"

"No Mother. We were warm enough, but it's just started to snow again, so I invited Harry to come in for a cup of tea. Mother, this is Harry Roberts."

"I'm very pleased to meet you, Mrs Evans. You have a lovely home." Just then a young woman appeared at the door to what Harry thought must be the kitchen. She was like an older version of Bronwen, with the same dark eyes and black curly hair. She wasn't as beautiful, in Harry's eyes, though.

"Hello, you must be Harry. Bronwen hasn't stopped talking about you since last night." She had a twinkle in her eyes as she said this.

"Dilys, you're terrible!" Bronwen was blushing fiercely, "Don't listen to her Harry. She's always teasing me. I hope you've got the kettle on Dilys."

"Of course I have. I put it on as soon as I heard the front door go. How do you take your tea, Harry?"

"Before the war I used to have two sugars, but since rationing started I've tried to do without the sugar, so just milk please."

"Ok, I won't argue with you because we have all given up sugar in our tea, and we're saving our rations to make apple pies. We have an apple tree in the back garden and we had a good crop this year. We've tons left to use up. You'll have to come again and have a taste of Bronwen's apple pie. She makes them much better than I do."

"Thank you, I'd love that." Harry replied.

Bronwen's mother urged Harry to sit next to her and bombarded him with questions about his family, what Manchester was like and whether he liked South Wales.

"I really like it here," he replied, smiling across at Bronwen, "though I haven't really had much time to explore. The army keeps us very busy. I believe there are some lovely bays beyond Swansea. I'd like to go over there when I get a full day off."

"Yes, it's called the Gower and there are several bays. Bronwen will take you there, although it's not as pleasant now, with all the barbed wire along the coast. You can walk along the cliffs though, and the buses still go that way." Even though she wasn't going out, Bronwen's mother was up to date with everything that was going on in the outside world. She encouraged visitors and enjoyed lively discussions about anything and everything, and she avidly listened to the news on the wireless. All this Harry discovered while he was drinking his tea.

It was getting darker and Bronwen got up to put the light on. Harry looked at his watch. "It's nearly four o'clock, the afternoon has flown by. I need to get back to camp to report for duty tonight. Most of the raids are coming at night time, so we have to be ready for them."

Bronwen saw him to the door. "It's been a lovely afternoon," she said. "Thank you for being so understanding about my father."

"I'm glad I was able to help. I'd love to see you again. Do you go out to work?"

"No, I'm just looking after Mother at present. I expect I'll have to do war work at some point. I'd like to be a nurse, like Dilys, but I can't start training until I'm eighteen, in March, but, until I'm called up I want to continue looking after mother."

Harry knew how old Bronwen was and the date of her birthday, but he feigned ignorance as he said, "My birthday's in March too. I'll be twenty two on the fifteenth."

"How amazing, my Birthday's on the fifteenth too!" she replied.

"What a coincidence, maybe we could celebrate together." Harry said. Already he was expecting to see a lot of Bronwen and he hoped she felt the same way. It seemed that she did, when she answered.

"Oh Harry, that would be lovely!" She reached up and kissed him on his cheek. "When are you off duty again?"

"I'm free most afternoons at the moment, as we're manning the guns at night. Shall I call here tomorrow?"

"Oh yes. I may not be able to go out as Dilys is working tomorrow, but at least we can have a cup of tea and a chat. It will depend on how Mother is. Will that be alright? You might want to do something more interesting."

"That'll be fine. I'm happy with simple pleasures. I would really enjoy a cup of tea and a chat."

As it happened, the next day Mrs Evans was feeling quite bright and a friend had come to visit, so Harry and Bronwen went out. Bronwen wanted some shopping, so they went for a walk first and ended up at the local shop where Mrs Evans's ration book was registered. The shop was full of people, and they all knew Bronwen, so she had to introduce Harry to everyone. He was creating a lot of interest in Skewen.

"I'm sorry about all the attention. Everyone knows everyone else here. There's no privacy." She apologised as they were walking away.

"That's ok; it's a bit like that in Newton Heath too. If I took you there everyone would want to know you."

"Oh, I thought Manchester was a big city, like London?"

"Well, the city centre is very busy, and you're not likely to meet anyone you know there, but Newton Heath is a suburb. It has its own shops like you have here, and a market. If I was to walk through the market on a Saturday I'd be saying hello to almost every other person. It's very friendly, and very nosey!" He laughed and she responded with her delightful, tinkling laughter. Harry could sense that she liked him, and he had to admit to himself that he already loved her. He so hoped that she would come to love him too.

oOo

For the next two weeks Harry saw Bronwen whenever he was free. Sometimes they stayed in the house chatting to Mrs Evans, but as often they went out, if Dilys was there, or they had visitors. One day Harry was off duty all day until evening so they went into Swansea and Harry bought a silk scarf for Bronwen, for Christmas, and she helped him to buy presents for his Mum and sisters. He managed to get some good quality tobacco for his Dad's pipe too. They had a meal at a little cafe and then saw the matinee at the pictures. Harry was so happy to be in Bronwen's company that he hardly remembered the film.

He was looking forward to seeing his family, but he knew that he would miss Bronwen desperately while he was away.

On the day he was travelling home his train wasn't until late morning, so he called round at Bronwen's first to say goodbye. She was alone in the living room and had a parcel for him. "I made some welshcakes for your family. I hope they like them."

Harry was delighted. "I'm sure they will; thank you." He leaned across to kiss her on the cheek, but she offered him her lips. It was the first time they had kissed properly and it was the sweetest kiss ever. Harry felt it tingle right down to his toes. As they broke away Harry looked into her eyes, and he couldn't help himself saying, "I love you, Bronwen. I know we haven't known each other long, but I know. I've never felt like this before." He didn't need an answer; he could feel that she loved him too. This was a time when his gift was a blessing.

"I love you too," she whispered, and he kissed her again.

"I don't want to leave you, but I must go and see my family. It's only a week, but it will be the longest week of my life. I hope you have a good Christmas. Give my regards to your mother and Dilys."

"Dai will be here too. We got a letter from him this morning. I can't wait to tell him all about you. Happy Christmas my love." There were tears in her eyes, but she was smiling.

"Bye bye lovey." He didn't realise that he was using his Mum and Grandma's term of affection. It just seemed natural to him.

oOo

Harry was shocked to see the damage that the blitz had already done in the centre of Manchester, but he was relieved to see that Newton Heath was untouched. He got home to a tremendous reception. The whole family was there, including Auntie Elsie and Uncle Tom with their youngest, Sally. Harry's sisters hugged him so tightly he could hardly breathe. Alf was there too, along with Audrey and Susan, though Bobby was on duty. Harry was hoping that he'd see Bobby at some time while he was home. It was quite a party.

Audrey was still hanging on to Harry's every word, which made him feel very uncomfortable. He determined to tell her about Bronwen as soon as possible and in the kindest way that he could. He got the opportunity very soon, as she followed him when he went out, ostentatiously to look at the back garden, but really to get away from all the attention.

"How are you liking it in Wales?" Audrey asked

"When I'm not working I'm really enjoying it. I've met a lot of nice people."

"Any girls?" she tentatively asked.

"Actually, yes, I've met a girl that I like a lot. Her name is Bronwen."

"Oh ... I'm pleased for you." Audrey looked anything but pleased. Harry took her hand.

"Audrey, I think a lot of you, I do, but I don't think of you in the way that you'd like me to. I'm sorry."

"I know," she said "I've known for a long time, but I suppose I hoped

that things might change. I'm glad you told me about Bronwen though."
Her eyes were glistening with tears, but she smiled up at Harry. "Have
you seen your Dad's new hen house?" She quickly changed the subject,
and Harry went with her to look at the hens.

oOo

It was as well that they had a party on Harry's first day of leave, because
Christmas that year turned out to be Hitler's party. For the two nights
from 22nd to 24th December, Manchester had the worst bombing of the
blitz. Venturing out of the Anderson shelter in the back garden, in the
early hours of Christmas Eve, Harry saw the sky to the west was just a
mass of flames. It looked like the whole of Manchester was on fire.
Christmas Eve was a very sad day for everyone in Newton Heath,
although the nearest bombs had fallen in Miles Platting, just a couple of
miles away. Harry went to see if he could help the ARP workers nearer
to town. They were clearing rubble from a bomb site. Local people were
standing, looking grey-faced with shock. An ARP warden came to talk to
Harry. "They've lost their home," he said, "but they are more concerned
for their next door neighbour, an elderly lady who refused to go into the
shelter. We think she is under here."

Harry set to, to help move the rubble brick by brick. Every so often
everyone would stop to listen, in case the old lady was still alive, but
they heard nothing. Then Harry sensed, rather than heard, something.
He knew that people wouldn't understand, so he said, "I think I heard
something over there." They all rushed to the area he indicated. There
was a wooden beam holding up the rubble. They quickly cleared the
rubble and it took four men to lift the beam. They saw the old lady, lying
on her side, cradling a cat! It was the cat's distress that Harry had picked
up on. The lady was unconscious, but when they gently lifted her out
they found that she was still alive. The ambulance took her away, but
the cat stayed by Harry, mewling piteously. He picked it up and checked
it for injury, but it seemed alright. The old lady had protected it from

harm. He carried it over to the neighbours. "Do you know the cat's name?" he asked.

"It's called Missy, but we can't look after it, we're homeless now!" said the woman, and she burst into tears. Harry thought the tears were probably a good thing to relieve a little of the tension. "Don't worry, I'll take it home to my Mum. If I give you our address would you let the old lady know where her cat is?" She nodded, and someone produced a pencil and paper for him to write down his address.

Harry returned home to be greeted by the smell of mince pies baking. "I didn't feel like celebrating Christmas, after the last two nights," said Alice, "but then I thought that we've still got to eat, and I made the mince weeks ago, so we might as well make the most of it. What's that you've got there?" she saw the cat put its head out from under Harry's coat. He told her about the old lady.

"Oh no, the poor thing! How is the lady?"

"She was unconscious when they took her in the ambulance, but they were hoping it was just concussion. I've left our address with the neighbours. They said they'll visit her when they get settled. I think they said they were going to stay with relatives."

Alice put a saucer of milk down for the cat, which it lapped up rapidly. "Go up to the pet shop and see if they've got any cat food, Harry. I'm not sure about rations for animals, but if you call at Alf's on the way, his mum will know, as they've still got Ginger."

Harry returned later with several tins of cat food. "Luckily the pet shop man had been stockpiling cat and dog food since the first hint of war, and tins last forever. It's not rationed, yet, anyway," he said.

While Alice was in the house alone, Harry took the opportunity to tell her about Bronwen. She was the only person who knew about his recurring dream, "Mum, I've met my dream girl." Alice looked up at him.

"You mean the girl....?"

"Yes, the girl I've been dreaming about for almost eighteen years. Her name is Bronwen, and I love her. She's the girl I'm going to marry."

"Oh Harry, I'm happy for you. I was never sure if she was a real person, but I hoped, for your sake, that she was. Let's put the kettle on and you can tell me all about her." Harry laughed; whatever happened, good or bad, Mum would always put the kettle on for tea.

oOo

5 MORE CHANGES

Harry wrote to Bronwen on Boxing Day, to reassure her that he and his family were safe after the devastating Manchester blitz. During the two days he had left of his leave he went to see Mr Marshall, who was looking worryingly frail, and he managed to see Bobby for a couple of hours. Bobby was exhausted after working on the anti aircraft gun during the raid and he was glad of a couple of hours in the pub with his best friends. Alf was also working long hours at the railway sheds but his time off happily coincided with Bobby's. They caught up with all that had happened since they last saw each other. His friends were very interested to hear about Harry's girlfriend, especially as he had never had a proper girlfriend before. He enjoyed describing her to them.

Alf's mother had started war work at Frankenstein's factory, sewing battledress for the troops. She only had Ted and Alf at home now, as all the other boys were married and in the forces and the girls were married too, so she had decided to do her bit for the war effort. Alice had twelve year old Jenny to look after, but even she was working part time at Frankenstein's, as was her best friend, Dorothy. Audrey and Norma had been working there since before the outbreak of war, both in the typing pool. Frankenstein's had originally produced rubber products, but they had now branched out into all sorts of clothing and equipment for the troops. Another product they produced was parachutes and some of the women were using the offcuts of silk to make knickers, so they could use their clothing coupons for other things.

Susan had been allowed to continue working for Mr Marshall for the present. It seemed that the powers that be were unsure whether hers was a reserved occupation.

oOo

Harry's seven days leave was soon over, but he was happy to be going back to Bronwen. He had missed her dreadfully. He wondered if he could take her home with him next time he had leave. It would depend on her mother's health, of course, but he could hope.

Back at camp little had changed. The men who had been on guard duty over Christmas were still moaning about it, but they would be getting leave for New Year, so nobody listened to them. Swansea had been relatively quiet. It seemed that Hitler had been too busy targeting Manchester. Harry was sure that Swansea would be hit again though.

He was on guard duty as soon as he got back, so he was unable to see Bronwen straight away. Chalky had the afternoon off though, and he was going into Skewen, so he agreed to take a note to her.

Harry finally got to see Bronwen in the afternoon of New Years Eve. He was on duty in the evening, so he wouldn't be able to see the New Year in with her. When she opened the door she threw herself into his arms. "Oh Harry, I've missed you so much!" they stood in the hallway for quite a while, enjoying the closeness, until they heard Mrs Evans's voice from the front room. "She's been quite poorly," said Bronwen, "come in and talk to her, she'll be pleased to see you."

Harry was quite shocked to see how Mrs Evans had deteriorated. She was sitting up in bed and her face was as pale as the pillow. She gave him a smile though. "It's lovely to see you Harry. Sit yer and talk to me while Bronwen makes a pot of tea. How was your family?"

Harry told her of everything he had done while with his family. She was particularly interested in the rescue of the old lady and her cat. "How kind of your mother to look after the cat for her. Did you find out how the lady is getting on before you came back?" she asked.

"Yes, I went to see her in the hospital. She had a broken arm and concussion, but no other injuries. She's an amazing lady. The nurse said that she was a 'tough old bird' and she laughed at that. Of course, she has no home to go to now, but her niece is going to take her in when she leaves the hospital. I got the impression that she didn't get on with her niece, but she doesn't have a good chance of being rehoused, so they may have to put up with each other for a while. The niece won't take the cat either, but Mum doesn't mind keeping her for as long as it takes."

"How kind she is," said Mrs Evans again. Her voice was becoming fainter, and she had only drunk a little of her tea, so Bronwen suggested that she and Harry went into the living room to give her Mother a rest. "Yes, cariad, I'll have a little sleep now. It was good hearing all your news Harry." They quietly left the room, Harry carrying the tea tray.

"I'm so worried about her, Harry." Bronwen whispered when they had left the room. "She was fine while Dai was here. Having him home gave her a boost, and we had a lovely Christmas, but then she found out that he may be going overseas soon, and, as soon as he had gone, she cried and cried. It seems to have taken all the energy out of her."

Harry pulled her to him and held her in his arms. "I'll be here as often as I can, lovey. I'm no nurse, but I'm good at making conversation, if that's a help?"

"Oh yes, just you being here is a help, my love. I'm so glad I've got you." They went into the kitchen and Bronwen put the kettle on for more tea.

"What exactly is wrong with your Mother?" asked Harry.

"The doctor says it's her heart. I sometimes wonder if she has a broken heart. She adored Daddy, and when he started to be ill she was devastated. We didn't notice anything wrong with Daddy for a long time, probably years, but the last three or four years of his life he couldn't walk or speak properly, and he finally couldn't swallow either. He just wasted away. Mother hasn't been well since he died."

"How old is she?" he tentatively asked, unsure whether she would think it intrusive, but she responded straight away.

"She will be forty two next week."

Harry tried to hide his shock. Bronwen's mother looked at least sixty! It was obvious that recent years had taken their toll.

Bronwen nodded, "Yes, I know, she looks a lot older." She burrowed into his chest and he was glad he was there to give her some comfort. The whistle of the kettle made them both jump.

"I'll make the tea, you go and sit down, lovey," he said, and she gratefully accepted.

Harry had to go soon after they had finished their tea, as he was on duty in the evening, but he promised to be back the next afternoon. "Happy New Year, lovey," he said, and kissed her with more passion than he had intended. She responded with as much passion and it was difficult to break away, but they finally managed it. Bronwen watched him as he walked down the road. Every time he looked back she was still there, and he would wave again.

oOo

Mrs Evans seemed to improve a little after this, and she was delighted with the beautiful bouquet that Harry brought for her birthday. She was sitting in the living room again and Dilys was there too. Bronwen had made a sponge cake and they had quite a little party.

Although she was still very frail, and she never went out, Mrs Evans was always sitting in the living room when Harry visited, and life seemed to go on in a gentle fashion. If Dilys was at home, or one of Mrs Evans's numerous friends were there, Harry and Bronwen would go out for a walk, or to the pictures. They were blissfully happy, despite the war. On a beautiful, clear day in early February, Harry had a full day off, and they took the bus to Oxwich Bay, on the Gower coast. They couldn't go right down on to the beach, as it was protected by barbed wire, but they had a beautiful view of the whole bay from the top of the path. Harry was enthralled! He had only been to Blackpool and Southport, where there was a flat expanse of beach and not much else in the way of scenery. They had a flask of tea and packs of sandwiches, which they enjoyed, sitting amongst the marram grass near the top of the path. It was an idyllic day.

It was as well that they made the most of that day, because it would be a long time before they would have such a happy day again. Harry was extremely busy at the camp and on the gun. When he got time to see Bronwen he found her distraught because her mother had again taken a turn for the worse. Dilys was there as much as possible, but the hospital was full of air raid victims, and less acute patients were being evacuated into the country. Then, on the night of the 19th of February, Swansea had its worst night of bombing since the war began. The waves of bombers were never ending all night, Harry was kept busy with the gun crew, and they all fell exhausted into bed the next morning, with ears ringing and heads aching. They dragged themselves back to the gun site on the evening of the 20th, hoping for a little respite only to find fresh waves of bombers coming over. The gun was boiling hot from constant use. Swansea suffered badly from the raids of these two nights, but, again, there was little damage to the docks. The hospital was overflowing with casualties and the mortuary was full.

Harry set his alarm clock for early afternoon so that he could go to see if

Bronwen and her mother were alright. He dragged himself out of bed, shaved quickly and set off down the road to Skewen. He was relieved to see that Bethlehem Road looked unscathed, but the look on Bronwen's face when she answered the door told him that there was something drastically wrong.

"My Mother's dead!" she cried, and threw herself into his arms.

Holding the sobbing girl in his arms, Harry couldn't believe how much grief he felt for the woman he had known only a few short weeks. He felt like crying too, but he held himself together while he murmured comforting words. Finally he said, "Come on lovey, let's make you a cuppa and you can tell me all about it," and he led her into the living room and sat her down on the settee. While he was putting the kettle on he wondered where Dilys was. Surely she should be here with her sister? He brought in the tray, poured two cups of strong tea and added sugar, despite the fact that they had both given up sugar.

"Now, first of all, where is Dilys?" he asked.

"She doesn't even know yet. I ran out to the phone just before the raid started last night, to tell her that Mother was very ill, but, when I finally got through they told me that she was in theatre helping with the worst casualties and she couldn't come to the phone, so I left a message. Then I phoned our doctor, and his wife said that he was out on emergencies but she would send a boy to tell him. She said he would come as soon as he could, but he may be a long time. I got back to Mother and stayed with her all night. She was too ill to go in the shelter and I wasn't going to leave her. The doctor came after nine this morning, but she was unconscious by then and he said there was no more he could do for her. He stayed with me to the end though. He looked really tired, he'd been up all night, so I made him some tea and a sandwich and we both sat and watched her. She died at a quarter past eleven. The doctor said he would send a nurse to lay her out and he would inform the undertaker. The nurse has only just gone. She looked exhausted too. Oh Harry, all these people dying, it's just too much!" Bronwen related all this so fast that she hardly drew breath. She sat back and took a great gulp of hot tea. "Harry, what am I going to do without my mother?"

"Well, first of all we have to tell Dilys, and then your brother. Shall I go up to the hospital?"

"No, don't leave me! I want to go with you, but I've got to wait for the undertaker. Goodness knows when they will turn up, after the night we've just had."

"Well, what if I go to the phone box and phone the hospital? I can try and speak to someone who can break the news to Dilys. Then I'll ask the operator if I can be put through to the Welsh Fusiliers headquarters to get a message to your brother. Do you know his unit or division, and his personal number?" This gave Bronwen something to focus on, and she went to get the details for him. While she was doing this they heard the front door open. "It's Dilys, thank goodness!" Bronwen cried. Dilys didn't need to be told what had happened. As soon as she walked into the room and looked at her sister's ravaged face she started to cry, and the two girls clung to each other, saying nothing, just weeping. Harry went into the kitchen to make a fresh pot of tea and give them some privacy. When he returned they had composed themselves somewhat and Bronwen was telling Dilys all that had happened.

"I'm so sorry that I wasn't here, cariad," said Dilys. "I didn't get your message until an hour ago. The nurse who should have given the message to me last night was called to casualty just after she answered the phone. She never stopped all night, and neither did we in theatre. We were all having a late breakfast when she remembered. I was just about to go to bed. Anyway, matron has given me the day off. I don't need to be back until tomorrow morning. I may get more time off when I tell her what has happened."

Harry left them talking while he went to the phone to get a message to Bronwen's brother, Dai. It was remarkably easy. The operator knew straight away which number was wanted, and Harry spoke to Dai's commanding officer, who promised to break the news and arrange compassionate leave. Harry thanked goodness that Dai hadn't been sent overseas yet.

When Harry got back the undertaker was there. Bronwen left Dilys dealing with that while she let Harry in. She clasped Harry's hands. "I'm so glad you came when you did my love. I don't know what I'd have done without you today."

"I'm glad I was here lovey, and I'll be here for you whenever I can."

oOo

Harry was able to get time off for the funeral although he wasn't strictly a member of the family. He told the sergeant that he and Bronwen were engaged, which wasn't strictly true, but Harry knew that they soon would be engaged. The little chapel was so full, there were people standing in the aisles. Mrs Evans had been a very popular lady and everyone wanted to show their respects. Dai looked so young and vulnerable as he said a few words about his mother. Of course, Harry thought, the lad was only nineteen, and seemed even younger in his grief. Bronwen sang her mother's favourite hymn, "All Things Bright and Beautiful", and when she threatened to break down during the last verse, everyone joined in. It was a beautiful service, for a beautiful lady.

Several people came back to the house after the funeral, and Harry eventually found himself sitting with Dai. It was the first time Harry had been close enough to really look at Dai. Like his sisters he had dark brown eyes and black hair, though his hair was so short that the curls couldn't be seen. Harry could sense that Dai felt completely lost and empty. He knew that feeling, like a part of you had been torn away. He wondered how he could make things better for Dai, and he remembered what his mum had said after Billy had died. "The empty feeling will ease, a little, after a while," he said, and saw that Dai was taking notice. "Just now all the thoughts of your mother are painful, and that's natural, but gradually the pain will be easier to bear. It never completely goes away, how could it, when someone you love so much is taken from you? Eventually, though, you'll be able to remember the good times and be able to smile."

"How do you know all this? You're not much older than me, but you sound like you've been through it too." Dai looked confused.

"I have been through it, though I still have my mother, and I can't imagine what life would be without her, but I lost my brother when I was a child, and we were very close."

"What happened?" Dai, for a moment, seemed to forget his own pain. Harry told him about the tragedy that took his brother away and also told him about his grandma and his dog.

"I'm not saying that the loss of my dog equates with your loss, but it added to mine. I'm so glad that I met Bronwen. She has brought happiness back into my life, and I'd do anything to try and lessen her pain, and yours and Dilys's. Anyway Dai, I know it's something that everyone says at these times, but if there's anything I can do, anything at all, please ask."

"Thanks Harry, if you can just be around to support my sisters when I go back to my unit, that will make me feel better."

Harry took Dai's hand and shook it firmly. "I will definitely do that, as long as I'm in the area. I'm hoping they keep me here for a long time, but, even if I'm posted I'll still do my best for them." Dai returned the handshake and managed a weak smile.

oOo

Dai returned to his unit and Harry continued to see Bronwen at every opportunity. As their joint birthday approached Harry discussed with Bronwen how they should celebrate. They were sitting in the living room, drinking tea, as usual.

"I don't feel like celebrating at all, how can I enjoy myself when my Mother is no longer here?"

"I understand, but your Mother wouldn't want you to avoid your birthday altogether. What if we take a picnic to Oxwich bay, if the weather isn't too bad? It's such a special place." Harry replied.

"I suppose that would be alright, and, if the weather is horrible we can have the picnic in the house. Yes, I think I can cope with that."

Harry smiled, and then mentioned something that had been on his mind. "Have you thought about what you are going to do now?"

"Yes, I think I'll train to be a nurse. I've asked Dilys about the training in Swansea, and she said there'll be a new intake of students in July. I'll have to have an interview with the matron. They're desperate for nurses so I should be accepted."

"What will you do about the house?"

"We're going to keep it on. It's still our home and it means we can come here on our days off and Dai can come when he's on leave. The rent isn't high, so we can manage it between us and we can keep our mother's furniture and things. Dilys has already applied to get both our names on the rent book."

"That's a good idea. I hope you get taken on for training, although I'll be worried about you being in Swansea with all the raids going on."

"You are sweet Harry, but you know nowhere is safe really. Look what happened to Sidings Terrace last September. We're not immune here in Skewen. They say that if your name is on it, you'll get it."

"I suppose so, but I wish I could wrap you up in cotton wool, somewhere far from the bombs. I love you so much, Bronwen, I don't want anything to happen to you." Bronwen laughed at this, and Harry was pleased to hear her laugh, even though it was a bit strained. He hugged her and kissed her with a passion that she reciprocated. For a while they could forget about the war and their losses.

oOo

The fifteenth of March was a lovely, crisp, sunny day. Harry called for Bronwen and they were in good spirits as they walked to the bus stop. After changing buses in Swansea, they were soon looking down on Oxwich Bay. It was just as lovely to Harry as the first time and it seemed to enhance his love for Bronwen. She was a beautiful young woman in a beautiful place. His heart was full.

After they had eaten their picnic Harry said, "I've got a present for you, Bronwen, I hope its ok." He opened a tiny box containing a solitaire diamond ring. Bronwen gasped.

"Bronwen, I know we haven't known each other very long, but I love you with all my heart and I want to spend the rest on my life with you. Will you marry me?

Her eyes glittered with unshed tears. "Oh Harry, I feel the same. I feel as though I've known you all my life. Yes, I will marry you." Harry breathed a sigh of relief, although he had known her answer. Her emotions were like an open book to him. He could feel the love she had for him as though it was his own emotion. He didn't know how to tell her that he had, in actual fact, known her all her life. He didn't know if he would ever tell her. The only other person who knew about his recurrent dream was his mother. Although his closest friends knew about his strange ability to detect, and sometimes influence, other people's emotions, he had never told them about the dream. He didn't understand it himself, so how could he explain it to others?

He slid the ring onto her finger. It was a little loose, but the jeweller in Swansea had advised him to bring in his fiancée, once he had "popped the question" and the ring could easily be altered. They could call on the way back today.

While they were still sitting, overlooking the bay, they began to make plans. "You know I'll most likely be sent overseas, and it could be at short notice?" said Harry. Bronwen nodded sombrely, and their little bubble of happiness became deflated. Harry quickly went on. "Will they still take you on for nurse training if you are married? I was thinking that maybe we could get married before you start and we can spend all our off duty time together. What do you think?"

Bronwen was wide eyed with wonder. She obviously hadn't thought that they would be married so soon. Harry detected a mixture of emotions, happiness at the thought of the imminent wedding, doubt about whether she could take up her training, and sadness that her parents wouldn't be there to see her married. Eventually she answered. "I think that Dilys said there were some married women amongst the student nurses. They are allowing it because of the war. I'll have to ask her to make sure, but, if it is ok, I'd love to get married soon. What will your parents say?"

"My Mum already knows how I feel about you. I'm sure she'll be happy for us. I'm not so sure about my Dad, but if he doesn't like it, it's just too bad. Mum will talk him round anyway, and my sisters will be delighted. They'll probably want to be bridesmaids!"

"Oh my goodness, I hadn't thought about that! If Dai can get leave he can give me away, and Dilys can be my chief bridesmaid, otherwise my uncle Dennis can give me away. Oh, now I'm planning it, and we don't know yet about the hospital!"

"We might as well make plans. We have to think that it will all work out," Harry replied.

oOo

Amazingly it did all work out. Harry got 48 hours leave for the weekend of 21st of June, his dad, Bill, got railway passes for himself, Alice and the girls. Alf also got a rail pass, so he could be best man. Bobby was the only unlucky one who couldn't get leave. They were all accommodated by Bronwen's friends and family.

Dilys and Dai also managed to get the weekend off. Clothing coupon shortages could have been a problem, but Alice got a loan of dresses for the girls and Dilys also borrowed a dress. Hers was pale blue and Norma and Jenny's were pink, but they looked good together with their white floral headdresses. Bronwen was very lucky to have a new dress made out of material that her aunt bought, using coupons donated by friends and family. Bouquets, buttonholes and headdresses were made by the local florist. Harry was so glad that Alice had never needed his savings. He was able to pay for everything, including a professional photograph, and two night's stay at a boarding house at Oxwich Bay, their special place.

It was a wonderful ceremony in the chapel. Harry looked at his bride and his heart was overflowing with love. Her black curls encircled with flowers and her dark eyes sparkling with joy. Everyone was happy; Even Bill had a smile, although Harry could tell that he had reservations about his son marrying a "foreigner". There was an element of sadness at the absence of Bronwen's parents, but Dilys said that she was sure they would be looking down on them somehow. Dai proudly led his sister down the aisle, looking so mature and smart in his uniform.

The reception in the house in Bethlehem Road was a jolly affair, with just a quiet moment, when Uncle Dennis proposed a toast to Bronwen's parents, "who made a grand job of bringing up three fine young people. They would be so proud of you all. Gone, but never forgotten." Everyone responded with "hear, hear."

The food was plentiful, again due to the generous donation of precious rations. After everyone had eaten they had a sing-song around the piano, and Bronwen sang "We'll keep a welcome," after several requests. Her beautiful voice filled the little house.

Harry found time to talk to his family and Alf, who all said how lucky he was to marry such a lovely girl. "Not just lovely to look at, but a lovely nature too," said Jenny.

"Yes, she's been really kind to us, making sure we're comfortable," said Norma. "You'd think she would have enough on her mind with the wedding, but she didn't forget any of us."

Alf just said, "She's gorgeous, mate. Congratulations!"

Bill just shook his hand firmly and said, "Look after her, lad. She's your responsibility now."

"I know Dad, and I'll do my best, but, will you and Mum keep in touch with her if I get sent overseas?" Bill just nodded. He was a man of few words.

The bride and groom were showered with rose petals as they got into their transport, an army jeep driven by Chalky White, aided by their sergeant turning a blind eye. They couldn't have got to Oxwich by bus at that time on a Saturday anyway. It was a good job it was the longest day of the year, as it would have been treacherous driving through the blackout with only a small slit of headlights. It was still just daylight when they arrived, the bay looking even more beautiful in the moonlight. Chalky left them, with many a joke about the bridegroom's duty, as he drove away.

They had an idyllic weekend. When they finally emerged from their room they went for long walks along the cliffs, talking a little, but mostly just quietly enjoying the closeness and frequent kisses. It was over all too soon.

oOo

A few weeks of happiness followed. Swansea was bombed sporadically, but, thankfully, it was nothing like as severe as the February blitz. Bronwen moved into the nurses' home at the beginning of July. She was in the training school at first, which meant that she had every evening, and the weekends, off. Often Harry was able to organise his own time off to coincide with hers, and they had some nights together at the house.

Their happiness was brief. In August Harry was given 28 days embarkation leave. He was going overseas. The destination was a secret, but everyone thought that it would be North Africa. The Italians had taken over most of these countries, and were aiming for Egypt, which was still in Allied hands. The Germans were now involved, led by the notorious Field Marshall Erwin Rommel.

Harry wanted to spend some of his leave in Manchester, but he wanted to spend as much time with Bronwen as possible. Dilys was well respected at the hospital, and she managed to get permission from matron for Bronwen to have two weeks leave after her preliminary training, when she should have been on her first ward, so that she could go to Manchester with Harry.

oOo

Bronwen was wide eyed when they arrived in Manchester. The size of the city, combined with the blitz damage, was overwhelming. They went to get the tram in Piccadilly and Harry pointed out the shelters and vegetable plots where the gardens used to be. "It would normally be full of flowers and fountains," he said, "It's sad to see it like this, but it's understandable. Our safety and our need for food are more important than beauty."

Bronwen nodded, "yes, I suppose we are lucky to at least have the beauty of the coastline, despite the barbed wire on the beaches. I'm just glad we're alive." Harry hugged her in agreement.

As the tram took them down Oldham Road, Harry noticed even more damage than there had been the last time he was home. Newton Heath seemed to have escaped the worst, though. They walked up Church Street, Harry showing Bronwen all his favourite shops, the market and the church. He had a vivid memory of the first time Grandma Davies came up this street, with the four year old Harry showing her the sights. How the years had flown since then!

As they walked down Amos Avenue Harry saw Bobby cutting the privets at the front of his house. "Bobby!" he shouted, and his friend looked round with pleasure.

"Hiya Harry, your mum said you were due home today." He grasped Harry's hand, shaking it enthusiastically, and turned to Bronwen. "You must be Bronwen. I'm sorry I couldn't make the wedding but it's lovely to meet you." She smiled shyly at him.

"Are you on embarkation leave too?" asked Harry, hopefully.

"Yes, I've got a rail pass to Liverpool in September. Looks like we'll be together again, mate."

"That's great news," said Harry. Having his best friend near, even if they weren't on the same gun crew, made him feel so much better. "I'll see you later, Bobby."

"You will, because my Mum has organised a party at our house tonight to welcome you and Bronwen. So we can have a sing song. I believe you're a good singer, Bronwen?"

"Well, I do love to sing," she answered.

"Don't be modest, lovey," said Harry, "You're the best singer I've ever heard."

"And you are biased, cariad," she replied.

Harry laughed, "Yes, I am, but I'm right too."

"I can't wait to hear you," said Bobby, amused at Bronwen's blushes.

Harry looked down the road and saw his mum at the front door, obviously looking for them. He waved to her. "See you later Bobby." Bobby waved them away and turned back to his gardening.

Alice gave them a very warm welcome. "Come upstairs, I'm dying to see your faces when you see what I've done to your bedroom," she said, with a cheeky smile that Harry had never seen before. He was intrigued.

Alice opened the door to Harry's small bedroom and stepped back for them to see. Harry gasped! A double bed was pushed against the wall and it was covered with Grandma's old patchwork quilt, but the quilt had been cleverly extended to fit the bigger bed. The colours matched perfectly. "Dorothy and I worked together on it for your wedding present. Alf and Bobby brought the bed. It's second hand but the mattress is new. I didn't ask how they got it. I hope you like it."

"It's lovely, Mrs Roberts," said Bronwen.

"I hope that you can call me Mum. Though I know I can't take the place of your mother," Alice replied.

"I always called her Mother, so I would love to call you Mum, and thank you, Mum, for the lovely bedroom." She gave Alice a warm hug and Harry smiled at them both. He could feel the love between them and it gave him such a wonderful feeling, knowing that the two women he loved most were becoming more than good friends.

"I'm sorry it's such a small room, but the girls need the bigger room." Alice added.

"It's perfect, Mum. We'll be so cosy in here." Harry pulled his two women into a hug, his heart overflowing.

oOo

Harry was pleased to see all his friends and family at the Kerr house that evening. Even Jimmy Bates was there, and he seemed to be staying close to Audrey. Harry wondered if they were courting; the thought didn't alarm him much as it would have done in the past. He realised that Audrey hadn't written to him for quite some time. He had been so wrapped up in his love for Bronwyn that he hadn't noticed, and now he felt guilty. When he went into the kitchen to get another drink for Bronwen, Audrey followed him. There was nobody else in the room.

"I'm glad I've got you alone, Harry," she said. "I've got something to tell you, before Dad makes an announcement." Harry gave her a puzzled look. "Jimmy and I are getting married next Saturday. He's also on embarkation leave and he asked me if I would marry him before he goes. We've been writing to each other and he's spent all his leaves with me." Harry's puzzled look turned to one of amazement. His first thought was that Audrey couldn't be in love with Jimmy so soon after her obvious feelings for him, Harry. Then he felt extremely guilty for even thinking such an arrogant thing. He had Bronwen. Why shouldn't Audrey be as happy with Jimmy?

"I hope you'll be very happy," he said, and he couldn't help asking, "Are you sure about your feelings?"

She bristled with indignation. "He loves me. I'm sure about that!"

Harry was full of remorse. He noted that she didn't say that she loved Jimmy, but he didn't pursue it. He had no right to question her. "I'm sorry; I had no right to ask. Thanks for telling me. I hope you'll be as happy as I am with Bronwen." He kissed her cheek and quickly left the room before he could sense her feelings.

It was a proud Fred who got up a few minutes later, tapping his glass with a spoon.

"I would just like to make an announcement," he said, smiling across at his blushing daughter and an embarrassed Jimmy. "My beautiful daughter, Audrey, will be marrying Jimmy Bates next Saturday at All Saints, and you are all invited. Please join me in a toast, to Audrey and Jimmy!" Everyone repeated the toast and animated conversation broke out.

"Isn't that lovely, cariad?" said Bronwen. "Audrey seems a lovely girl. I've been having quite a chat with her. I'm sure they'll be as happy as we are." Harry agreed, and hoped that Bronwen and Audrey would become friends in the future, when this horrible war was over. He fervently hoped that all the people in this room would still be alive when it was over. It was difficult to be optimistic at a time like this.

oOo

Harry enjoyed showing Bronwen all the favourite places of his youth. They were often accompanied by Bobby and Susan, Audrey and Jimmy and also Norma and Alf. Bill had at last acknowledged that his daughter was growing up, she was now eighteen, and he had given her and Alf his permission to start courting. On one particularly fine September day all eight of them walked to Daisy Nook with a picnic. They sat at the side of Crime Lake, laughing and joking and making the most of their time together. Although they were all acutely conscious of the fact that three of them were going to war in a couple of days, they were determined to ignore it on this beautiful day. Nobody mentioned the future. It seemed that they had an unspoken pact to live for the moment. They didn't start for home until the sun was almost setting. It was quite dark when they arrived at the Roberts' house, where Alice had invited them all back for tea.

Jenny was typically disgruntled because she hadn't been able to go with the others. At the age of thirteen, she was still at school, and Alice wouldn't allow her to have a day off. "It's not fair!" she complained.

"Just because they're a few years older, they get to have all the fun. I didn't learn anything new at school today anyway. It was cookery this afternoon and I can already cook better than that stupid teacher! You taught me, didn't you Mum?"

"Yes, but you might learn different things at school, things that I don't cook. Anyway, what subjects did you have in the morning?"

"Maths and geography; Ok, the geography was good, because we've got a map of the world showing where all the action is." She looked at Harry. "I think you boys are going to North Africa. That's where all the action is now. I wish I was going!"

Bronwen looked shocked, not yet knowing what Jenny was like. "Jenny, you wouldn't like to be in the middle of a war zone, would you?"

"Yes I would, the boys have all the fun!"

Harry intervened. "It won't be fun, Jenny. In the desert it'll be hot and sandy, with flies everywhere. We'll be eating corned beef and tinned rice pudding and water will be rationed, and that's before the fighting starts."

Jenny looked sullen. "Well, I'd still like to fight for my country," she said, quietly, but she didn't say any more.

The other girls were all close to tears. The magic of the day had been dispelled, and Norma gave her sister a thunderous look. "Come on Jenny," she said forcefully, "let's go and help Mum with the tea." A subdued Jenny followed her into the kitchen.

After a hearty meal of shepherd's pie with lots of home pickled red cabbage, everyone's spirits had lifted. Audrey suggested that they go back to her house so that she could play the piano for a sing song.

"Oh yes, and Bronwen can sing that lovely Welsh song for us," said Norma, who couldn't get enough of Bronwen's singing.

It was their last get together for a long time. Two days later the boys were on the train to Liverpool. Harry had put Bronwen on the train to Swansea an hour earlier. It had been a very painful parting.

6 OVERSEAS

The SS Mendoza was docked in Liverpool, along with the other ships that were going to form a convoy. Harry, Bobby and Jimmy met up with their Royal Artillery friends, some of whom they hadn't seen since their training days. They were shown to the deck where they would eat and sleep. They would have to sleep in hammocks suspended above the tables where they would eat, and store their kitbags underneath. Harry and Bobby were on the same deck, almost at water level. Jimmy was on another deck with the anti tank gunners, but they saw him often.

They had eight tedious weeks on board ship. Harry was mortified to find out that he was the most seasick of all the gunners. It took him almost two weeks to get his "sea legs" and to get used to sleeping in a hammock, and he had to put up with all the jokes, like "Did you forget to check which way the wind was blowing when you threw up? You've got bits of carrot all over your face," and, "Don't put your kitbag near Robbie, lads. He thought mine was a sick bucket!" He was too miserable to laugh with them. As well as feeling constantly sick he missed Bronwen so much that he thought his heart would actually break. It was a constant ache. When he finally felt well enough he wrote to her every day, but he had to keep all his letters together until they reached a port.

They docked at Dakar to refuel and, although they weren't allowed to leave the ship, they could give their letters in for posting. Sadly they didn't get any letters from home here. They probably wouldn't get any until they reached their destination. Harry continued to write letters to Bronwen every day. He told her every little incident that happened on the ship, though not about his seasickness or the fact that gale force winds had made their lives a misery for a while. He did tell her, on every page, how much he loved her and missed her.

It was after they left Cape Town, having had four pleasant days of rest, that Harry began to have the dreams of Bronwen again. Since he had met her he hadn't had the dreams. He hadn't needed to, when he had the real girl by his side, but now that he was at last beginning to sleep properly, his sleeping mind found its way to her once more.

She was working night duty at the hospital and she looked exquisite in her uniform, with her white starched cap holding back her raven curls. He felt as though he could reach out and touch her, but the dream only allowed him to look at her and long for her touch. She was talking quietly to a patient who obviously couldn't sleep. She smoothed back the lady's hair and they exchanged smiles. Harry smiled too, at his lovely, lovely Bronwen.

After this Harry visited Bronwen in his dream most nights. Sometimes she was sleeping in her room in the nurses' home, and sometimes at the house on Bethlehem Road. Often she was working and one time she was at a dance with Dilys and her friends. He was glad that she could get out and enjoy herself once in a while, but, seeing her dancing with another man was a pain difficult to bear.

oOo

At long last the journey was over. They docked at Suez and marched to a camp ten miles from Alexandria, where they were under canvas and they were reunited with their AA guns and equipment. It was incredibly hot and many of the men suffered stomach ailments. It was fortunate that they didn't start active service immediately, as it took most of them some time to acclimatise.

The food could be monotonous, but those who weren't suffering from dysentery were training so hard that they ate everything that was put in front of them. Harry was intrigued to see the "Compo boxes", that their supplies came in. These boxes were packed by girls in factories in the UK, and some of them had little notes in for the soldiers. Each box contained a day's rations for fourteen men, or fourteen days rations for one man. All the food was in tins: tinned bacon and tomatoes, stew and vegetables and tinned potatoes, corned beef and rice pudding or semolina. Tea, sugar and milk came in cubes that you threw into a bucket or teapot of boiling water. There were also boiled sweets or chocolate, and cigarettes. Harry didn't smoke, but he used his cigarettes as currency, swapping them for sweets or writing paper, and sometimes the local Arabs would do tasks in exchange for cigarettes – polishing boots or mending clothes or making tea. Water came daily on the water cart, one bottle of water per man per day.

Now part of the eighth army, they had a few weeks of training in desert warfare before they marched on. By this time the anti tank guns had moved away from the artillery, as they were working with the tank regiment. Jimmy waved goodbye to his friends. "See ya lads. No doubt we'll meet from time to time!" he shouted as they drove off. Harry felt that he and Bobby would miss him, their childhood animosity now completely forgotten. They had got to know him well on the journey, and of course he was now Bobby's brother in law. Harry fervently hoped that Jimmy would stay safe.

They were now getting regular mail from home, which helped to keep their spirits up. Harry read his letters from Bronwen over and over. He didn't mind that they were all very similar, descriptions of her work at the hospital and telling him how much she loved and missed him. She never mentioned the air raids or the number of people injured in them, for which he was thankful. Similarly he didn't mention some of the first aid training that he was undergoing, which was quite graphic at times and made him realise the sorts of injuries he may receive, or have to deal with. He told her all the funny things that happened, and about the heat, but not about the flies and the dysentery. Of course he wasn't allowed to say where he was, but he knew that she would guess anyway.

He received a letter from Alice every week, often containing a message from his sisters or from Bill. Mr Marshall rarely wrote now, but Susan's regular letters to Bobby often contained news about him. It seemed that Mr Marshall wasn't very well and was leaving most of the work to Susan and Ted. Harry tried not to worry about him.

He soon didn't have time to worry about anything else but the war, as they began to move towards the enemy. As AA gunners they were never in a forward position. They were generally protecting the camps and ammunition and fuel dumps, which were the targets of the Luftwaffe. They needed all their concentration to plot the height and speed of the incoming planes and aim the shells, with a timed fuse, to explode at the right height and position. Each man on the gun crew had to know his task and everyone else's; so that they worked in perfect timing with each other. They could also take over the task of another gunner in the event of that man being injured. Mostly they were successful in preventing the destruction of their precious supplies. When the bombardments were finally over, they were so exhausted that they just had time to eat their stew and rice pudding before falling into bed.

Most nights Harry was so tired that he fell into a dreamless sleep. In many ways he was glad that he wasn't dreaming, because the realities of war were the stuff of nightmares. Thankfully Harry and his friends had, up to now, been spared the really horrific injuries that the "poor bloody infantry," (PBI) were subjected to on the front lines, but the sheer noise and heat and the screams of the guns, added to the persistent flies, the lack of water and the stink of unwashed bodies, were bad enough. He missed his realistic dreams of Bronwen, while feeling glad that he didn't see anything bad happen to her.

oOo

For months they slogged on through the desert. In December they got closer to Tobruk and managed to relieve the troops who had been besieged there since April. They then continued to Benghazi, and beyond, but it was only for a short time. Field marshal Erwin Rommel's army were well trained. The allies were soon retreating, and over the next few months they were gradually driven back through Libya and into Egypt. By the time they got back to El Alamein everyone was physically and mentally exhausted.

oOo

It was the end of July 1942. Harry and Chalky were resting in the shade of their AA gun. They had cleaned and greased every bit of the gun and it was ready to fire at a moment's notice. They had been battling constantly for a month to keep Rommel's army from taking El Alamein. Now it seemed like they were going to have some rest, as they had just heard that they were to regroup and resupply. There were rumours that Rommel's supplies and reinforcements had been sunk in the Mediterranean.

"What a relief!" said Chalky. His eyes were red and sore from the heat and the sand, and his skin was red raw. Harry was no better. He wished for a cold bath, but water was rationed, so they couldn't even have a shave. The only men without a beard were those too young to grow a beard.

"I wonder if we'll get a chance for some R&R in Alexandria?" said Harry. "I've heard that some men are getting leave."

"Ooh, that'd be good," Chalky replied. "In the meantime let's have a brew. It's your turn Robbie."

"Are you sure? I thought I made it last time. Harry looked at Chalky's grinning face. "Oh, alright, I make a better brew than you do anyway." He wiped the old tealeaves out of the teapot that Chalky had bought from an Arab. In fact it was two of Harry's cigarettes that had paid for it, but Chalky had done the deal, so he reckoned he had bought it. Chalky had also acquired the can of petrol that they used to boil the water for tea. Harry didn't ask where it came from. Sometimes it was better not to know these things. They had a little hollow in the sand, lined at the base with a stone. Harry poured a little petrol into it and lit it with a match, poured some of their precious water into an old pan and it was soon boiling. He poured this over a couple of cubes of compo tea in the pot. It was sweet and strong, and tasted like nectar. They drank it quickly before the flies could take over, although they weren't successful. They both spit out flies that had landed on the edge of their mugs. "Filthy things!" Harry complained. He knew that he would never get used to the flies.

The sergeant came over. "Post, lads!" he called. Harry had two letters, one from Alice and one from Bronwen. He saved Bronwen's letter for later, when he could be alone. Alice's letter contained an amazing piece of news. Audrey had given birth to a baby boy on the first of June. Jimmy was a dad and Bobby was an Uncle!

"I have to go and find Gripper," Harry told Chalky. He still found it strange, using Bobby's nickname, but everyone knew him by that name, so Harry had to use it too.

It didn't take him long to find Bobby, who also had a letter, from Dorothy, and he was waving it in the air, shouting, "I'm an Uncle. I've got a nephew!"

Harry was laughing with him. "Anyone would think that you were the dad, the way you're dancing about! I didn't even know that Audrey was pregnant, did you?"

"No, apparently she told Mum not to tell us until the baby was born. She was worried about the air raids, because she had heard rumours of girls losing their babies, through shock. Mum said it was a load of rubbish, but she promised to keep it secret anyway. Jimmy knew, but she didn't even tell him until recently. She didn't want to get his hopes up. He'll be full of it when we see him. Fancy, he must have got her pregnant on their wedding day, the randy sod!"

Harry laughed, but it made him think sadly of Bronwen. She had wanted to try for a baby before he went away, despite her nurse training. She'd said that she would give up the nursing if it meant she could have his baby. He had convinced her that it would be better to wait. He didn't want to leave her with a baby to look after alone, but now he wondered if he had made the right decision. What if he was killed? Would it have been better for Bronwen to have a baby, a part of him? He knew that his Mum would have supported Bronwen in that event. No, he thought, stop thinking like that! He looked so grim that Bobby looked alarmed.

"What's up, Harry? You look like you've lost a bob and found a penny!" he asked.

"Oh, sorry Bobby, I'm really happy about the baby. I just started thinking about Bronwen. Just ignore me."

"I know mate, I'm constantly thinking of Susan and wondering if we'd made the right decision in waiting to get married. What if she finds someone else? I wouldn't blame her. We've been here nine months now with no sign of an end to the war. What if it goes on for years?"

"Well there's one thing I know, Susan will be waiting for you for as long as it takes. She's potty about you, has been since she was ten. I think, I hope Bronwen will be there for me too."

"Of course she will. Now, let's go and find the daddy while we've got a quiet time."

Almost all of the eighth army were camped in the same area at El

Alamein, and they knew where the armoured division's tents were, though it took them quite a while to get there. They knew that Jimmy had also had a letter as they approached. He was in the centre of a crowd of men, all congratulating him. His face was as red as his hair and he had a grin from ear to ear!

"Hey, Robbie, Gripper, I'm a dad, I've got a son!" Harry and Bobby reached him through the crowd and shook his hand.

"Congratulations Batesy. Has the baby got a name?" said Harry.

"Yes, John – Johnny, he was born on the first of June, weighing six pounds ten. That's a good weight, isn't it?" he looked sombre for a moment. "I've missed his Christening. I would have loved to have been there. Alf and Norma are his godparents. Johnny was born on Norma's birthday, you know."

"Yes, I realised," said Harry. "I sent her a letter for her birthday. I couldn't get a card. I got a letter from my Mum today. She said Norma had got my letter, but she didn't give me all the details about the baby. I'm so pleased for you, Jimmy."

"Me and my mates are going into Alex tonight to wet the baby's head. Are you coming? We've organised transport, so there'll be room for you. We can go to the bath house first and get a good wash and shave."

Harry and Bobby smiled. "Sounds good, it should be ok; we'll just need to ok it with our sergeant. We've got plenty of Arab money and Harry's cigarettes," said Bobby.

"You still not smoking? I don't know how you do it. I'd die without a fag!" Jimmy exclaimed.

"I don't know, I've just never fancied it. Anyway, my fag rations come in handy. Most Arabs prefer tobacco to cash."

"That's true, anyway, I'll see you later," said Jimmy.

oOo

They had no trouble getting passes for the evening. Nobody had been able to leave camp for a month, so, now that it was quiet for a time, anyone who wasn't on guard duty could go out for the evening.

Ten men went out in two jeeps. Harry, Bobby and Chalky were with them. They had a great time in Alexandria, most of them ending up inebriated. Only Harry and one of the antitank gunners were fit enough to drive back. Harry still didn't really like the taste of alcohol, so he drank very little and was content to keep an eye on his mates. He almost had to lift Jimmy, the proud father, into the jeep. Most of the others managed to drag themselves in, helpless with laughter.

Just as Harry had got all his passengers into the jeep, he suddenly had a sense of someone in pain. He looked at all his mates, but they were all giggling at a joke. They obviously weren't in pain. There was an alley nearby, and the feeling led him there.

"Hey, Robbie! Where you going?" shouted Bobby.

"Just going for a slash!" he replied. That produced more inane laughter.

He edged down the alley with his back to the wall. He didn't want to be ambushed. Some unsavoury locals had been known to attack allied soldiers just for their cigarettes if they ventured anywhere alone. He decided that he would only go as far as he could get while keeping the jeep in sight. Luckily he found the source of the feeling just a few yards in. There was a horrible stench coming from what looked like a pile of rags. He gagged, and thought he was going to be sick, but he managed to hold it back.

As he leaned closer, he realised that it was a dead body, but why could he sense someone in pain? He pushed at the body with his boot and heard a yelp. It was a small dog, trapped under the body. He eased it out, trying not to hurt it further, as it was obviously in pain. It stank almost as much as the body, which must have been there at least a day, judging by the smell. He carried the dog out of the alley, having no qualms about leaving the body for someone else to discover. The man was in Arab dress, so he obviously wasn't a member of either army. Harry was more concerned for the living dog. He had never been able to resist an animal in need.

"You poor thing," he said, as he gently felt all its limbs. It yelped, but nothing seemed to be broken. He stroked it and it burrowed into his body, spreading its smell onto his uniform. So much for having a bath and shave! He'd have to clean his uniform with petrol tomorrow. He wondered how the dog had become injured; being trapped beneath his master wouldn't have caused all that pain. He gazed into the dog's eyes, remembering how Bess had transferred visions to him, though he didn't know if it would work with a foreign dog. It did work; he got a vision of the Arab being badly beaten by three other men, the little dog barked at them and tried to nip one of them, he got kicked in the ribs for his trouble and then he was thrown against the wall. His master fell on top of him and the three men ran away..

"Robbie! C'mon mate, we're getting bloody cold here!" It was Jimmy shouting, so Harry picked up the dog and put it in Jimmy's lap. "Pooh, what's this? It stinks!"

"It's a dog, and it's hurt, so just hold it 'til we get back to camp," Harry replied.

"Oh, trust you, Robbie, always a sucker for a stray."

Harry had already started the engine and set off. Jimmy was so drunk that he fell asleep holding the dog. All the other men were already asleep, leaning against each other, so nobody else complained about the smell.

oOo

The little Jack Russell soon became a mascot for the gun crew. He was such a pleasant little character that nobody could resist him. He was never short of food, taking the last bit of everyone's stew and vegetables, he would eat anything. Typically they called him Jack. The sergeant was as daft about him as the gunners, and the officers turned a blind eye. Apparently, they weren't the only group to adopt a dog. What would happen when they left North Africa, Harry didn't know. He preferred to cross that bridge when he came to it.

Wherever the gunners went, Jack was with them. During this relatively quiet time they were able to go to the beach and swim in the sea. It helped to heal a lot of the skin ailments that many of them had developed, as well as boosting morale. Jack would be running up and down the water's edge while they were swimming. It seemed that he didn't like to go in the deep water, but he enjoyed getting his feet wet.

oOo

In August the men heard that the eighth army were getting a new commander, Field Marshal Bernard Montgomery. He was a charismatic man and he soon instilled a devotion in the men, who called him 'Monty'. He made a point of visiting every unit and his Australian type bush hat became well known. His speeches improved morale no end.

While they were waiting for reinforcements, Monty started a system of training designed to harden up the troops for the coming battle. The PT exercises were the most intense that any of them had endured before, and they also had to undergo more training in their weapons. Harry thought that his crew already knew their weapons, but he had to admit that the training honed their abilities to a precision unknown before. It was October before Monty declared that they were ready for an offensive. He told the troops that they would win through, and they all believed him.

On 23rd of October the offensive began, under cover of darkness. Harry's gun crew, along with the other light AA guns provided the light for the infantry and tanks to move forward, by firing tracer shells along fixed lines, so that they could keep to their bearings.

It was a fierce fight over several days and by 3rd of November, the battle of El Alamein was won. Rommel's army were retreating. Churchill was so pleased that he had all the church bells rung in Britain for the first time since 1939.

Over the next few months Harry had no time to think about anything but the war. Bronwen was a presence always in the back of his mind, and he looked forward to her letters, but he had none of his dreams for quite a long time. He didn't dream at all. Life was one long round of maintaining, cleaning and firing the guns, eating and sleeping when possible, moving on, and then cleaning and firing the guns again. Little Jack followed the AA gunners wherever they went. He seemed to be immune to the noise, though he always pushed himself into a corner of the sandbag walls while a bombardment was going on, emerging with his tail wagging as soon as it became quiet.

There were no serious injuries to any of the AA crews, though some of them had shrapnel wounds. When he saw Bobby, he noticed a bandaged arm, but it was apparently not serious. Of Jimmy they saw nothing. The AT gunners were always far ahead, so they hoped that no news was good news. They knew that there had been many deaths but, as yet, nobody they knew had lost their life.

On 23rd January 1943 the eighth army reached Tripoli and this became their headquarters. Harry and the rest of the gun crew were relieved to stay in one place for a time. They set up their gun, surrounded by sandbags and prepared to protect Tripoli from air attacks. The Luftwaffe tried to raid several times in February, but, every time, they were beaten back by the efficiency of the anti aircraft crews.

Harry's friends had time to wash and repair their uniforms, helped by the Arabs, who would do invisible mending for a couple of cigarettes or a tin of corned beef. Everyone wrote letters home, and the incoming mail caught up with them. It was the end of March when Harry began to dream again.

oOo

He was on Bethlehem Road in Skewen when he heard singing. It was the discordant singing of a group of drunken people, apart from one sweet voice that soared above the others. Harry's heart pounded as he recognised his wife's beautiful voice. Several people were coming up the hill. He recognised Dilys, and the blonde hair of Rhiannon, who lived further up the road. They were with three men in RAF uniform, and each man had an arm round one of the girls. They were all singing, "We'll keep a Welcome," and they were all, even Bronwen, quite drunk. Harry was sad and angry at the same time. Bronwen rarely drank alcohol, she preferred lemonade. Why had she started to drink? He got his answer by listening to their talk. They got to Bronwen and Dilys's house, and Dilys struggled to get her key in the door. She finally fell into the hallway, giggling. Bronwen and the two men followed her, with Harry close behind. Rhiannon continued up the hill with the third man.

"Just a cup of tea, and then you leave!" Dilys was trying to be stern, but she was laughing too.

"Ok darling, we heard you," said one of them. He followed Dilys into the kitchen.

Bronwen flopped down onto the settee and put her head into her hands. "I shouldn't have had brandy; it's gone right to my head. I feel so dizzy."

"You needed it," said her companion, "after the trauma you've both suffered."

"Well, it was a shock, Mr Jones all smashed up in the road!" she started sobbing.

He put his arm around her, and Harry felt like hitting him. How dare he comfort my wife, it should be me! Harry tried to move towards them, but he found his insubstantial self unable to move. He was so frustrated that he wanted to scream. He could only stand and look.

Dilys brought in the tea tray and gave a cup to Bronwen and the two men. "Thanks for bringing us home; neither of us is used to strong drink. How many brandies did you give us?"

"Only three, the landlord said there wasn't any more. As it was he got the bottle from under the counter, and it cost us a fortune!"

"Three double brandies? Goodness, no wonder we could hardly walk. Here, Bronwen, drink that tea while its hot. It's good and strong too."

Bronwen looked up through tear filled eyes. "I don't think I can drink it. I feel sick," and she jumped up and staggered to the bathroom. When she came back she seemed a bit less drunk. She sat on the settee, leaned back and drowsily said, "I think I'll just sleep here." She leaned on the shoulder of the man and fell asleep.

Dilys, the worse for wear herself, said, "I think I'll just leave her there to sleep it off. We're not working tomorrow anyway. It's time for you boys to go. Thank you for rescuing us."

"We've got a problem," said one of the men. "We can't get back to base now the buses have stopped for the night, and it's too far to walk. I don't suppose we could stay here?"

Dilys seemed unsure, but Harry could see that she didn't want to throw the two men out, after they had been so helpful. "Well, my mother's bed is still in the front room, I suppose you could sleep there?"

"Oh thanks Dilys, you're a lady. You won't hear a peep from us."

"No no no!" shouted Harry, but of course they didn't hear him. He drifted away from the dream, hoping that Dilys and Bronwen would be ok. He wanted to stay in the dream until morning, but his stupid subconscious brain wouldn't let him. What was the use of having this so called "gift" if he couldn't protect the person he loved most?

The next night he couldn't wait to get into bed. His mates were going into Tripoli for the evening, but he complained of a headache and said he was going to get an early night.

His sleeping mind took him straight to Bronwen, and he breathed a sigh of relief to see her and Dilys sitting in the living room together. There was no sign of the RAF men.

"How do you feel now?" asked Dilys.

"I'm ok, I think. I'm glad those men have gone though. They seemed good fun when we were in the pub, but I wasn't so sure afterwards."

"I know what you mean. I'm glad they were gone when I got up, and you were in the bath. Didn't you see them go?"

"I think I was awake earlier. I seem to remember that one, Dave, I think, saying good bye. It was strange, I felt, I don't know – I didn't like him. I felt dirty after he'd gone. That's why I went for a bath. I hope we don't see them again."

Dilys gave her a hug, "So do I cariad. We'll both hope together. Now, let's get an early night, we're back at the hospital first thing."

oOo

7 MOVING ON TO ITALY

The war in North Africa was over in May 1943. Rommel's army retreated to Italy and the allies were left to clean up, rest and lick their wounds.

Some of the infantry and armoured divisions of the eighth army moved over to Sicily to force the Germans from the island in the summer of 1943. Most of the light AA guns stayed to protect Tripoli, so Harry and his mates had a relatively quiet time.

On 8th September the Italians surrendered to the Allies, but the Germans remained in Italy, determined to fight.

During this time Harry dreamed of Bronwen almost every night, and he was relieved to see her either working or spending time with Dilys or her other friends. There was often another girl at the house in Bethlehem Road, and Harry gradually realised that she was Dai's fiancée. Bronwen hadn't said where Dai was posted. He wondered if Dai was still in Britain. He asked about Dai in his next letter to Bronwen.

They were getting post much more quickly now. Monty had emphasised the need for soldiers to be in touch with their families, and air letters were now common, so, in less than two weeks Harry had his answer:

My dearest Harry,

It's lovely to hear from you so quickly now. I feel that you are very close and your lovely letters make me feel as though I could reach out and touch you. You don't know how much I want to touch you, or, maybe you do know, because you always seem to know how I feel. I miss you so much cariad. I wonder when this horrible war will end.

You asked about Dai. He is in the Royal Welch Fusiliers and, up to now, his division are still in Britain, I'm not allowed to know exactly where, guarding the country. So we see a lot of him, and he is engaged now, to a lovely girl called Maggie. She spends a lot of time with us, even when Dai isn't here. She is from North Wales, but she is in the land army, based quite near here, so she spends her off duty time with us. We've given her a key to the house so she can let herself in any time. They are getting married in two week's time, which seems very quick, but I can tell you, as one of the family, that they are expecting a baby.

Maggie is going to live here when she has to give up the land army. She seems quite happy about it. I think the land army is a lot harder work than nursing.

Dilys is well and working hard. She is on the maternity unit now, and she will be going into the countryside soon, where they have evacuated the new mums, so I'll only see her on her days off then. I'll miss her, so it will be good to have Maggie here.

Dilys doesn't seem to feel the need for a boyfriend. She says that there'll be plenty of time for that after the war. I wonder if she'll ever marry, she loves her work so much.

Well, that's all my news cariad. I love you more and more. Please keep safe, I couldn't live without you.

All my love,

Bronwen.

oOo

It was October when the gun crews got word that they were moving to Italy. The Allies had taken Sicily and the Germans had retreated to the mainland.

Harry had a dream of Bronwen the night before they left. It wasn't like his usual dreams, in that he wasn't exactly sure what was going on. Dilys and Bronwen were having a very heated discussion, which was strange in itself, because they rarely disagreed, and it was obvious that Bronwen was distraught. She was sitting, hunched up in the armchair, he could only see the back of her head, and Dilys was on the settee opposite.

"You have to tell me, exactly what happened that night. I need to know!" urged Dilys. "You must remember what you did, look at you!"

Bronwen was sobbing so much that Harry could hardly tell what she said. "I thought it was Harry. I was dreaming about him, and I woke up to find .... you know. I thought it was Harry! I felt terrible!" She dissolved into more tears and Dilys went over to her and hugged her.

"Its ok cariad, you'll be alright. It'll work itself out, and I'll look after you."

"But what about Harry? What will I say?" sobbed Bronwen.

"For now, you say nothing. Harry is fighting a war and he doesn't need to worry about something we can't change. You love him don't you?"

"Yes, with all my heart, you know that."

"I do, and I know that he loves you too. It will all work out for the best, you'll see."

Harry was so sorry that Bronwen was hurting so much. He couldn't imagine what the girls were talking about, but it must be something that Bronwen did, something that he wouldn't like. I didn't matter what Bronwen did wrong, he would always love her. He couldn't think of anything that would change his love. "I love you Bronwen," he said, but, of course, she couldn't hear him.

oOo

They shipped out the next day. Harry couldn't bear to leave little Jack behind, so his friends took most of his clothes in their kitbags, and Jack went into Harry's, and in that way they managed to sneak him onto the ship. It was harder when they transferred on to the landing craft. Jack didn't like the movement at all and he was constantly whimpering. Chalky and Bobby started to sing very loudly and, when the sergeant asked them what they were playing at, they said that they were just trying to keep up morale. "Well, do it a bit quieter then," he said. Thankfully, by this time, they were nearly at the beach and the sound of the waves crashing on the shore covered up any other sounds.

They had to camp very near the shore as the preceding infantry and tanks had come up against fierce opposition and had only managed to proceed a short way inland. Little Jack was glad to be released and was running all around the camp.

"Where did that dog come from?" shouted one of the sergeants.

"I don't know sarge, he just turned up, probably hungry," said Harry. The gun crew sergeant came over then and immediately recognised the dog.

He winked at Harry. "You'd better give him some food then gunner Roberts."

"Yes sarge, right away." He knew that their sergeant was a dog lover too and, although he couldn't have allowed them to take the dog on the ship if they'd asked, it was obvious that he was pleased.

"Keep him out of trouble gunner!"

Harry smiled, "Yes sarge." He opened a tin of corned beef for the dog, whose tail was wagging so much his whole body was shaking.

oOo

For weeks they slowly moved on in the wake of the infantry and armoured divisions, who were suffering heavy losses. Harry was glad that they were not too near, as, even at this distance he was getting feelings of pain and anguish projected from the casualties. Worst was the feeling of helplessness, that he couldn't do anything to ease them.

As they worked their way northeast they were busy harassing the enemy to take their attention from the "poor bloody infantry". They had no leisure and Harry fell into an exhausted, dreamless sleep every night. During this time he had two letters from Bronwen. They were unlike her usual letters. She seemed very subdued, telling him very little, but repeating over and over how much she loved and missed him, and hoping that he would still love her when he came home. He couldn't understand why she would think he could ever stop loving her.

oOo

In December three things happened to send Harry into a pit of depression. Why did bad things always come in threes?

Harry and Chalky were just making a brew when Bobby came running up. Before he said anything Harry could sense agitation and grief from him.

"What's up, Bobby?" he asked, quickly sitting his friend down on a compo box.

"It's Jimmy, he's badly injured. A messenger came to ask if I could go to him, but he's asking for you too, Harry. They've just moved him from the casualty clearing station to the field hospital. My sergeant has Ok'd it, and I've got use of a jeep. Can you come?"

It didn't take long to get permission, and they shot off in the jeep. The last thing Harry wanted to do was visit the hospital, but he had to do it for Jimmy's, and Audrey's, sake.

They found out which tent he was in and they both stood in horror at the entrance. Harry was so overwhelmed by the sensations of agony and weakness that he nearly passed out. He must have looked bad, because a sister rushed forward and grasped his arm.

"Are you alright, laddie?" she asked in a lilting Scottish voice. "Sit down for a minute."

Harry felt really embarrassed. "I'm ok now, I think. We've come to see gunner Bates." Harry made an effort to pull himself together.

"He's my brother in law," explained Bobby. He was looking almost as pale as Harry.

The nurse looked grave. "Now lads, you'll have to prepare yourselves. He's very badly injured. He's lost both his legs and he has internal injuries. I'm sorry, but we don't think he'll make it."

"Oh no! Do you know what happened?" said Bobby.

"We don't get to know all the details here, we just patch them up, but I think it was a mine." She led them to a bed far up the ward, near the nurses' station – a group of wooden boxes used as seats and desk. The other sister was writing up notes there.

They wouldn't have recognised Jimmy, only for his red hair, looking even redder against the pallor of his face. They tried not to look at the lower part of the bed, where the absence of his legs was obvious. Tears came to Harry's eyes, and he could feel that Bobby was close to tears too. They knelt down on the ground at the side of the low bed. Jimmy sensed them there and opened his eyes.

"Hiya lads," he whispered, "Thanks for coming. I want to say ..." he swallowed painfully, "... sorry, for how I was when we were kids."

"That's all forgotten mate," said Harry. "You've proved that you're not a bad 'un, and Audrey loves you, and you've got a smashing son now. You'll have to get better for him. They'll send you home now, so you'll be able to see him." Bobby just nodded; it was obvious that he didn't know what to say.

"No, Harry, I won't be going home, I know that. Something's broken inside. I can feel it, and the doc said as much." He swallowed again and shut his eyes. Harry thought that Jimmy was too tired to say any more. He tried to think of something positive to say.

"Don't talk like that Jimmy; it could take a long time, but you'll get better."

Jimmy shook his head and then grimaced at the pain that small movement caused. "Listen lads, I want you both to promise me that you'll look after Audrey and Johnny."

"That goes without saying," said Bobby, finding his tongue at last. "They won't want for anything as far as I'm concerned, and I know Alf and Harry, and all the family will look out for them, but Jimmy, you've got to try and get better."

Jimmy looked really weary and just shook his head again. The sister came up then and said, "Time to go lads, he needs his rest. Come back tomorrow if you can."

They never saw Jimmy again. They got word the next day that he had died during the night. They were both deeply saddened, but not really surprised, after seeing the state he was in. Harry started to compose a letter to Audrey.

The same day Harry had two letters, one from Alice and one from Susan. As soon as he saw Susan's writing he knew it was bad news. She only wrote to Bobby normally. He opened his mother's letter first.

Dear Harry,

I'm so sorry to give you this bad news. Mr Marshall died of a heart attack last week. As you know, he had been unwell for some time, but I think that Ted being called up was the last straw for him. He couldn't cope with the extra work, even though Susan tried to take on as much as she could. She has been trying to run the business singlehandedly since then. His sister has moved into the house and she has arranged the funeral. I don't think Susan likes the sister very much, but I'll let her tell you more, because she is going to write to you too.

Have you been getting regular letters from Bronwen? I don't know if we have done anything wrong, but we haven't heard from her for quite a while. She used to spend all her leave with us, but we haven't seen her for months, and she hasn't answered my last letter. I know your Dad can be a bit abrupt, but I don't think he said anything untoward last time she was here. I hope she's alright. I expect she is just very busy at the hospital.

Norma and Jenny are fine and both working at Frankenstein's. Jenny, of course, wants to join the ATS when she's old enough, but I'm hoping the war will be over before she has a chance. It's bad enough worrying about you all the time.

Little Johnny is beautiful. It looks like he'll have ginger hair like his dad. Give my love to Bobby and Jimmy, if you see them.

That's all my news lovey. We'll go to Mr Marshall's funeral in your name.

Keep safe,

Lots of love, Mum.

Harry wanted to go somewhere private and have a good cry, this news on top of Jimmy's death was just too much, and what was wrong with Bronwen? There wasn't anywhere private in an army camp, and you were expected to keep a stiff upper lip and carry on. Tragedies were happening every day, but this was the closest Harry had been to personal tragedy since the war began. Chalky was looking anxiously at him.

"Bad news Robbie?" Harry nodded. "I'll put the kettle on then."

Harry sat on a box and opened Susan's letter. It was evident from the start that she was very angry.

Dear Harry,

I know that your mum has told you the bad news. I left my letter a couple of days so that you'd get hers first. Just in case though, I have to tell you that Mr Marshall has died.

Did you know that he had a sister? No. Neither did I. She never came to see him when he was alive, but she moved into his house the day after he passed. Not a word of explanation! I didn't realise that he owned the house, but she obviously did. He didn't leave a will and she's his only relative, so she'll get everything and she's not wasting any time.

I went into work yesterday and she was moving everything around in the shop. When I asked her if she was going to run the shop she said, no, she's closing it down!

She's already got another hardware shop to buy all the stock. She said that the shop is going to be her parlour. Snobby cow!

I asked her about the wirelesses that are rented out. She said to ask the customers if they want to buy them, otherwise I've to bring them back so she can sell them. The bitch!

She's given me a week's notice and told me to sort the wirelesses out quickly because she's got a buyer for the van.

Well, I'm joining the ATS, and if they'll have me quickly I won't work my notice. What a horrible woman. Her brother isn't in his grave yet.

I'm so sorry Harry, I was happy to keep your job for you, for after the war. That bitch has spoiled it all. Sorry to rant about it too. You've probably got enough to worry about.

Keep safe Harry. And keep my Bobby safe too.

Love, Susan

Harry sat down heavily on a box and Chalky handed him a mug of strong, sweet tea. "Thanks Chalky," he said. Taking a huge mouthful that burned his tongue.

"Want to talk about it?" said Chalky.

Harry nodded. "We found out this morning about Batesy kicking the bucket, and now I've been told that my old boss has died and his sister is closing down the business. Gripper's girlfriend had been keeping the job open for me. I'm not too bothered about the job, I can't think beyond the end of the war anyway, but I really liked that old man. He'd built the business up from nothing and I've been working for him since I was twelve. The other thing is that my wife seems to be in some kind of trouble, but she won't tell me what it is. The thing is, bad things always come in threes, and I'm terrified that my wife is ill. I couldn't bear that."

"I didn't know you were superstitious Robbie. You don't believe all that rubbish, do you? I bet your wife's fine, she's probably just fell out with her sister, or someone at work. Women can make a mountain out of a molehill. You'll see, she'll be ok." Chalky slapped his back and took a slurp of his tea.

"Probably you're right," said Harry. Of course Chalky knew nothing of Harry's insight into other's feelings, and nobody knew about his accurate dreams of Bronwen. He knew that there was something badly wrong, but, from then on, he kept his worries to himself.

oOo

Towards Christmas there was a lull in the fighting and the men had time to write letters and make repairs to uniform, and they could all sleep better.

It was the 22nd of December when Harry visited his dream, after an absence of several weeks. He had a massive sense of déjà vu as he viewed the scene that took him back over twenty years.

It was the same room, and even the same bed, but the woman in the throes of labour wasn't Bronwen's mother. It was his beloved wife herself, and Dilys was delivering her baby! Harry was shocked to the core of his soul as he watched Dilys hand the baby to Bronwen. She was sobbing uncontrollably as she held the baby girl. The baby was the image of Bronwen at that age, with dark curls and dark eyes.

Harry wanted to run away from the scene, but his fickle subconscious kept him there watching.

"Bronwen looked down at the baby and said, "My lovely girl, you should have been Harry's." Her tears dripped onto the baby's face.

Harry's tears were flowing now. "Bronwen, how could you do this to me? I thought you loved me as much as I love you. I never believed you could do something like this, it shouldn't be possible. He watched in anguish as she sobbed over the baby, until Dilys reached to take the baby.

"I need to wash her now cariad, then I'll make you comfortable and then we can have a nice cup of tea." Bronwen gave up the baby reluctantly, still sobbing her heart out.

The scene faded and Harry found himself back in his camp bed, with the sounds of snoring men all round him. It was still barely midnight. He lay awake for a long time, trying to make sense of what he had seen.

"How did I not notice she was pregnant before?" He asked himself, and then he realised that the last time he had visited the dream she had been sitting in the deep armchair, talking to Dilys. Before that she may not have been showing. He thought again of the conversation she had with Dilys that night. She had said, "I thought it was Harry. I was dreaming about him, and I woke up to find .... you know."

Harry was angrier than he could remember ever being before, and grieving - grieving for his lost love. He lay awake the rest of the night, just going over it again and again, trying to understand, and trying to decide what to do. Should he stop writing to her, could he pretend that he hadn't seen what he had seen? No, he couldn't ignore it, but, could he forgive her? There was one thing; he couldn't talk to anyone about it. How do you explain that you've seen your wife having someone else's baby in a dream? No, he had to work this out himself. He was heavy eyed when he dragged himself out of bed, thinking, "I was right, bad things always come in threes."

oOo

Over the next few weeks Harry was unusually morose. If they hadn't been actively fighting, and moving on every few days, his friends would probably have questioned his mood. As it was, they were all too tired to think of anything but surviving, eating and sleeping. Harry was glad of the activity as they slogged through the mud and slush of the Italian winter. More than once their gun on its trailer was bogged down and had to be rescued by a tank.

A few times Harry visited Bronwen in his dreams. It was absolute agony to see her with her baby, the agony only slightly alleviated by the obvious fact that she was as unhappy as he was. He wished that he could control his dreams at this time.

He hadn't written to Bronwen since the birth, though he'd had two letters from her, the second one begging him for a reply. She was obviously worried about him, and he was sorry that he was giving her the worry, but he didn't know what to write. He couldn't reveal that he knew about the baby. How could he explain how he found out? In the end he sent her a short letter so unlike his usual letters, without the usual terms of endearment, that he knew she would wonder what was wrong. At least she would know he was alive.

oOo

They had been moving westward across the mountains for some time. The rumours were that the fifth army, who had been fighting on that side, had encountered fierce opposition and had enormous losses. The eighth army were to join them near a place called Cassino. They needed to take the top of a mountain in order to free the way north. The Germans had possession and were obviously reluctant to give it up.

By the time the artillery arrived on the lower slopes the infantry were dug in further up. Harry noticed a horrible stench in the area.

"What's that smell? It's atrocious!" he said. Chalky and Tug were also wrinkling their noses.

The sergeant came over and said, "It's rotting carcasses, not human, I hasten to add. I've just been talking to the officers and they told me that the only way to get supplies to the lads dug in on the slopes is to take them up by mule at night. The poor mules get shot at, and sometimes just fall off the narrow paths. It's too rocky to bury them so they're just left to rot."

"Oh, the poor things!" said Harry. For the first time in weeks he had sympathy for another creature. Little Jack came up to him just then and he picked him up to give him a cuddle. The dog could always make him feel better.

It was the 11th of May, almost midnight, when all the artillery guns, over a thousand, bombarded the Germans who were holed up in the monastery at the top of the mountain. Under cover of this fire, the Polish infantry worked their way towards the top. It took until the 17th of May for them to be successful, and many of them died in the process, but it meant that the Allies could at last get further north.

Harry's gun crew didn't have to move on immediately, so they had time to rest and explore the area, if they were so inclined. Harry didn't feel like doing anything, but Chalky had different ideas.

"Let's go down into the town," he said, one morning. "We might find a bar, or something."

Harry looked down the steep mountainside at the ruins of Cassino. "It doesn't look like there's anything left of the town," he replied. "I think I'll just stay here.

"No you won't, you've been too miserable lately, you need a change. Look, here's your mate, Gripper, he'll come with us." Bobby and two of his gun crew appeared. "Are you up for a trip into town lads?" said Chalky.

"We were just thinking the same. There must be some of that Italian wine somewhere down there," said Bobby.

Harry tried to refuse again, but Bobby wouldn't take no for an answer, so he followed them reluctantly. He looked round for little Jack, but he had disappeared, probably hunting rabbits. They set off down the winding track.

They were nearing the town when they came across one of the unfortunate mules, lying at the foot of a rock face. The smell was horrendous. They all hurried past, trying not to breathe in, when Harry suddenly stopped.

"Come on Robbie, let's get away from this stink!" shouted Chalky.

"I won't be a second; I just want to check something." Harry had sensed something alive. He was sure that it wasn't the mule, which was decomposing. There was a pile of rubble nearby, obviously brought down when the mule fell. Harry could see a body partly covered. "Lads, there's a man here and he's still alive!" he shouted. They all ran back to see. Harry was already moving the rubble. When they uncovered him he didn't look too injured. His head had been protected by a big rock suspended across a gap. The man groaned as they gently moved him. Harry took his water bottle and wetted a hankie to wipe the man's filthy face. His eyes slowly opened. "Grazie," he said. Harry held the water bottle to his lips, and he drank greedily.

"Can you move?" asked Harry.

"English?" asked the man.

"Yes, do you speak English?"

"A little."

"Good, because we don't speak any Italian," Harry replied. "Let's see if you can sit up." Harry and Chalky lifted him into a sitting position. He cried out, and they realised that his left arm was broken. They checked his legs before they tried to stand him up, but, although they were covered in bruises; they didn't seem to be broken.

"Do you think you can stand?" asked Harry.

"I'll try," he replied. Avoiding his left arm, they managed to help him up. He was swaying and looked very pale, but he stayed on his feet. The men were amazed that he wasn't more badly injured. He had been very lucky.

"We could take him back to camp," said Bobby, looking up the track.

"No, no! Take me home, please. It just down there," he pointed to a farmhouse about half a mile down the track. "My daughters will be worried."

With difficulty they took off his shirt and used it to bind his arm to his body, and then replaced his jacket on his good arm and fastened it round him to provide more support. With one man on each side of him and one at his back, they made their slow way down the track.

As they approached the farmhouse a dog started barking and two young women came out. When they saw who it was they came running, shouting, "Papa, Papa!" The man seemed to lose his strength when he saw his daughters. His legs gave way and it took the efforts of all five young men to carry him into the house.

The girls were asking questions in rapid Italian. Harry finally interrupted them and asked, "Do you speak English?"

"Oh yes, I am so sorry. I should have realised. My name is Carla and this is my sister Sofia. Thank you for helping my father. May I ask your name, and then may I ask what happened?"

Harry hadn't looked properly at the girls while they were getting their father into the house, but now he looked at Carla and he got a shock. She was so like Bronwen, it was uncanny. The same raven curls reaching her shoulders, the same dark brown eyes and straight nose in a heart shaped face. His heart missed a beat! He realised he had been staring for so long that his friends were looking at him strangely.

"Oh, sorry, I'm Robbie, this is Chalky and Gripper, Johnny and Spud" He used all the nicknames that they were used to. It was too much to explain their real names. "As for what happened, we found your father under a pile of rubble on the track back there. I'm afraid he probably fell when his mule fell. The mule is dead, I'm sorry."

Carla looked puzzled. "We don't have a mule; it must be one of the Cypriots. They've been using mules to take supplies up the mountain, but they stopped two days ago"

"Oh, there wasn't anyone else there," said Harry.

"No, the mule driver would have had several mules. If that one was shot, or falling, he would have cut it free to save the others, but how did my father get there? Papa ..." she asked her father what had happened, in Italian." He looked sheepish, but he answered in English for the sake of the soldiers.

"After you went to bed last night I went for a walk up the track. I'm sorry," he turned to the soldiers, "I thought you had all left. I was going up to your camp to see if you had left anything, petrol or tins of beef. I saw the mule, and I was looking to see if it still had a pack. I heard the rocks fall, and then nothing. The next thing I noticed was you kind men helping me. I must have been unconscious for a few hours."

"Oh, Papa, you could have been killed!" cried Carla.

"I know, it was stupid of me. I'm very grateful. Will you stay for something to eat, and some wine? We have plenty of wine anyway," he offered.

"What about your arm? It needs setting," said Harry.

"My daughter, Sofia, is a nurse." The younger girl blushed. "She will bind it and then take me to the doctor in town, but first, we must eat."

"Yes, we have chicken and pasta. At least we still have a few chickens, and I have made bread," said Carla. "You are all welcome. The thought of fresh bread brought a smile to everyone's face. They hadn't had bread for a long time. Carla sent two of the men down to the cellar for a few bottles of wine, while Sofia dressed her father's arm. Harry went with Carla into the garden to pick salad. "The chicken is already cooked, and the pasta takes no time at all. The salad will just finish it off"

Harry held the basket while Carla picked tomatoes, lettuce and basil. He couldn't take his eyes off her. She even smiled like Bronwen. "Why you keep looking at me?" she asked.

Harry was embarrassed. "I'm sorry; it's that you are so much like my wife. I haven't seen her for two years."

"Ah, you miss her very much."

"Yes – yes I do." He missed her with a pain that was sometimes hard to bear, and it was now mixed with a feeling of betrayal and loss. Would she want him back, now she had someone else's baby? Did he want her back? Yes, as he thought about it, he knew that he did want her back and he would fight for her. He didn't know how he would feel about the baby, but he knew that he didn't want to live without Bronwen.

"You hesitate?" said Carla, "but you do miss her?"

"It's a long story, but yes, I do miss her, more than anything." He replied.

"Maybe you could tell me this long story? I am a good listener." She gazed at him with those eyes that were so like Bronwen's.

"Ah, I don't think it's a story that can be shared, but thank you for caring."

She smiled sympathetically. "Let us take the salad in. You boys must be very hungry."

When they returned to the house the others had already started on the wine. Sofia was giggling and her father was smiling broadly, despite all his aches and pains.

"Robbie, you should see the wine cellar. There's hundreds of bottles!" shouted Chalky. Harry laughed.

"Well, dozens, anyway," said Carla's father apologetically. Harry realised that they hadn't asked the father's name.

"Sorry, we didn't ask your name, Senor?" he said.

"My name is Carlo Granelli; my daughter was named after me. Please call me Carlo," he replied.

"Oh, there's a Louis Granelli who has an ice cream shop in Manchester, where I live," said Harry.

Carlo answered with a big grin, "That is my great uncle. His family have been in England for many years. When you go home you must tell him that you have met us. I think he will be very interested."

"What a coincidence! When I write to my mother I'll ask her to call in and tell the Granellis about our meeting," Harry answered. It was good to have something pleasant to write about.

They were soon all sitting round the kitchen table enjoying the delicious chicken and pasta in a rich sauce, which they mopped up with fresh crusty bread. The lettuce and tomatoes were the best that Harry had ever tasted. It was a wonderful meal.

Harry had never tasted wine before and he found the Italian red wine delicious, much more palatable than beer. For some reason he had never really enjoyed the taste of beer, but he would drink a small amount just to be sociable. He drank two large glasses of wine and felt a lot happier than he had for some time.

Carla started to clear the table and Sofia turned to Carlo. "Papa, we must go now, your arm," she said.

"Ah yes, I suppose so," he laughed, and Harry thought that Carlo had had more than two glasses of wine, judging by his red cheeks and the glazed look in his eyes.

"We'll go with you into town," said Chalky. "You might need some help, and we were heading for the town anyway. Are there any bars still open in the town?"

"Oh yes, there is Luigi's. He would stay open even if his roof was blown off. We can show you where it is, it's not far from the doctor, and then I can join you after my arm is set," said Carlo, laughing again.

"Papa, you should come home after your arm is set. You need to rest," said Sofia.

"We'll see, we'll see," he replied, "I will need to thank these boys for all they've done, and we can all come back in the wagon. One or two glasses of wine won't harm me."

Sofia just shrugged; it seemed she knew her father well. "Come then, we need to go." Two of the soldiers helped Carlo out of his chair and they made their way to the door.

"I'll stay here and help Carla to clean up," said Harry. He wasn't in the mood for merry making with his friends. He just wanted to sit quietly and enjoy the warm feeling that the wine had given him.

"Oh yes?" said Spud, "I hope you haven't got designs on the lovely Carla."

"No, he's married to the lovely Bronwen. There's no way he would look at anyone else. You're quite safe Carla," said Bobby. Nobody seemed to think it strange that Harry didn't want to go on a drinking spree. They all knew him to prefer reading and writing letters in his free time and they all accepted that, especially as he was generous with his cigarette ration.

Harry and Carla stood at the door as Spud helped Sofia to hitch the horse to the wagon and they all helped Carlo up into the seat. They waved merrily as they left.

After they had washed and dried all the dishes, Carla poured two more glasses of wine.

"I'm not sure if I should have any more," said Harry, "I don't have a head for alcohol normally, but this wine is tasty."

"It won't harm you, we drink it all the time," she replied. "Come, let's sit outside."

They took their glasses out to the garden. At the back of the house there was a stunning view down the valley. If they turned to the right they could avoid the sight of the ruined town and forget about the war for a while. There was a stone seat, but Carla led him to a grassy bank and they sat on the soft, warm grass, enjoying the heat of the late afternoon sun.

They sat in companionable silence for a while, and then Carla said, "About your long story?"

Harry was startled out of his reverie. He realised that he would like to tell someone about his dream. Could he share it with Carla? He wondered if the wine was making him more open, or was it that Carla seemed to be so sympathetic? He would like to know more about her, anyway.

"What about your story, Carla; why is such a beautiful woman still at home with papa?" Immediately he felt deep waves of grief emanating from her. He felt sorry for bringing up bad memories, but she replied.

Taking a deep breath, Carla said, "I wasn't always at home with papa. I was married at age seventeen, to Angelo. He, I had known since a small child. We wanted children, many children, but it didn't happen. It seems I was not destined to be a mother. When the war started Angelo went into the army and he was sent to North Africa. He was killed at El Alamein." She said this so bluntly, but Harry could feel her grief and sorrow.

He was stunned. Angelo was one of the enemy at that time, and many, on both sides, were killed. Harry couldn't avoid feeling guilty for Carla's loss.

"I'm so sorry," he said. "So many were killed at that time. I am deeply saddened that your husband was one of them."

"Robbie, I didn't tell you this to make you feel guilty, or sad, just so that you would know me better. I came back home when Angelo went away, partly to escape from my lonely apartment and partly because Sofia went to train as a nurse. Papa needed someone to keep house after mamma died."

"How long since ....?" began Harry.

"Mamma died in 1939, just before the war started. I'm glad that she didn't have to see the destruction of our town, and especially the monastery. It would have broken her heart."

"I understand, I was devastated at the destruction of my own home town, Manchester," Harry replied. Carla nodded and squeezed his hand in sympathy. They didn't need to say anything else.

Harry looked at his empty wine glass. How many had he drunk? It didn't seem to matter any more.

Carla picked up both glasses. "I'll get us some more wine and then you can tell me your story."

Harry smiled; He felt ready to talk now. When she returned he started. "I have to tell you that nobody else knows of this. Even my wife, Bronwen, doesn't know the truth, and that's because the whole thing seems unbelievable. Somehow, I think that you will believe me, and it will be a relief to share it." He took a sip of his wine and continued.

"My wife had a baby girl, last December. She is not my baby, because I have been away for over two years. I love my wife deeply, but I don't know what to do with this knowledge, how to react. You see, Bronwen doesn't know that I am aware of the baby. She hasn't mentioned it in her letters, although she declares her love for me, and yes, I know that she still loves me as much as I love her, as much as she ever did."

Carla was shocked. "So, how did you find out, did someone else write to you?"

"No, and this is the part of my long story that you will find difficult, if not impossible, to believe. I dreamed of the birth. I saw the baby being born, as it actually happened. I've been having these dreams of Bronwen all my life."

"But, if you dreamed it, how can you know it is true?" Carla was perplexed. Harry could sense her confusion.

"I can explain how I know it's true. As I said, it is a long story. When I was four years old, on my fourth birthday, I had a realistic dream of the birth of a baby girl. I had never seen the mother of the baby before, but I knew, even at my young age, that I was seeing something real. I knew this baby girl was important to me, that I would meet her some day. After that I had regular dreams of the girl growing up. I grew to love her even before I met her, and I did meet her ..."

Carla interrupted him, her eyes sparkling with amazement. "... and it was Bronwen, Your wife?"

Harry smiled, knowing that Carla believed him. "Yes, she is four years younger than me, born on my fourth birthday. We were destined to be together."

"How, wonderful!" said Carla. "Thank you for sharing this with me. You must truly love her, and she, you."

"Yes, and that's why I find it so hard to accept that she had another man's baby. I want to forgive her, and I hope that I'll be able to accept the baby as my own, but I don't know if I am strong enough."

"I think you are strong enough, and you have much love in you to give to that child. I think that your Bronwen has made a mistake that she deeply regrets, and she must be terrified that she will lose you. That would be a big loss, because I can tell that you are a wonderful, loving man." She took the empty glass from his hand and laid it on the grass beside her own, and then she very gently kissed his lips.

Harry responded with a passion that he had not felt for anyone but Bronwen. It was as if his body was no longer connected to his mind. He was powerless to stop. He returned her kiss deeply as she gently pushed him back until they were both lying on the grass, and she was unbuttoning his shirt and shorts.

In the heat of the Italian May they wore very few clothes, and these were soon on the grass beside them. They both indulged in lovemaking that their bodies had missed for many months, neither of them really conscious of what they were doing. It was only when they were lying, exhausted and replete, that Harry realised what they had done.

"Carla, I'm so sorry!" he cried, grabbing his shorts. "I don't know what came over me!"

Carla smiled. "Don't say sorry; we did what our bodies needed to do. It doesn't alter your love for Bronwen, or mine for Angelo. Also, you may now be able to understand how Bronwen came to make her mistake. Our bodies have a way of taking over our minds sometimes."

"How did you become so wise?" he asked.

"I think it is living with our loss that makes us wiser. We have to take what life has to offer. Being with you today has been wonderful, a memory to treasure."

"I'll treasure it too, Carla. You have made me feel so much better. Oh, but we didn't take any precautions! What if you have a baby?"

"Robbie, you forget, I tried for five years to have a baby; I am barren."

Harry could feel her grief and felt sorry for reminding her, after sharing such pleasure.

She was soon smiling again, though. "Come on, I'll make some coffee. Your friends will be back soon."

"Oh yes, my goodness, we're lucky they didn't come back sooner. That would be embarrassing, to say the least."

"Oh, I knew they would not be back yet. Papa would have to drink at least one glass of wine with Luigi, and tell all his friends about your rescue of him."

In fact they had time for two cups of coffee and a long chat about their respective lives, during which time Harry told Carla his real name and described his family in Newton Heath.

The sound of Harry's friends returning up the track with Sofia and Carlo was reverberating around the valley. They were all singing "O Sole Mio; Sofia's true soprano blending with the deeper voices of the men. It ended in raucous laughter as they came through the gate. The horse came to a stop by the door. Harry was glad, for the horse's sake, to see that only Carlos, Sofia and Chalky were in the cart. The others were all walking alongside, still laughing. Obviously they had found Luigi's bar well stocked.

"Hey Robbie!" shouted Chalky. "You missed a great time. That Luigi is a great comedian, and generous with his vino."

"Well, I'm glad you thought of the horse, anyway. He would have had a hard time pulling you lot up the hill," Harry responded.

"Oh yes, Sofia only let me sit in the cart so I could support Carlo. She didn't want him to damage his plaster, and she was driving. I think she fancies me," he whispered so loudly that everyone heard and started laughing again. Sofia blushed furiously.

Harry helped them all down off the cart. Even Sofia had been drinking wine at Luigi's, so Carla ushered them all indoors for coffee, while Harry unhitched the horse and gave him hay and water. He hadn't had much experience with horses, but he had an affinity with all animals and could tell what was needed.

He was just about to go into the house when he heard his name called.

"Hey Robbie!" It was Tug Wilson, coming down the track with little Jack at his heels. The dog was overjoyed when he saw Harry.

"Sergeant wants you all back, now," Tug said when he reached Harry. "We've just had word to move out at first light tomorrow. The PBI have met up with Jerry again and they need our back-up. Seems like the other AA gunners are having a hard time of it, so we have to catch up as soon as possible. Where is everyone?"

"They're inside, and all the worse for drink. Come and meet the locals," Harry replied.

oOo

Harry found it hard to say goodbye to Carla. He knew that he would never see her again, and he could never thank her enough for her understanding, and for the physical relief he now felt, without any regret. Her wise words had negated any shame he might have felt. He could hardly believe how much had happened in the short space of one day.

He looked back several times as he and his friends made their way back up the track in the early evening. Each time Carla was still at the gate waving, until a bend in the track hid her from view. He was quiet the rest of the way to the camp, while Chalky and the others regaled Tug with ever more exaggerated reports of the rescue of Carlo and the trip into town. Little Jack trotted alongside Harry, looking up at him now and again, wagging his stumpy little tail.

oOo

That night Harry dreamed of Bronwen. She and Maggie were sitting together, feeding their babies. He drank in the sight of his beloved wife, and he realised that he loved her more than ever. Carla had made him realise that Bronwen's mistake could so easily have been his own mistake. Why had he only realised that now?

He looked at the baby girl in her arms. She was much bigger now, of course. He thought back to the day she was born. December 22nd was etched on his memory, so she was now five months old, and a perfect miniature of her mother, her dark eyes dancing with intelligence. She was just as beautiful as Bronwen, and he felt the stirring of affection for her.

He hadn't been taking any notice of the conversation between the two young women, but a comment from Maggie made him listen.

"You never said how it happened, how you came to have Sian. Is it too painful to talk about?"

Bronwen looked at Maggie with eyes brimming with tears. "I don't mind telling you, Maggie. It might help you to understand how I feel. Dilys knows the whole story, of course. We didn't tell Dai, in case he let his temper get the better of him."

"It was that dreadful night when poor Mr Jones was killed and the two RAF men helped us. They took us to the pub and Trevor brought out a bottle of brandy from under the counter. Well, you know that I don't drink as a rule, but it was the shock, you see? I know that I had at least two large brandies, maybe more. I vaguely remember singing on the way home, and then feeling really tired, and then not much else until later. Dilys told me that I refused to go to bed and so she put me on the settee. I had no idea that the two men stayed the night too, in mother's bed. I was dreaming about Harry, and it was so real! We were both on the settee and he was telling me how much he loved me, and then we were making love. There was something different about his lovemaking; he wasn't as gentle as usual. It was then that I realised there was something really wrong. I woke up to find this man on top of me. I pushed him off, and he jumped up and started saying 'sorry, sorry, I got carried away!' I was only wearing my petticoat, and the blanket that Dilys had put over me was on the floor. I felt sick! The man rushed out of the room and I heard him talking to the other one and then they both left. I felt so dirty, I went up and had a hot bath, thank goodness we had hot water, but I still felt dirty afterwards."

"I couldn't accept that I was pregnant for a long time. It was only when Dilys noticed and confronted me that I told her what I remembered of that night. She has been so good, looking after me and not blaming me." Bronwen dried her eyes and looked up at Maggie.

"It's a good job Dai doesn't know the whole story," Maggie replied. "He would want to kill that man!"

"He doesn't have to, the man is dead." Bronwen stated, bluntly. "His friend came to the pub and told Trevor. He was shot down on his next sortie. I'm sorry he's dead, but I'm glad I don't have to face him."

"So, Sian doesn't have a dad," said Maggie. "Bless her; at least she has a good mother."

"No, she does have a daddy. I have to believe that Harry will accept her when he comes home. I know you'll think I'm crazy, but I feel that he is her daddy, in spirit. My mind, and body, were totally with Harry when she was conceived. That man just provided the seed. Harry is a wonderful, loving man. I believe that he will accept her."

Harry listened to this conversation with wonder. It didn't escape him that Bronwen had described him in exactly the same words that Carla had used. He didn't feel that he had been wonderful and loving recently, though. He felt ashamed that, for the past five months he had been thinking badly of Bronwen and grieving for his lost love, when she had been going through a terrible trauma. He had never lost his love. She had been steadfast in her love for him while feeling tremendously guilty, and terrified that she would lose him. He needed to write to her as soon as possible and reassure her that he would never leave her. How to do that without revealing that he knew about the baby, he was unsure, but he would find a way. Maybe when he started to write, the words would come to him.

He awoke to the sounds of the camp in the early dawn. There would be no time for letter writing today, that was certain.

oOo

There was very little time for letter writing over the next six weeks, though Harry did write short notes to Bronwen and Alice from time to time. He kept his letters optimistic and full of love, but he hadn't yet found the right words to reassure Bronwen that he would return to her no matter what had happened in the interim.

The eighth army travelled 225 miles north in those six weeks, continually harassing the Germans, while the fifth army, consisting of mainly Americans and led by an American General, took Rome, and consolidated the Allies position in Italy.

The Germans didn't get reinforcements because Hitler was throwing his best troops and tanks and the Luftwaffe at the eastern front and in France, where the D Day landings on 6th June, in Normandy had formed a second front.

The eighth army infantry and tanks had many casualties, and weren't getting reinforcements, while the AA gunners had very little to do. Some gunners were recruited into the infantry, but Harry and his mates were luckier, being given other tasks, driving, cooking and assisting the sappers in setting up camp.

Harry finally had the time to compose the letter that had been on his mind for so long.

Dearest Bronwen,

I'm sorry for the short notes I've been sending recently. You will understand that I can't tell you any details, except that we have been very active, and moving on almost every day. In any case, I and my mates are all well, and we've now got a bit of respite, so I can write a proper letter.

I am missing you more than ever and I can't wait until this horrible war is over and I can be back there with you.

Lots of things have happened because of the war, things that wouldn't have happened otherwise. Some of my mates have done things that they would normally think were very wrong, like stealing. Not that I have been stealing, well, apart from grapes and tomatoes that were lying unpicked in fields. I've seen nasty things done to the enemy too, and not always with good reason, but it's because they are not thinking straight. I've decided that I am not going to judge anyone for what they do while the war is on. I've been lucky, in that I haven't been put in a position where I've had to do things against my conscience, except one thing that I'll tell you about when I see you. Don't worry, I haven't done anything nasty, or against the local people, in fact I've found them very friendly and generous. It's just something I wouldn't have done if I'd been at home with you.

I'm sorry to make such a mystery of it, but you'll realise when I tell you, and hopefully you will understand that it was because of the war. I imagine you have experienced things that you will need to forget about when this is all over too.

I love you more and more every day, my darling girl. I'm looking forward to the day when we'll be together and we can put all these things behind us.

All my love,

Your Harry xxxxx

oOo

8 INTO AUSTRIA

The eighth and fifth armies were working their way through Northern Italy towards Austria by the spring of 1945. The Germans were surrendering in their thousands and the Allies had to decide what to do with them. Harry came into direct contact with German soldiers at this time when he, Tug and Chalky, along with several other gunners, were ordered to escort a group of prisoners to a recently vacated POW camp in Vercelli, which was a two day march away.

It was the end of April and already quite hot as they made their way west. The prisoners were naturally subdued, talking quietly amongst themselves for the most part, and not giving any trouble. Harry sympathised with them, realising how easily the positions could have been changed. "They are just ordinary lads, like us," he said to Chalky, who agreed with him. There was one British soldier though, who saw this as an opportunity to be nasty to the prisoners.

A stranger to Harry, he was an obnoxious little man, about five feet four, with mean looking eyes and a face that a Mediterranean tan hadn't improved at all. He was constantly prodding the prisoners with his rifle and calling them "Jerry bastards" or "stupid Krauts". The prisoners were trying to ignore him, but they were getting increasingly riled. Harry asked the man to tone it down, but he just sneered and called Harry a "Jerry lover". He was careful not to do any of this when the sergeant was near, of course. It came to a head as they stopped for a rest in a village where there was a large stone water trough with cold, fresh spring water issuing out of a spout.

The prisoners were queuing up at the trough to drink and splash their hot faces. One of the Germans was a massive man, at least six feet seven with broad shoulders. Just as he approached the trough the obnoxious man prodded him with his rifle and said, "Come on, get a move on, bastard!" the gigantic man turned to him and grabbed him by the seat of his pants and the neck of his shirt and threw him into the trough, where he came up spluttering and swearing. Everybody, British and German alike, cheered and whooped. The tense situation was immediately relaxed.

The sergeant came up to see what the commotion was, just as the soldier was rescuing his rifle out of the water. "Sergeant, look what that big bastard has done to me!" he shouted, but he was drowned out by laughter. The sergeant took in the situation and said, "It looks like you deserved it, gunner. You'd better stay up front where I can keep an eye on you." Mister obnoxious didn't like that one bit, and glared at the sergeant's retreating back, but there was nothing he could do, so, with his boots squelching, he followed, wincing at the continuing laughter.

oOo

They stopped for the night shortly after the water episode. They didn't have tents, but each man had been issued with a blanket and minimum rations. They made themselves comfortable in a field.

Harry and Chalky were on guard duty first, with two others. The prisoners were all wrapped in their blankets, getting ready for sleep, and the atmosphere was relaxed. Nobody seemed interested in trying to escape. Harry and Chalky were leaning against the field gate, drinking tea and talking quietly. The other two guards were at the far end of the field. The sky was ablaze with stars and all was peaceful. "You wouldn't think there was still a war on, would you?" said Chalky.

"No, Italy is a beautiful place when you're not fighting or climbing mountains," Harry replied.

They were quiet for a while, and then Harry got the sensation that someone was in pain, a sensation that he was all too familiar with, and which he dreaded. As he tried to pinpoint where the sensation was coming from he realised that it wasn't physical pain he was sensing, it was deep, emotional pain. Someone was desperately trying not to cry. He started to walk towards the nearest prisoners, who all appeared to be asleep.

"What's up Robbie?" whispered Chalky.

Harry had to think quickly, "I thought I heard someone groan, as though they're in pain," he whispered back. By this time he was standing over the gigantic man who had entertained them earlier. "Are you ok mate?" he asked. The man turned over and Harry could see his face was wracked with grief. "Come and have a brew," Harry said, miming the action of drinking. The man nodded and got up.

"Get another mug Chalky, we've got company," said Harry. They still had the teapot that they had acquired in North Africa. It had given them many a life saving brew. The three of them squatted over the tiny fire while Chalky made fresh tea.

"Do you speak English?" asked Harry.

"A little," was the reply.

"Let's start with names then. I'm Robbie and this is Chalky."

"Pleased to meet you," he said, politely. "I am Hans."

"Would you like to tell us what is bothering you?"

Hans gulped; he was obviously holding back tears. It was strange to see this in such a big man. "Mine brother died. I just found out today, from one of the other men. His tank was blown up two weeks ago. We were twins."

Harry was horrified. He had seen what a tank could look like after it was blown up. Sometimes the men inside were cooked alive. He was sure that Hans would have seen similar sights. He felt deeply for Hans, especially as he also had lost a brother, albeit in different circumstances. He handed the mug of tea to Hans. "I'm so sorry, Hans, no wonder you feel bad. Drink your tea, and maybe you'd like to tell us about your brother?"

Yes, thank you. Franz, mine brother, was my identical twin. We did everything together."

"Bloody 'ell," said Chalky, "there was another as big as you? I bet nobody bullied you at school."

Hans gave a weak laugh. "You are right, nobody bother us, but we did not take er, advantage, of our size. We had lots of friends, and we could use our size to help people. Franz especially was very kind. We were learning to be carpenters before the war, and he loved to mend the houses of our family and friends. We wanted to be together in the army, but they wouldn't allow it. Now I'm glad, I wouldn't have liked to see him die, and at least now my mother has still got me. I don't know how I'll tell her though."

"You'll find a way to tell her, and you will be able to comfort each other. Do you have any other brothers or sisters?" asked Harry.

"No, my mother had no more children after us. She joked that carrying the two of us was enough for one woman. My father also is not with us. He died just before the war."

Harry patted his arm. He didn't know what to say, but Hans seemed grateful for the gesture.

They talked for some time, Harry and Chalky telling Hans a bit about their lives. By common consent, they didn't discuss the war. They all knew it was nearly over, but it was too painful a subject. Maybe they would never talk about it.

When Harry and Chalky were relieved by two more guards, Hans went back to his blanket, giving them a grateful smile. This was one time that Harry was glad that he had this 'gift'. It didn't feel like a curse tonight.

oOo

They reached the small POW camp the next afternoon. Apparently it had been used to house allied POWs who were working on the surrounding farms. Those prisoners had all dispersed now. There were vastly more German prisoners, and Harry wondered how they would fit them all in. He was glad that it wasn't his problem.

There were lorries waiting to take Harry and the other guards back to their camp. It was a relief not to have to march back.

Before they left Harry looked for Hans among the prisoners but, even though he should have towered over the others, he wasn't in sight. He hoped that Hans would be alright.

oOo

The camp was in a turmoil of packing up when they got back. They were on the move again, this time through the mountains to Austria. The eighth army was much smaller now. Many divisions had been sent to other areas, but it was still a substantial number of troops that marched through the Plocken Pass. The war was all but over, and this small remnant of the eighth army was needed to tidy up one of the areas that had been devastated by the war. On the 8th of May, when the war officially ended, they entered the town of Klagenfurt, in Southern

Austria, where they were destined to stay for some time.

The town was badly damaged, having suffered many air raids, and there were hundreds of refugees. The eighth army leaders had a lot to sort out.

There followed a time of routine for Harry. He was a gunner no longer, but was now a private in the Service Corps, doing something he had always enjoyed, cooking. Chalky and Tug had been sent elsewhere but Bobby, still known as Gripper, was using his talent as a carpenter, helping the sappers to erect wooden huts in place of the tents that they had been living in. They were soon enjoying the luxury of a roof over their heads and real beds, and Harry was working in a well equipped kitchen.

Little Jack was still an adopted member of the camp. Everybody knew him, but he spent most of his time with Harry. He wasn't officially allowed in the kitchen, but he had a makeshift bed just inside the door and, as long as he didn't get in anyone's way, he was tolerated, and he never went hungry.

Harry got to know the area over the following months, spending a lot of his spare time walking with little Jack, and often helping the locals to repair their homes. On the whole the Austrian people seemed pleased to have the British troops there. Most of them were friendly and grateful for any help.

He also wrote many letters, to Bronwen and Alice, of course, and also to Audrey, Alf and his army friends, who were now scattered across Europe. He was happy that the tone of Bronwen's letters seemed more relaxed, a fact that was confirmed by his dreams.

In his dreams he followed the progress of the baby, Sian; She was now a delightful toddler, often far too energetic at bedtime, running around with Bronwen giving chase but laughing at the child's antics. But most of the time she was already asleep when Harry was visiting in his dreams. He would stand over her cot and gaze at the beautiful face that was so like her mother's. He knew that he was falling in love with this baby, and it was with a shock, one night, that he realised that he was thinking of her as his own daughter. He was watching Bronwen tucking her in and bending down to kiss her goodnight, and his heart was full to overflowing with his love for them both. He yearned to go home.

He had applied for home leave several times, but had been told to be patient. Europe was still in turmoil, transport was difficult and only for the most urgent cases. The casualties and POWs were the first to go, of course, and then you had to have a better reason than anyone else to jump the queue. He got forty eight hours leave in Vienna in the September with a group of his mates, which he enjoyed up to a point, but he had never been one for drunken nights out. He did manage to get some presents for Bronwen and his family. He wanted to get a present for Sian too, but he wasn't supposed to know of her existence. At the last moment he decided to buy her a beautiful doll in Austrian national costume. He thought he could keep it for when she was older.

oOo

It was shortly after returning from Vienna that Harry was walking towards Lake Worther with little Jack. The dog was excitedly running ahead and rootling through the bushes. Suddenly the dog came running back to Harry. He could feel that the dog was agitated. "What's up Jack?" he bent down to look into the dog's eyes. Jack gave him a vision of a man and a girl in the bushes. At first he thought it was just a couple doing what came naturally, but then he realised that Jack knew the man, and Harry thought he knew the girl, and he didn't think that she was enjoying what was happening. Jack turned and ran back to the bushes and Harry sprinted after him, forcing his way through the undergrowth.

It was Mr Obnoxious. Harry now knew he was called Pierce. He had his left arm across the girl's chest and his hand over her mouth. His right hand was struggling to undo his flies. The girl was obviously terrified.

Harry saw red: He grabbed the back of Pierce's shirt and dragged him to his feet, while Jack grabbed his ankle and clung on with his teeth.

"Ow, get that dog off me!" Pierce shouted. "What's up with you anyway? She's just a Jerry bitch!"

Harry was head and shoulders taller than the other man and a lot more bulky. He gave him such a hard uppercut to his chin that he flew several feet and landed on his bum. His look of outrage would have been comical if the situation hadn't been so serious. Harry was so furious that he felt like kicking the man too, but he restrained himself. He had never hit anyone in anger before and he didn't like the way it made him feel.

"You are a horrible little man, and a rapist, and this is an innocent young girl. She is fourteen years old!"

"How do you know how old she is? You've probably had her too!"

Now Harry did kick him. "How dare you! She is the daughter of a friend, a farmer who has provided a lot of the fresh meat that we eat; Meat that you've probably enjoyed eating. You are a pathetic, obnoxious man. Get out of my sight, but be sure I'm going to report this!"

Pierce picked himself up, giving Harry a glare full of venom, and then something in Harry's eyes made him turn away, and he rapidly left. Harry helped the sobbing girl to get up. "Are you alright, Anna?" he asked. "Did he hurt you?"

"No, I am fine now. You came at just the right time. Thank you Harry."

"Thank Jack too," said Harry, "He was the one who found you, and he did a good job of chewing that man's foot."

Anna only understood half of this, but she bent down and ruffled the dog's coat. "Thank you, Jack," she said. The dog wagged his stumpy tail and licked her face.

"Let's get you home," said Harry.

When Harry told Anna's father what had happened, he was ready to go after the man with his carving knife, but Harry managed to calm him down.

"Don't do that Jan; you'll only get into trouble. I'm going to make sure that man is sent away. This isn't the first time he's done something nasty. I know what to do."

Harry went straight to the sergeant who had been in charge of the POW escort. He had got to know this sergeant since they had settled in Klagenfurt, and he knew him to be a good man who wouldn't tolerate the abuse of women. When Harry told him what had happened he said, "Leave it with me private Roberts. This isn't the first I've heard of that man. I'll make sure he's posted.

Harry never saw Pierce again, and he wasn't sorry.

oOo

Harry spent Christmas in Klagenfurt and managed to have a good time, despite missing his family dreadfully. It seemed unfair that the war had been over for months, and yet he still hadn't had home leave, and demob seemed like a distant hope. He sent home the presents he had bought in Vienna, apart from the doll, and he received two enormous boxes from home. The one from Alice contained a big Christmas cake as well as knitted socks and mittens and scarves, and several books. Bronwen sent a batch of Welsh cakes and a blanket made up of dozens of knitted squares. The squares had been knitted by Bronwen, Maggie and Dilys and the wool had been donated by all the local women, because "we heard that it gets very cold in Austria in the winter". Harry laughed at this. It did indeed get extremely cold. Despite the war damage, Klagenfurt looked beautiful under the layers of snow, and Harry was grateful for the warmth of all the things knitted with love by his family.

He finally got the good news that he was being given 28 days leave towards the end of February. Bobby also got leave at the same time, so they were able to travel together. There was an airfield at Klagenfurt and they were to be flown from there to an airfield near Calais, where they would then get the ferry to Dover. The good news was that their 28 days only started when they reached home soil, and would finish when they got back to Dover. Harry sent a letter to Alice to tell her that he was going to Bronwen first, and then they would both come up to Manchester after a few days. He didn't tell Bronwen at all. He wanted to surprise her.

oOo

Harry got off the train in Skewen and made his way up Bethlehem Road. It looked exactly the same as when he left, over four years before. So much had happened since then. He was nervous. Had he made the right decision to surprise Bronwen? What if she wasn't there?

He didn't have a key, so he knocked on the door. Maggie answered, holding a little boy in her arms. He hadn't met Maggie, but he knew who she was, and she knew him too. Her face was a picture of surprise.

"Hello Maggie, I'm Harry, it's lovely to meet you at last. Is Bronwen in?"

"Yes – yes, she's in the living room." Maggie stood back to let him pass, but didn't follow him into the room. Bronwen was sitting on the settee and Sian was playing on the floor. The child looked up and said, "Daddy?" Bronwen gasped, and was obviously going to say something, but Harry spoke first.

"Yes lovey, I'm your Daddy." He crouched down and held out his arms, and she threw her tiny arms around his neck. "Hello lovey," he said, tears running down his face. He looked at Bronwen, whose face was a picture of astonishment.

"Don't I get a kiss from my wife?" he asked, and stood up, still holding the child to his chest. Bronwen, now weeping too, stood up to receive his embrace, and the three of them stayed there hugging for a long time, until Maggie said, "Shall I put the kettle on?"

oOo

Much later, when they were in bed and lying contented after the most perfect lovemaking, Bronwen asked, "how did you know, about Sian? I know Dilys would never have written to tell you. I'm baffled."

"I know lovey, and I have to tell you now, something I should have told you a long time ago, something you are going to find very hard to believe."

He then told her everything, from the first dream when he was four years old, through the years, how he knew her when he met her, and how he worked out what had happened when Sian was conceived. Bronwen was dumb with amazement. He ended by telling her about Carla.

Bronwen moved away so she could look at him. "Harry, I can hardly believe what you are telling me, but I know you wouldn't lie about a thing like this. It's a bit scary, Harry; do you mean that you can come to me in your dreams, whenever you want?"

"No lovey, not whenever I want. I have no control over it. Sometimes it would be months between, and then, like when you had Sian, it could be two or three nights running. I saw you coming home drunk with the airmen, but I didn't see what happened afterwards, thank goodness. I think I would have gone AWOL if I'd seen that, made my way back from

Africa so that I could beat him to death. I can't help how I am Bronwen. I hope you can accept that its part of my strange brain."

"And I hope you can forgive me for what I did with Carla. It's something I would never have done if I was at home with you. I could blame the wine, and the stress of the war, and missing you so much, but I can only blame myself."

Bronwen looked at him. "I believe what you've told me, I always thought that you were very perceptive, how you seemed to know things before I mentioned them; it all makes sense now. I see what you meant in your letter, about having done something wrong. I read that letter over and over, but couldn't think of a thing that you'd do wrong. It did help, though, to feel a little less guilty about what happened to me."

"How can I blame you for what you did, when I did something much worse?" she continued. "In any case, I should thank Carla: From what you tell me, she was instrumental in changing your mind about me, that I hadn't really been unfaithful to you. I also could blame alcohol for my actions, and I was dreaming about you when that horrible man took advantage of me, but maybe I had been too friendly to start with. We should never have invited them into the house. I am so ashamed, but I'm not sorry about Sian. I love her so much, as much as I love you, only in a different way. I meant what I said when I felt that she was the child of your spirit." She snuggled back into him.

Harry smiled and held her closer to his chest. "So, we've both made mistakes, and our beautiful daughter has come from one of those mistakes. She is truly a treasure, so let's forget the past and concentrate on bringing up that lovely little girl."

"You really see her as yours, Harry? I'm so happy, but I have another confession to make. I promise that after this there are no more confessions. When I registered Sian's birth I put your name as her father. I didn't want her to have 'father unknown' on her birth certificate. Even then I hoped you would accept her."

Harry burst out laughing. "How wonderful! So she really is mine, in spirit and legally on paper. You clever girl! But I have to ask you something now. Why did Sian call me daddy, when she'd never seen me before?"

It was Bronwen's turn to laugh. "It's because she was calling Dai 'daddy'. She had heard Dai's son, Gareth, call him daddy and she thought that was his name, so I told her to call him uncle Dai, and that her daddy was still a soldier. She has seen soldiers, so when she saw you in uniform, she must have thought, 'this is my daddy'. She's a clever girl."

"She must take after you then," Harry laughed. "Now I've got two clever girls!"

oOo

They had five wonderful days, despite the terrible weather. One day they went to Oxwich Bay on the bus. They followed the path down to the beach and they walked the full length of the bay, now free of barbed wire, with Harry carrying Sian on his shoulders. Their happiness was palpable.

Harry had written to Alice to let her know when to expect them. Bronwen was very reluctant to go. "What will they think when they see Sian? Maybe you should go alone first and tell them." She was obviously very apprehensive.

"No, I don't want to give them time to think anything. They'll have to accept that Sian is my daughter now, and if they don't like it they'll have to lump it. Anyway, I know my mum will be ok, once she gets over the surprise, and my sisters will be delighted with her. My dad might not be too happy, but he'll have to accept my decision. I'm not a kid any more! My friends will be pleased for us both, you'll see."

"I hope you're right Harry," she replied.

Bronwen was very quiet in the train, but Sian made enough noise for all of them. She was so excited, she had never been in a train, and she was going to see 'grandma and grandad and two new aunties'. She had inherited Bronwen's love of music, and she was singing 'twinkle twinkle little star' and 'baa baa black sheep', so many times that even Harry was relieved when she fell asleep, about ten minutes before they arrived in Manchester.

London Road station was as busy as ever, so Harry didn't see his mum and sisters fighting their way through the crowds until they were just a few feet away. Jenny screamed, Harry, Harry!" and threw herself into his arms, closely followed by Norma and Alice. Bronwen stood back, holding the sleeping Sian in her arms, nervously observing the group hug. Finally Harry pulled away from his family and drew Bronwen to his side. "Mum, this is our daughter, Sian," and he gently took the toddler into his own arms, waking her in the process."

"Daddy, are we there?" she asked, sleepily.

"Yes lovey, and this is your grandma."

Alice was stunned, but she had to respond when Sian held out her arms and said, "Hello grandma," confident that she would be welcome.

"Hello Sian," said Alice, as she took the child. There were tears in her eyes, and Harry could sense the mixed emotions.

Jenny came to the rescue, saying, "Oh, she's lovely! Can I hold her?" She took the child from Alice and said, "Hello Sian, I'm your Auntie Jenny. I've never been an auntie before," she started laughing and Sian giggled too. It was obvious that she liked Auntie Jenny.

Norma was as hesitant as Alice had been, but she soon fell under Sian's spell. She was such a delightful child that she was loved by anyone who met her. Harry hoped that his dad would be equally captivated, though he didn't think it would happen immediately.

"Shall we go for a cuppa before we go home?" he suggested. He thought that they should get the explanations out of the way as soon as possible. Everyone agreed with that, and they were soon sitting round a table loaded with tea and cakes. Sian had been given a cup of milk, which she drank with relish, leaving a white moustache. Alice automatically got out a hankie to wipe the child's face and Harry smiled. Things would work out with his mum on his side.

It was Norma who brought up the sensitive subject first. "Well, we can see that Sian is the image of her mother, but, Harry, You've been away over four years. You can't expect anyone to believe ....."

"I don't expect anyone to believe anything, Norma. Everyone can make their own minds up. What I do want, though, is for everyone to accept that Bronwen, Sian and I are a family. To accept that bad things happened during the war to many people, but the bad thing that happened to Bronwen while I was away resulted in this beautiful, innocent child who loves everyone she sees. You see, good things can come out of bad." Harry could feel the love and understanding coming from his sisters and Alice.

"Well said, Harry," said Jenny, "there are enough children around now who have lost their dads, or never had one. They all need the love of a family."

Harry looked at his little sister. She had been a child when he last saw her, now she was a young woman of almost eighteen, and wise beyond her years. Her resemblance to his lost brother was a lot more obvious now. Billy's bright blue eyes shone in her face. He wondered what Billy would have thought of this situation, and then he knew. Billy would have thought it hilarious. He would say, "I can't wait to see me dad's face!" Harry laughed.

"What's so funny?" Jenny asked.

"I was just thinking about our Billy. He would have enjoyed this situation," Harry replied.

Alice laughed too, Harry could tell she was more relaxed now, "Yes, Harry, Billy would have loved it, in fact he is probably looking down on us right now and saying, 'I can't wait to see me dad's face!'"

Amazed, Harry said, "That's just what I was thinking. You took the words right out of my mouth, Mum." The tension was eased and they all laughed, even Bronwen laughed with relief, and Sian laughed because she was two years old and everything was fun.

oOo

By the time Bill got home from work the tea was ready and Sian was asleep on the settee. He came in through the back door and met Harry in the kitchen. "It's good to see you home son," he said, and shook hands vigorously.

"It's good to see you too, Dad. There's something I need to tell you ..." but Bill was already on his way into the living room and he caught sight of the child.

"Who is that?" Harry could tell that Bill was adding two and two and coming up with five.

Harry quickly summed up the situation and said, "Bronwen, take her up to our room." Bronwen scooped up her daughter and almost ran up the stairs.

"Her name is Sian, and she is our daughter, mine and Bronwen's." The determined look on Harry's face was matched with a thunderous look on Bill's.

"She's not your daughter, and I want that woman and her bastard out of my house, right now!"

The two girls gasped and Alice cried, "Bill, she's an innocent child!"

"But the mother isn't, and I'm not having her in my house!"

Harry stopped him saying anything more, "Dad, you don't know what Bronwen has gone through, and I'm not going to explain, unless your attitude changes, but I'll tell you this. If Bronwen is not welcome here then neither am I, and you'll never see me again. That little girl is my daughter as much as any other child we may have in the future. I have accepted her as mine and that's the end of it." Harry said all this with a calmness that he didn't feel. He prepared to go upstairs to pack, but Alice stopped him with a hand on his arm.

"Let me have my say now," she said. "If Harry and Bronwen leave this house, then so do I. I won't stay a moment longer!"

"That goes for me too," said Jenny.

"And me!" Norma added. Harry wondered where they could all go.

Bill looked around at his family in astonishment, his anger suddenly deflated. Harry sensed that Bill couldn't believe that his meek wife would turn against him, but he knew that she was in earnest. She never said anything she didn't mean. He sat down heavily in his chair

In despair, he said, "but I'm in the right. She broke her marriage vows. How can you condone that?"

Alice answered for them all. "How she came to break those vows I don't know, and I'm not going to ask, but the fact that Harry has come home safe and has accepted the child is enough for me. As far as I'm concerned Sian is my grandchild and I'm happy to be her grandma." Harry's love for his mother soared. He wanted to pick her up and swing her around for sheer joy.

Bill continued, in a much quieter voice, "but what about our friends and neighbours, and your brother and sister in law? They know how long Harry has been away, and they can all count. What do we say to them?"

Harry could tell that Bill was coming round to accepting the fait accompli. "Anyone who cares about us will accept Sian as I have. Anyone who sneers or comments, well, they don't care about us, so they don't matter. They'll soon find something else to sneer about. We can just ignore them." Harry knew that it wouldn't be easy, for any of them, but if they stuck together as a family they would come through it.

Bill sighed, "Alright then, I can see I'm outnumbered. I still don't like it, but I'll say no more on the subject. Let's have our tea. I've been working all day and I'm starving."

Alice went over to him and kissed his cheek. It was the first time Harry had ever seen any affection between his parents. They usually kept their feelings private. He thought it was a good sign.

Harry called Bronwen down for tea. Sian was sound asleep on her makeshift bed in their room, so they left her to sleep. Bill didn't speak to Bronwen at all, in fact he didn't speak to anyone, but the girls and Alice kept up a barrage of questions about Harry's time overseas. He kept his answers light and entertaining, they didn't need to know the realities of war, and so the evening went well. They particularly enjoyed the story about the giant German who threw the obnoxious little man into the water trough. By the time they were all ready for bed Harry could sense that the female side of his family was happy and Bill was now calm and beginning to accept the new situation.

oOo

The next day was Sunday and they all, except Bill, went to church in the morning. Harry noticed lots of inquisitive stares from people that he knew. Some people came over after the service to welcome him home, and he introduced Bronwen and Sian to those who hadn't met her before. Some looked puzzled, but nobody questioned the fact that a soldier who had been away four years had a daughter aged two. He also noticed those who deliberately didn't come over to speak, and he knew why, but he didn't care. He was delighted to see Alf, who came over to stand by Norma.

Alf smiled at Norma and said, "Have you told Harry the news?"

"No, I thought I'd wait until you were here, and anyway, Harry had big news of his own," and she nodded at Sian. Alf looked at the child, then at Bronwen and Harry.

"Is this your daughter? You kept that quiet." He bent down to Sian and said, "Hello, I'm your uncle Alf." He took her tiny hand and shook it solemnly. She smiled up at him.

"This is Sian, our daughter," said Harry, smiling at Alf. He knew that Alf had taken in the situation immediately and approved. Alf looked up at Harry and Bronwen and gave them a big wink.

"Bronwen, your daughter is nearly as beautiful as you. You must be very proud of her."

Bronwen was delighted, "Yes I am; very proud." She replied.

Harry looked quizzically at Alf and Norma. "Come on then, what's your news?"

Norma was beaming and Harry noticed that Alice and Jenny were smiling too.

"We're getting married next week, in a double ceremony with Bobby and Susan," said Alf. "We decided we'd waited long enough and, when we got the news that you and Bobby were going to be on leave at the same time, we arranged it. Susan is based in Manchester now and should be demobbed soon."

Jenny was jumping with excitement, "We got parachute silk for the brides' frocks from Frankenstein's, and I'm being bridesmaid and Audrey is being matron of honour. We got some lovely blue material off the market for our frocks." She turned to Norma. "I think that Sian should be a bridesmaid too, if we can get her a frock."

"What a lovely idea," said Norma. "There's bound to be someone with a child the same size that's got a frock we can borrow. There's been so many weddings recently, with all the boys coming home."

"Well, that's wonderful news," said Harry. "We'll have to call on Bobby and Audrey on the way home. How is Audrey? She doesn't give much away in her letters."

Norma answered. "She seems to have accepted now that Jimmy has gone, and she absolutely adores little Johnny. She is going to stay living with her parents. Joe is married with a baby daughter, and now Bobby and Susan are getting married, Johnny can have his own bedroom. Susan has already found a house on Culcheth Lane, and we've got one on Daisy Bank, so Jenny will be able to spread out in our bedroom."

Jenny piped up, "If you and Bronwen are coming back to Manchester when you're demobbed, Harry, I don't mind having the little room, seeing as there's three of you."

Alice looked really pleased as Harry replied, "That's really generous of you Jenny. We haven't actually discussed where we'll live, but I would like to come back here," he looked at Bronwen, "that's if you don't mind, Bronwen?"

Alice jumped in before Bronwen had time to answer. "We would love to have you, and you might get a house near us eventually." Harry could sense the hope in his mother's heart that she would have all her family nearby.

"I would like to come here," Bronwen answered. "In fact, I don't mind where I am as long as I'm with Harry. No doubt Dai and Maggie will be pleased to have more room in the house, especially as they are expecting their second baby."

"More babies!" exclaimed Jenny. "I expect there will be an explosion of babies now that all the boys are coming home. Well, Mum, don't expect me to settle down any time soon. I plan to have some fun before I start having babies." This set off everyone laughing. They were still chuckling when they turned into Amos Avenue and made their way to the Kerr house. Alf came along with them, as he had been invited for dinner, and he wanted to see Bobby and Susan.

They all crowded in and Dorothy said, "I'll put the kettle on," which was what they all expected. Audrey's son, Johnny, was playing with his toy cars on the floor and Sian immediately went over to watch. He looked at her and said, "What's your name?" she told him and he said, "Sharn, that's a funny name!"

"It's a Welsh name, Johnny," said Audrey. "Sian comes from a long way away, so I expect it isn't a funny name where she lives." Audrey bent down and said, "Hello, Sian, it's lovely to meet you." Sian smiled shyly.

"D'ya like playing with cars? You can play with me if you like," said Johnny.

"Yes, I play cars with Gareth," Sian replied.

"Ooh, don't you talk funny!" Johnny said, but noticed that Sian looked upset. "But it's nice, funny. I like it," he added. This brought a smile, and they both settled down to play.

Audrey turned her attention from the children. "Hello Bronwen, it's lovely to see you again. I wondered why you hadn't been to see us for a long time, but I can see you've been busy. Sian is beautiful, you must be proud of her." Harry felt an outpouring of love and gratitude towards Audrey, who was sensitive enough to not question the fact of Sian's existence, but just accepted her, making Bronwen feel comfortable.

Dorothy, coming in with the tea, was just as accepting as her daughter. It was obvious that Alice must have put them both in the picture, and Harry wondered when she had found time to do it.

He didn't wonder for long, because Bobby and Alf were looking at him with big grins on their faces. He just said, "what?"

"We want to know if you'll be our best man," said Alf. "Seeing as we are all best friends, we don't want anyone else as our best man, so we thought you could do the honours for both of us. The vicar said it's alright."

"Well, if the vicar says it's alright, then it's alright by me, but do I have to make two speeches?" Everybody laughed.

"Well, you can do one speech if you like, but you better make it a good 'un," said Bobby, causing more laughter.

oOo

When they got back home there was the welcome smell of roast chicken coming from the oven. The vegetables were all prepared, so Alice shooed everyone out of the kitchen, saying she could manage it all. Norma and Jenny started to set the big table in the living room while Alf was chatting to Bronwen. Harry took Sian out into the back garden, where Bill was planting early potatoes.

"Want any help, dad?" Harry asked.

Bill looked up. "You could hand me those seed spuds while I drop them in the holes, if you like."

Harry was just reaching for the sack of potatoes when Bronwen came to the back door and called, "Harry, could you come and help Alf to lift the table into the middle?"

"Yes, just coming," he called back, and put down the sack. He went back into the living room with Bronwen and helped Alf with the table.

"We could have done it, you know," said Jenny, "but Alf has turned all gentlemanly on us, now he's marrying our Norma,"

"It is a very solid table. I didn't want you girls to hurt yourselves," Alf replied.

"You want to try working at Frankenstein's for a bit. You'd soon see how strong we are." Said Jenny, and they all laughed.

Harry suddenly realised that Sian hadn't followed him into the house. She was still in the garden with Bill. Although he knew that his dad wouldn't hurt the child, he was apprehensive as he went out again. He needn't have worried; Bill and Sian were working their way down the row with the child handing him a seed potato out of the sack each time he asked for one. They didn't notice Harry at first.

"Grandad, why are you putting potatoes in the ground?" Sian asked.

"To make more potatoes, you see these little lumps on them?" she nodded, "Well they will grow and grow in the ground and each one will make a new potato."

"That's clever, Grandad." She looked up and saw Harry. "Daddy, Grandad can make lots more potatoes out of these. Isn't he clever?"

Harry could sense that Bill was enjoying working with the child. "Yes, Sian, grandad is clever. Do you want to come and wash your hands for dinner now?"

"Yes, are you coming too, Grandad?"

"Yes, I'm ready for my dinner." Bill stood up and took the child's hand. "She's a good talker for a two year old," he said to Harry.

Harry was bursting with pride. "Yes, she's very bright," he replied.

oOo

The wedding was wonderful. All Saints church was full to bursting. Most of Alf's large family were there, and Susan's family was almost as big. By comparison, Bobby's and Norma's families were quite small.

The two brides were beautiful in their white dresses. It was a yellowish white, the colour of the parachute silk, but nobody minded. Audrey and Jenny, along with Susan's sister, were in pale blue, and they had borrowed a delightful little blue dress for Sian, who was overjoyed at being a bridesmaid. She had white flowers in her dark curls and carried a little basket of white and pink carnations. There were lots of 'aahs' from the congregation as she walked down the aisle, holding Jenny's hand. The only person who looked disapproving was Harry's auntie Elsie, and she didn't matter, because Harry knew that she was so disapproving of almost everything that nobody ever took any notice of her.

Nobody had a house big enough to hold the reception, but Fred Kerr had found out that there was a really posh room above the co op on Graver Lane and, more importantly, it wasn't very dear to hire it. Fred's lorry came in handy for the catering. Everyone pooled their ration coupons and the women made mounds of sandwiches and jellies at home. Fred then took all the food in boxes on the back of his lorry. The only thing missing was a wedding cake, but they used a cardboard one for the photos.

The landlord of the Culcheth Gates was very happy to provide a couple of barrels of beer for the men and bottles of sherry for the ladies. There was also a tea urn in the room, so nobody went thirsty.

Audrey was delighted to find that there was a piano in the room. She played all the favourite tunes and Bronwen sang along. Those who hadn't heard Bronwen sing before were captivated by her beautiful voice. Auntie Elsie commented loudly from her seat in the corner, "I don't know what they are all marvelling at. Her voice sounds quite ordinary to me!" Harry noticed that Auntie Elsie didn't offer to sing though, and he was thankful. He had painful memories of her drunken voice at other family gatherings.

oOo

Harry, Bronwen and Sian spent two weeks of his precious leave in Newton Heath. They visited all of Harry's favourite places, including Daisy Nook and Brookdale Park. They had a day in Town, though there was very little to buy in the shops. Sian couldn't get enough of the pet shops in Tib Street. "Can we have a dog, Daddy?" she asked.

"Maybe, when I come home for good," he replied. He wondered if there was any way he could bring little Jack home, but he didn't think it was feasible, with the quarantine laws. He hated the thought of never seeing that little dog again. He tried to push it to the back of his mind and just enjoy his leave, though it was difficult.

On the last day they went to Philips Park Cemetery to visit the graves of Billy and Grandma, and the newer grave of Mr Marshall. They left Sian with Alice, and Harry was glad they had, because he couldn't stop the tears from falling, and wouldn't have wanted Sian to see that. Bronwen's arms were a great comfort. As they walked sombrely up Briscoe Lane, Bronwen asked, "Have you thought what kind of work you'll do, now that Mr Marshall has gone?"

"I have, actually, what would you think if I trained to be a teacher? I've heard that they are doing emergency teacher training courses for ex-servicemen. It's something one of my teachers said I'd be good at when I was at school, but we couldn't afford for me to stay on at school then. It would mean being on a grant instead of a wage for over a year, but I've still got savings, and if we're living with my Mum and Dad it won't cost a lot."

I think that's a marvellous idea Harry. I could see you as a teacher; you're so patient with everyone. Maybe I could get a part time job too, if I could get someone to mind Sian."

"It's a thought, but we should manage alright even if you don't work. I'm quite excited about becoming a teacher now I've told you. I just hope it all works out."

"I'm sure it will, Harry. I think you could do anything you set your mind on." Harry smiled at Bronwen's confidence in him. It boosted his confidence in himself too.

oOo

There was quite a crowd seeing them off at the station. It was a Saturday, so Norma and Jenny were off work, and Alice was no longer working, since the war ended. Alf, who was now an engine driver, had a day off; he stood proudly beside his new wife, and Audrey had also come along with Johnny, who wanted to wave goodbye to Sian, his new best friend.

Alice clung on to Sian until the last minute, handing her up to Harry as he stood in the carriage doorway. He knew that Alice was going to miss her new grandchild.

"I feel as though I've known her all her life, instead of just two weeks," Alice said, and smiled up at Bronwen, who was leaning out of the window. "Bring her back soon, Bronwen; don't wait until Harry is demobbed. You can move in with us whenever you like, and then you can get your name on the housing list." Bronwen promised that she would.

Bronwen sat back in her seat while Harry held Sian up to the open window to wave.

"Bye-bye Grandma, bye-bye Johnny, bye-bye Auntie Jenny, bye-bye Auntie Norma and Uncle Alf, bye-bye Auntie Audrey!" Sian was leaning so far out that Harry had to hold her tightly round her middle. She was in danger of falling right out of the train. He let her watch until she couldn't see the family any more.

"Come in now lovey, we'll have to close the window now or Mummy will get cold," Harry looked at Bronwen, and there were tears in her eyes. "Sad at leaving, lovey?" he asked her, though he could tell that she was really quite happy.

"Partly," she said, "though I'm happy to be seeing Dilys, Dai and Maggie, and little Gareth, but I'm crying with happiness, at being with you, and gratefulness at how your family have accepted me and Sian. It could have been a lot worse."

"I knew they would be ok, well, maybe not my Dad, but even he came round quite quickly, with a push from my Mum and sisters, of course. They were fantastic. I knew they would be on my side, but I never guessed that they would threaten to leave my Dad. For a few seconds I was visualising us all crowding into your little house with Maggie and Dai!" he laughed, and Bronwen joined in.

"Well, you would have all been welcome, but I'm so glad everything turned out fine." She sank back into the seat. "I'm exhausted now. Do you mind watching Sian while I have a nap?"

"I'd love it, shall we play insy winsy spider, Sian?"

oOo

Their last week together passed far too quickly, and there were more tears when Harry boarded the train for Dover, where he would be meeting up with Bobby. He kissed away the tears from the faces of his two best girls. "I'll write as soon as I get back to camp," he said, "and I won't be away anywhere near as long this time. I'm bound to get my demob papers soon. Bye-bye my lovely girls. Be good for your Mummy Sian."

"I will Daddy," she replied, and kissed him one more time. The whistle blew and he finally had to get on the train.

"Bye-bye Daddy, bye-bye!" his last view was of a little hand, madly waving a white hankie, and then they were gone.

oOo

9 Home, at Last

Harry and Bobby got back to camp at the beginning of April, and settled into their routines. Harry noticed that Jack wasn't in his bed by the kitchen door, but he didn't worry, as Jack liked to wander all over the camp and everyone knew him. He did worry the second day, though, when Jack hadn't been back for food.

"Has anyone seen Jack?" he asked the room in general.

"He's not been here for a few days," one of the men replied. "That young girl, Anna, has been taking him out sometimes. Maybe she knows where he is."

"Oh, right, thanks," said Harry. He had some time off in the afternoon of the next day, so he went over to Jan's farm. He saw Jack straight away, playing fetch with Anna. Jack ran across and made a big fuss of Harry when he saw him, as if to say, 'where have you been all this time?' but then he grabbed the ball and ran back to Anna.

"Hello Robbie, did you have a good time on your leave?" said Anna.

"Yes, thank you. Has Jack been good?"

"Yes, he has stayed here quite a lot. I think he was missing you. Come in and see my father. I will make some coffee."

Harry spent some time chatting to Jan and then got up to go back for his evening shift. He called Jack over. The little dog ran to him and Harry said, "We're going back to work now, Jack." Jack wagged his tail, but he stopped and looked back at Anna. He seemed reluctant to go with Harry.

Harry felt hurt. He had rescued the dog from certain death in Africa, and then smuggled him over to Italy. How could Jack transfer his affections to someone else? Then he began to think. The dog didn't know why Harry had been away for a month, and he had turned to the girl who obviously loved him. How could Harry resent that?

Actually, it was the perfect solution to the dilemma of what to do with the dog when Harry was demobbed. He crouched down and looked into the dog's eyes.

"Do you want to stay with Anna, Jack?" he asked. Jack knew Anna's name and so he knew that Harry was talking about her. He sent Harry an image of himself, sleeping on Anna's bed, looking very contented.

Harry looked up at Anna. He didn't need to ask her if she wanted to keep Jack. It was obvious in her body language as well as the sense of hope emanating from her.

"I think he should stay with you, Anna, if your father doesn't mind," said Harry.

Jan was beaming, "I am so pleased Robbie. It is what we wanted. We have much to thank this dog for and we both love him."

Harry walked away, his heart heavy at the loss of the dog, but with a sense of rightness too. He would never forget Jack, but he was glad that the dog would be happy with his friends.

He didn't have much time to mope. Three weeks later Harry and Bobby and two other privates were called to the commander's office. They all stood to attention, wondering if they had done anything wrong.

"Well, men, I've got good news for you," he said. "You are being transferred to Woolwich barracks as from tomorrow. You'll be there for a couple of weeks and then it'll be demob time for all of you. Thank you for your hard work and commitment. Private Kerr, I'm glad that all the huts are finished and well maintained. We'll miss your expert carpentry. Private Roberts, I will really miss your apple pie and custard. I hope you've taught Private Smith well?"

"Yes sir," said Harry, very pleased with the compliment, and overjoyed at being sent back to home soil.

The commander then said a few words to the other two men, and then they were dismissed. Harry made apple pie for the last time that night, and made sure that his assistant, Fred Smith, knew exactly how it was done.

oOo

The routine at Woolwich was the same as at any other camp. Harry did some cooking, and they still had to do PE, guard duties and "square bashing", but the men who were being demobbed also had an interview with an officer who was an expert in careers for ex servicemen.

"Private Roberts," he began, "do you have a job to go back to?"

"No sir," Harry replied, and explained about Mr Marshall's death and the closing of the business. He still felt very sad about that, and it showed.

"I'm sorry to hear about that. Do you want to try and get into the same kind of work?"

"Well, actually sir, I am hoping to get into teaching. I've heard that there are courses for ex servicemen."

The officer looked impressed. "Do you think you have an aptitude for teaching?"

"I don't know if I have an aptitude, but I've always enjoyed teaching. I taught one or two of the army lads to read and write, so they could write home and read their own letters. Some people didn't get the same schooling as I did, for one reason or another. I used to do the same at school, for kids who were struggling, and my teacher said that I could go to Grammar school, but we couldn't afford for me to stay on at the time. Now, I have savings, and my wife is very supportive. I am very keen to do it, if I can get a place."

"Where is your home town?"

"Manchester, sir."

"Well, let's see," the officer leafed through some files. "Ah, yes, here it is, Didsbury Teacher Training College. Do you know where that is?"

"I know where Didsbury is sir, I could easily find the college, and I could get there by bus or tram from home."

"Ok Private Roberts, here is the application form. Fill it in and send it off and let me know how you get on."

oOo

Two weeks later Harry and Bobby were on the train home. Harry was getting more and more excited as they got nearer to Manchester. Bronwen had moved into Amos Avenue the week before, and she had written to say that Jenny had given up the larger bedroom as promised, and Alf had brought a small bed for Sian. Harry smiled at the thought. Alf always seemed to be able to procure anything that was needed. He would make a good husband for Norma.

As they got off the train in Manchester, Harry could hear Sian's little voice almost before he could see her. "Daddy, Daddy, Daddy!" she shouted, bringing smiles to a lot of faces in the crowd. Bronwen was holding her up to see over all the heads, and Susan was standing with them, her eyes lighting up when she saw Bobby.

"At last!" said Susan, when they finally got together. "I thought that train was never going to arrive. Hello my love," she said to Bobby, and rewarded him with a big kiss. Harry didn't notice, because he was busy kissing his own wife.

"A kiss for me too, Daddy," Sian demanded. Harry gave her a kiss on her cheek, and changed it to a loud raspberry that made her giggle.

oOo

Harry and his little family settled in well. Alice was happy to have them close, and Jenny adored her little niece. Bill was still very reticent around Bronwen, but he had no defence against the charms of Sian. She loved everyone and expected to be loved in return. She was very interested in the garden, watching Bill's every move, and asking simple questions. She soon knew how to collect eggs from under the hens, and this became her job. Harry was amazed at how patient Bill seemed to be with the child. He couldn't remember his father being so patient with anyone else, except, perhaps, for Billy. Still, he didn't question it; he was just glad that everyone was happy.

On the 1st June it was Norma's birthday as well as little Johnny's 4th and it was a Saturday. Bobby and Alf were off work and Susan had 48 hours leave. Even Bill was free. They decided to have a picnic in Brookdale Park. Harry had some news and he decided to wait until everyone was together.

Despite the fact that most things were still rationed, the women got together quite a feast. Dorothy had been saving up dried fruits and her butter ration to make a birthday cake. The eggs that Sian had collected were very welcome, for this and for egg sandwiches, ("butties!" said Johnny).

They had eaten all the butties and Johnny had blown out the candles. Dorothy was cutting the cake when Harry said, "I've got some news. I've been given a place at Didsbury teacher training college."

Everyone exclaimed with pleasure and then Susan, smiling broadly at Bobby, said, "We've got some news too; we're having a baby!"

Norma started giggling, "So are we!" Alf's beaming smile was, if anything, broader than Bobby's

Jenny squealed with delight, "I'm going to be an auntie again!"

Harry looked around at all his happy friends and family. The happiness wrapped him in its warmth. Then he sensed mixed feelings from Bronwen.

She was blushing and there were tears in her eyes. "I didn't know how to tell you, Harry, I'm having a baby too, but you must still go to college. I can work for a few months, If Mum will look after Sian?" she looked earnestly at Alice.

"You won't need to work," said Alice. "We can easily manage, and it will be wonderful to have three new babies in the family." For, of course, she thought of Bobby and Susan as family too.

"Harry's eyes were full of tears too. "It's wonderful news lovey," he said to Bronwen. "I knew there was something you weren't telling me, but I knew it was nothing bad. Of course we'll manage." He threw his arms around Bronwen's waist and swung her round for sheer joy. Everyone was laughing and clapping; even Bill was smiling.

When they found out that all three babies were due in December,

Dorothy said, "That's what comes from having a month's leave in March!" the whole party erupted in laughter again. People walking through the park were looking curiously at the large group of people who seemed to be either drunk or off their heads.

Audrey had joined in the laughter, but Harry could feel that her laughter was tinged with sadness. He knew that she was thinking that she would never have another baby. He was glad that she had married Jimmy and had Johnny. At least she had that.

Audrey got up and went over to hug Bronwen. "I'm so happy for you," she said.

Harry realised that there was genuine affection building between the two young women, and he was glad.

oOo

Harry started at the college at the beginning of July. He soon got into the habit of studying, and was really enjoying the course. It was a thirteen month course, which had been condensed from the normal two year teacher's course. So the students' classes often extended into the evenings, and they had homework too, but they were all used to working hard in the forces, so they didn't mind. If they did well they would be qualified just in time for the new school year the following September.

Every Thursday the classes finished at 3pm, and Harry got into the habit of calling at the town hall housing department before going home. Bronwen had registered them on the council housing list before he had been demobbed, but housing was at a premium now that so many young people were getting married and so many houses had been damaged in the blitz. Bobby and Alf had been very lucky to get privately rented houses in Newton Heath, partly due to Alf's talent at procurement, but there simply weren't any more empty houses in the area. Prefabs were being built on every spare piece of land, even in Heaton Park and Boggart Hole Clough, but Harry wanted to stay in Newton heath if he possibly could. Every weekend he and Bronwen would have a walk around the estate, and then down Ten Acres Lane and through the teeming terraced streets, returning up Church Street. If they saw an empty council house, or spoke to anyone who had knowledge of a house becoming empty, Harry would make note of the address, and then pester the clerks at the town hall, begging for the house. No matter how many times they told him that he wasn't at the top of the list yet, he never gave up.

It was the week before Christmas that Harry got a breakthrough. He finished college early on the Thursday, the last day of term, and went straight round to Alf and Norma's house, where he knew he would find Bronwen and Sian. Norma had given birth to a boy, Billy, the day before. When he got there Bronwen and Susan were both sitting before the fire, both looking enormous and very contented. Sian was playing on the floor with Johnny. "Is Audrey here too?" Harry asked, unnecessarily, as Audrey never went anywhere without her son.

"She's upstairs with Mum and Alf's mum, all cooing over the baby," said Bronwen, "and she's got some news for us," she added, smiling secretly.

"Audrey's got news? What news?" Harry couldn't think what Audrey would have to tell them. He could see that Bronwen already knew, but he could also tell that she was hugging it to herself for a bit longer. Fortunately, Audrey came down just then.

"Oh Harry, I've got good news for you, well I hope it's good. Mrs Morris next door to us has been offered a cottage flat on Ascot Road. She's moving in after New Year. Her house will be empty; you'll have to get down to the town hall tomorrow."

Harry's heart soared. He wanted nothing more than to live on Amos Avenue, near his friends and family, and in a house just like the one he had grown up in. It would be wonderful for his little family. Normally optimistic, he felt that, maybe this time he would be near enough to the top of the list to be given the house. He mentally crossed his fingers.

"Oh, I so hope they let us have it," he said.

"They've got to Harry; we deserve it. That house was made for us." Bronwen's eyes were sparkling. Harry hoped she wouldn't be too disappointed if they didn't get it.

He went up to see his new nephew. Norma was blooming and Alf was proudly showing his son to everyone, saying, "Isn't he wonderful? Look at his little fingers, and his little nails, and his chubby legs. I think he's going to be a footballer. Look at his hair, he's perfect!"

"Yes, he is, and he looks just like you," said Harry. "The poor kid!" he joked.

"Hey you!" Alf retorted. "Anyway, he doesn't look like me. He's the image of Norma, so he's beautiful." Harry had to agree.

oOo

The next day Harry took Sian to town, ready to demand the house. Bronwen didn't go with them because she was close to her due date. It was Sian's third birthday on the Sunday, so he thought it would be nice to take her to Lewis's to see Father Christmas after they had been to the housing department, and to get her a birthday present.

Harry entered the housing office with trepidation. The last time he had been in he had spoken to a woman who was worse than any sergeant major that he had come across. "Mr Roberts, you have been told this several times now. We can't offer you a house until you are at the top of the list, and it's no use you coming in here with addresses of empty houses. We'll let you know when something comes up." She was already looking at the next person in the queue before he could respond. She might well have said, "Dismissed!"

He was in luck; he could see that it was a man at the desk. He looked vaguely familiar, but he had his head down as Harry approached. What a surprise when he looked up and said, "Hiya Robbie!" It was Chalky White!

"Hiya Chalky, fancy seeing you here? I would never have put you down as a desk job man. How long have you worked here?"

"I was a junior messenger here before the war, so I came straight back when I was demobbed and they put me in housing. This is the first time I've been on the public desk though. It's flippin' hard work, trying to please everyone. There's too many people and not enough houses. Anyway, Robbie, what can I do for you, and who is this lovely little lady?" He leaned over the desk and smiled at Sian.

"This is Sian, my daughter, and we've got another one due any day now."

Chalky gave Harry a calculating look. It was obvious he was counting the years they'd been away and looking at the age of the child, but he said nothing. Harry was grateful for his friend's tact.

"The reason I'm here is to ask if I can have this house," and he gave the address to Chalky. "The tenant, Mrs Morris, is moving out at New Year. Bronwen and I and nearly two children are sleeping in one room at my mum's. This house is just up the road from us. I really need this house, Chalky."

"Ok, well, let's have a look where you are on the list." Chalky had sheet after sheet of paper to look at. Thankfully, he found Harry's name on the first sheet, but nowhere near the top. "Hmm, you've got a second child now. That moves you up a bit." He grinned up at Harry and tapped the side of his nose. "Yes, I think we can offer you this house, Mr Roberts."

Harry got hold of Chalky's hand and pumped it up and down. "Thank you, thank you so much, Mr White. You'll be welcome at our house any time," and he shook Chalky's hand again. He wanted to chat further, but the queue was getting longer behind him.

"We'll be in touch when Mrs Morris hands in the key," said Chalky. He lowered his voice, "come in just before one o'clock next time and we'll get a bite together." Harry promised that he would.

He was walking on air as they left the town hall. They walked down to Lewis's, Sian skipping at his side. Sian enjoyed going up in the lift, with the man saying what was on every floor – "Second floor, ladies' fashions: Third floor gentlemen's suits and coats: fifth floor, Father Christmas Grotto – and she enjoyed the grotto, but she was unsure about the funny man with a white beard, even though he gave her a gift wrapped in pink tissue paper. When he asked her what she wanted for Christmas, she said, "a dog," and then turned to Harry and said, "Can we go to see the puppies now Daddy?"

Harry nodded to Father Christmas and took Sian back to the lift. When they got to: "ground floor, street level", Sian almost dragged him to the door.

They crossed the road and turned up Tib Street, passing the fruit and vegetable barrows on Church Street, and finally reaching the area where the pet shops were clustered together. Sian stood with her nose pressed up against the window where the puppies were all frolicking over each other. Harry understood her passion for dogs; it matched his own, to the point where he could believe Bronwen's hope that Sian was the child of his spirit.

Most of the puppies were black, and seemed to belong to one litter, but there was one puppy sitting aside from the others. He was mainly white with splodges of light and dark brown on his long coat, and one dark brown patch over his left ear and eye. He looked through the glass window at Harry and his eyes were full of intelligence. Harry fell in love with that little dog there and then. "Let's go inside," he said to Sian. She jumped for joy, and was inside the shop before he could move. She couldn't see the puppies because of the hardboard partition keeping them in the window, so Harry lifted her up.

"Look at the little white one Daddy, isn't he lovely?"

Harry put Sian down and reached over to pick up the puppy and had a good look at him to see if he was healthy. Definitely a boy, his eyes were clear and his long coat was smooth and clean. No fleas and no suspect sore patches on his skin. His feet were small, so he wasn't going to be a big dog. The dog looked into his eyes and seemed to be looking into his soul. He held the puppy out to Sian, and she took him gently. He covered her face with ticklish licks that made her giggle.

"Shall we have him?" Harry asked.

"Oh yes, Daddy, 'cos he loves us already, doesn't he?"

"Yes, he does," he turned to the man behind the counter. "How much?" he asked.

"Ten bob to you lad, the last of a good litter" he replied.

"Throw in a collar and lead and you've got a deal," said Harry. The man grumbled, but agreed. Sian chose a red collar and Harry helped her to fasten it round the dog's neck.

"I think we'll have to call him Patch, because of the patch over his eye," Harry told Sian.

"That's a nice name, but what's a patch?" Sian didn't really seem to understand his explanation, but she was happy with the name.

They caught the tram home, both supremely happy.

oOo

"You and your dogs!" said Bill when he came home from work. "We'll have a house full of kids and dogs at this rate."

Harry smiled; he knew that his dad secretly liked dogs, but he also liked to complain about things that he hadn't personally arranged. "Well, you won't have to put up with it for long, Dad, because we'll be moving out in the New Year." He sensed Bill's alarm at losing part of his family. "It's ok Dad, we're not going far, just to Mrs Morris's. She's got a flat and we've got her house."

"How did you wangle that? There's so many people looking for houses."

Alice, Bronwen and Jenny had already heard the story, so they went into the kitchen to finish preparing the tea.

"Well, it was a mixture of getting nearer the top of the housing list, knowing the house was coming empty, and finding an old army mate at the desk when I went to the town hall!" Harry was triumphant.

"You lucky beggar!" said Bill, but Harry could tell that he was pleased. He would never admit it, but Bill wanted his family nearby just as much as his wife did.

Tea was a very happy meal that day. Sian kept talking about the puppy and Harry was making plans for their house. Bronwen couldn't stop smiling; listening to Harry speculating where they would get furniture and wondering if Mrs Morris would be leaving anything. "What does she have in the back garden?" he wondered.

"Very little since old Mr Morris died," said Bill, who was interested in everyone's gardens. "She has got a good clump of rhubarb though, and the soil will be fertile. I can sort you out with some seed spuds in spring, and I've got a spare spade you can have. That'll give you a start, and we can borrow Mr Wallis's cockerel and put him with our hens, and then we can rear some chicks for you. Sian can help me with that." he smiled at the child, and Harry was grateful that Bill had taken to her, as everyone else had.

oOo

On Saturdays Bronwen usually went to the Market with Alice and Dorothy, often meeting up with the other girls on the way. This Saturday though, she said that she felt tired, so Alice went without her, leaving her resting in the rocking chair. Sian wouldn't go to the market either, because Harry said that Patch was too little to go that far, and she wouldn't leave him.

After making sure that Bronwen was alright, Harry took Sian and Patch out into the back garden to begin training the dog. They had great fun trying to get him to sit, and to "come here Patch". He was only a baby though, and they weren't very successful, but, by the end of the session, Patch obviously knew his name, and would go to whoever called him. When they finally got too cold to continue, they went inside and Harry put the kettle on for a welcome cup of tea.

Bronwen was dozing, but she woke when they came in, and said yes to a cuppa. Sian liked a cup of sweet milky tea too. Harry thought that this was because she liked to be like her mum. The three of them were sitting cosily by the fire when Alice came back, loaded down with shopping bags.

"Oh, Mum, I should have gone with you," said Bronwen.

"Nonsense, I managed fine. Anyway, I only carried them from Dorothy's. Bobby came with us. He's coming here shortly."

"Any news from Susan?" Bronwen asked.

Alice smiled, "well, I think Bobby wanted to tell you himself, but, seeing as you asked, she had a baby girl at two o'clock this morning."

"Oh, how lovely!" Bronwen looked down at her own bump, "Our turn next cariad," she said to Harry. Sian was so involved with Patch that she didn't hear what was being said. She had no idea that she was soon to have a little brother or sister.

Harry looked at his wife and sensed that she knew the birth was imminent. The midwife had said that it would be between Christmas and New Year, but, as he looked at her, he felt a tightening in his own stomach.

"Are you having ....?" he didn't say any more, looking down at Sian playing with the dog.

"Yes, I think so, but only slightly. I think it'll be several hours yet," she replied.

Alice looked concerned, but she just said, "I'd better get the dinner on. I'm sure everyone's hungry."

"I'm hungry, Grandma, and Patch is too," said Sian.

"Come and help me then," said Alice, and left Harry to talk to Bronwen.

"Shall I go for the nurse?" he asked.

"No, it's far too early, my waters haven't broken. I doubt we'll need her before teatime."

Bronwen was right. Bobby came with details of his new daughter, Linda, seven pounds of absolute joy. He left, and Jenny came home, and then Bill, and Bronwen was still sitting in the chair, squirming every so often, but seeming very calm.

After tea Harry took Sian and Patch to Dorothy's, ostensibly to show the dog to Johnny, but really to ask if Sian could stay the night, as she normally shared a bedroom with her parents. Dorothy, Audrey and Fred were happy to have Sian and the dog. Sian had never slept away from her parents, but she seemed quite happy with the novel idea, and Johnny thought it was a bonus to have his friend and a dog to play with. They were both sleepy and ready for bed when Harry left.

He got back to a house full of activity. Bronwen was now in bed and the nurse had been sent for. Alice had water boiling on the stove and Bill was sitting in his chair, puffing nervously on his pipe.

Harry was getting severe stomach pains as he ran up the stairs to his wife. She was holding on to the iron bedstead, her face a picture of painful concentration and sweat running off her brow. When the spasm was over she smiled at him. "I'm ok cariad, it's all going well."

He found a piece of towelling on the chair and used it to wipe her face. "Are you sure lovey? You looked in such pain." He didn't tell her about his own sympathy pains. She didn't need to know and, anyway, it would sound so pathetic.

"I'm fine. It's all normal," she replied.

He stayed with her until the nurse arrived. The pains were coming about every five minutes now, and Harry was finding it difficult to hide his own groans, so he was relieved when the nurse shooed him out, saying, "No room for fathers in here. This is women's work." He left meekly, passing Alice on the stairs, and then joined his dad in the living room. This was one time he wished that he smoked, just to give himself something to do.

"Sit down lad; let's listen to the nine o'clock news. It'll take our minds off it for a bit," said Bill. Harry looked at the clock. It seemed just a few minutes since teatime. Where had the time gone?

The next three hours went very slowly by comparison. It was two minutes past midnight when he heard a baby cry, and he breathed a sigh of relief.

Shortly after that Alice came down and said, "It's a lovely little girl, born on Sian's birthday. She'll be delighted."

"How are they; are they both ok?" said Harry.

"Mother and baby both doing well. You can go up soon, when the nurse comes down."

Harry crept into the room. Bronwen was sitting up holding the baby and looking absolutely beautiful. "Come and see your daughter," she said.

Harry leaned to take the tiny baby in his arms. He looked down at an exquisite little face, and then she opened her eyes and looked straight at him. The baby blue eyes seemed to see deep inside him, and he knew without a doubt that this little girl had the same gift of perception that he himself had. He gazed in wonder and he was absolutely, completely happy. Tears filled his eyes as he looked at his beloved wife.

"A house, a new dog and a beautiful new baby to join my other two beautiful girls. I'm sure now that good things also come in threes.

oooOOOooo

Harry's Dream

About the Author

Sheila Kelly was born and raised in Manchester as part of a close-knit working class family. She worked as a nurse, and then as a podiatrist, working in various areas of the NHS.

She has always been an insatiable reader, and enjoyed writing from an early age, so it was a natural progression, after retiring from the NHS, to write her memoirs. These were published in two volumes in 2017, and their modest success gave her the confidence to write this novel.

The story of Harry Roberts had been in her mind for at least thirty years, so it was quite a relief to commit her ideas to paper.

Sheila lives in Yorkshire with her husband, John.

Printed in Great Britain
by Amazon